Seven Kinds of Rain

River Saga · Book One

A NOVEL

Seven Kinds of Rain

River Saga · Book One

a novel by

K. Lyn Wurth

True to Story Publishing

Seven Kinds of Rain
River Saga, Book One
Copyright © 2016   K. Lyn Wurth
True to Story Publishing
ISBN-13: 978-1-945217-00-5
ISBN-10: 1-945217-00-6

Available from Amazon.com, barnesandnoble.com
and other retail outlets.

Permission requests:
"Attention: Permissions Coordinator," at
truetostory@klynwurth.com
More author information at www.klynwurth.com

for Beverly,

my first and deepest reader,

with love

I will open my mouth in a parable,
things we have known from of old,
things our ancestors have told us.

Psalm 78

December, 1909

The hotel window, caked with years of street dust, lets in only a gold haze of sunset light. In Evelyn Rose Grady's imagination, though, the window and its wall draw back like a curtain, revealing rows of purple, velvet-upholstered opera house seats. The wall between her and the next hotel room, between her and her husband's lover, is a paper stage set. Hundreds of blurry ladies and gentlemen study her as she hovers over her husband's table, arranged in her mind's eye with china, stemware and rich food. She fills her husband's glass with more whiskey and laudanum. This is the role of her life.

Sipping her home-concocted Vin Mariani, wine and laudanum, she glances at the little girl asleep on a blanket in the corner. She feels vaguely sorry for the child, but doesn't miss the motherly guilt she's exchanged for euphoria. With Titus in love with their act's pianist, the wronged wife consoles herself from skull-and-cross-boned pharmacy bottles bought along the vaudeville tour.

Her husband thrusts out his empty glass. If she refills it often enough with whiskey and laudanum, whichever mattress he falls onto tonight will hold his final rest. Will the audience judge her? She hesitates, fearing the hisses and boos of the ones she loves, then fills it to the brim.

This rot is making me dizzy, Titus mutters, shoving the table, almost tipping it over.

Hurrying to his side, she lifts his arm to her shoulder. He looks beyond her, as if through the wall, to where Miss Lila waits, but lets his wife lead him to bed. She tucks the blankets around him. When he shoves her away, someone in her audience gasps, The rogue, and, No gentleman, he.

He snores. Evelyn Rose slouches at table for half an hour, gulping laudanum straight from the bottle, her breaths growing shallow. In her hazy euphoria, she pours laudanum elixir into another glass and sets it and a hunk of cheese on the floor beside her sleeping girl. It would be a kindness, she thinks, for the girl to die with her mother.

Margaret sleeps on the pallet as if no drama unfolds in the room, as if this isn't the last act of her family life. Forgetting her, Evelyn Rose settles on the bed beside Titus, fading beyond the crowd's judgment or pity.

Disturbed by long silence, the girl pushes away the blankets and rubs her eyes. Wrinkling her nose at her mother's lethal offering, she wishes for her big dancing partner, Cedric. Mama said, He's too black to stay in this hotel, but Margaret wonders, Where does he sleep? Maybe Miss Lila knows. She'll have something better to eat and drink. She might even teach me a new song and dance.

Margaret Rose Grady, four years old, exits stage left from the scene her mother set.

∞

The red-haired girl next bed over asks, What's that tune you're humming, Margaret Rose?

Nobody.

That's a funny name for a song.

It's a funny song.

Will you sing it? Dance, too?

I tell her I'll get a licking if they hear me. They'll make me swab the double privy out back. But the other girls beg, too. I always dance when they ask me.

Winter pours like ice water off the glass. I'm shivering sad, but I don't want to get under the covers yet. Between those raggedy-thin curtains, the moon makes the snow look blue as ink. The shaggy spruce trees and fence shadows are black as the scabs on my knees.

I get water burning in my eyes and blink it away. We got enough crybabies around here.

Nobody's asleep. The blankets are thin as hankies and the radiator bangs cold. The girls sniffle, moan and cough from the grippe we pass around. Some of them huddle two or three on a bed, throwing arms around for heat, but if they fall asleep that way and Mrs. Geisel finds them, they'll get switched for sleeping together. It's some kind of sin. We don't know which one because there are too many to keep straight. The Germans must keep a list.

I squeeze my bare feet into my cold, cracked leather shoes, missing my pretty red stockings. Shuffling on the gritty plank floor, I get the feel of it under the pinch. I've been remembering already, so it's easy to fall into the piano music playing in my head, the shuffle-tap-step and the sway.

Just like that, I'm in the time before. Before Cedric carried me over the snow to the wagon with the black horse.

3

Before the bumpy ice road all night and half the next day to give me to this Lutheran orphanage.

I lay one hand across my forehead and frown like an actress. The girls sit up on their squeaky springs to watch, and when I know they're mine, I pick a low note to build the song.

When life is full of Clouds and Rain, and I am filled with nought but Pain

Who Soothes my thumpin, Bumpin Brain? Nobody!

I wipe a tear, sniff like I'm sorry for myself and set hands on my hips.

When winter comes with snow and Sleet, And me with hunger and cold feet

Who says, here's two bits, go and eat? Nobody!

While they nod and laugh, I stretch out both arms and duck-shuffle over the wood, soft-tapping and sliding like Cedric, like my body's only air and my feet tell a story to the floor. I picture him dancing alongside, taking my hand in his warm one to spin me, here between the rows of musty ticking stuffed with straw. His face is dark already, but like mine, it's black with burned cork. His silver pocket watch swings like keeping time on a grandfather clock. Even though I almost forgot Mama's and Daddy's faces, twisted with fights, I keep every wrinkle by Cedric's eyes and his smile. I follow the beats, his feet. I belt out the song how he taught me, how the girls like it, even if Mrs. Geisel hears me downstairs, because I got to do it right.

I ain't never done nothing to NOBODY, I ain't never got nothing from Nobody, no Time

And until I get something from somebody, sometime, I don't intend to do nothing for nobody, no time.

Two more verses, one about beer and steak so the girls lick their lips and rub their tummies and one about dynamite to make them snort in their red hands. Then I take a bow. Instead of shouting and clapping, the girls jiggle on their mattresses, squeaking the wires underneath.

On my way back to bed, I touch hands with the little ones and they whisper, Thank you, good night. The big girls pat my cheek or ruffle my hair and after I slip off my shoes, the biggest girl, Lois, pulls her warm stockings on my cold feet, tucks me in and kisses my cheek.

Hard footsteps knock up the attic stairs and I hold my breath, picturing that old lady in the doorway, her bun pulling her eyes back tight while she looks over all of us for something wrong.

After her shoes clomp down, we sleep. With the cold night drawing frost leaves on the windows, we dream of blankets and families.

Stone Woman waits without pushing, not caring if the afterbirth comes out. She looks away as her own mother cuts the pulsing blue cord that binds her to her boy. The day mourns with her. Wind rattles the window frame. Snow sifts over the sill, dry pellets skittering and tangling like panicked, fleeing creatures across the plank floor, before stumbling over knots and falling through the cracks. She pictures following them into that root cellar under the shack.

If she'd birthed in a round Kitkehahki riverside lodge the way her great-grandmother, She Who Holds You, had done, Stone Woman might have dreamt a true name for her firstborn. A name strong enough to defeat the ordered number and random name the reservation man would assign. In those circular earthen houses, with posts as big around as a woman's waist, the people sat and slept and ate on the packed, swept ground, with no fear of what vermin or spirits scurried under the floor. No wind to freeze their feet. No void to draw them down.

Her mother told of it so often that even though Stone Woman was born in this same White-engineered plank house fifteen years ago, she never feels it as home. It clamps her with angles and menaces her with corners and because of the house, the boy's rightful name eludes her. Here in Oklahoma, her people are like corn scattered and left uncovered, with no chance to thrust a root into the ground.

Crooked Walk, the boy's adopted father, broods in the next room. Stone Woman hears him muttering to his dead wife the way he always does, even here, in Stone Woman's maternal home. When her mother carries the baby away, Stone Woman rolls to face the wall.

Crooked Walk knows it's the right thing, to claim his youngest brother's just-born child, but the squirming, silent infant feels heavier than a dead badger in his trembling arms. Stone Woman looks nice enough and works hard to keep his home, but he doesn't want a new wife or children. Since his first woman died, Crooked Walk has only wished to follow her. But because his youngest brother was a fool, always looking for fights and finally finding one that killed him, now Crooked Walk has a child-wife and a son. It isn't what a sorrowful widower wants at fifty-five years of age.

Crooked Walk holds the newborn at arm's length and wonders, if this child was destined to be his, why didn't the boy come through the wife he loved for forty years? He looks into its wrinkled plum face and feels only obligation. It will have to be enough.

Their village is a broken arrow shaft, fallen away from the band since their doctor and two of the chiefs died in the same month. No one will step forward to fill that void. We live in a dark place, a dark time, he tells himself, with no promise for this fatherless child.

Walking to the snow-crusted grove, he clutches the shivering bundle to his chest to warm it, then blinks in surprise to find this much compassion in his hollow heart. He leaves the house to escape Stone Woman and her mother, peering out windows after him, prying into his confusion.

Sequestered behind a cluster of tree cholla, he sits on a stone and balances the swaddled boy on his knees. Closing his eyes, he hopes Tirawa might give a song or a sign for this boy. As if in reply, the wafting coal smoke from the house sweetens to something like burning cedar twigs.

As the baby frets, Crooked Walk clasps the leather bundle on a thong around his neck, then unties it. Taking the knife from his belt, he slices his index finger and then dips the blood-beaded tip into the earth and bone dust in the bundle. This soil he scooped from the Republican River bank, where White farmers have surely plowed up the old earth lodges. The bits of bone he pinched between his fingers from his grandfathers' burial mounds. Still young, he saved these two sacred things the day the American soldiers pushed his band out of Nebraska.

He tastes the bitterness, then thrusts his finger into the baby's mouth to paint his tongue. Startled, the boy grimaces, then sucks heartily, comforting them both. Crooked Walk feels a tremor in his chest, a hot rush like bleeding that he knows to be love. This is a strange medicine, a blood bond, and Crooked Walk hopes it carries power. He holds up the baby, who kicks free of his thin blanket. The man blinks back tears and murmurs in the tiny, coiled ear, I've given my blood and my fathers' bone. I have nothing else. I've done what I can for you, but you will walk sorrowful, alone.

Crooked Walk stands outside the kitchen window to tell Grandfather he won't chase me around the reservation again, that I'm too much trouble. The Indian school will straighten me out. All my friends are going there so I oughta go, too. That I'm eight years old and that's old enough.

Burnt Wolf tells him it's no good for the Whites to take me, that they won't let me talk Pawnee. They will cut my hair. Their hard shoes will make my feet grow into shapes like bird claws.

Then my father says he can't let me try to dig up my mother again, that she deserves to rest in peace after all he put her through. And he's too old to take care of a boy who won't listen.

Grandfather says, You haven't seen old.

I sneak out the front, careful not to let the wood screen door slam, and run to the North Indian Cemetery where my mother sleeps in a box under breaking-apart clods of dirt. They told me Stone Woman died a week ago. I saw her body stiff as a leather doll but I don't believe she's dead. It's a mistake and I got to dig her up so she can get air.

Crooked Walk never smiled at her, never touched her that I saw so he don't care if she stops breathing. That's why she cried and got no more children after me. She said he was no husband to her, not like my real father, who died before I was born. She never said that man's name, because he died angry and might come back angry if we say it.

She did teach me about our medicine bundle. About two feet long, it's rolled in bison hide and tied with strips of deerskin and ripped American flag. There's a long smoking pipe tucked in those strips and inside, my mother told me somebody wrapped arrows, a raccoon bone knife, stuffed birds, counting sticks, hawk bells and beaded leather. She kept it on the west wall of our house but Crooked Walk already took it down and I don't know where he put it. It's really mine but Crooked Walk keeps it from me.

Grandfather Burnt Wolf says my mother isn't in the ground but gone to a better place in the stars. When I asked how she got out of the box from under the dirt, he said, You ask too many questions. Then he told me again the story about Ku ruks la war' uks tl, Medicine Bear, that first part of my name before Sky Seeing, but I couldn't pay attention. It feels like I got flies buzzing in my head all the time.

All I can think about is my mother underground and how I got to get her out of that box.

The red and yellow dirt is still soft but it breaks my nails and makes my fingers bleed so I use a stick to dig. It gets dark and the moon floats up. After a couple hours, I got a damp hole the same size as me. I wore out both arms digging so I can't go deeper or pull myself out of the hole. I lay down and fall asleep on the bottom, my mother sleeping under me and a long black rag of stars over my head. The hole smells like rust and earthworms and the roots tangling down by my ears.

I sing to my mother the songs she sang to me and next thing I know, it's morning. My arms feel stronger but I don't dig no more. I pull myself out of the hole and fill it.

I sit by her. The sun climbs high and burns my arms, then falls again. I sit by her and nobody comes and I'm glad. I don't want to go back to that house. It's not my mother's now.

I oughta leave but I left part of me down in the hole where my mother sleeps. I call and call it back but like a dog who ate too much, it won't come. And if I get sent to a school far away, even if that dog gets hungry again, it won't ever track me down.

I press my hand against my chest where it aches and I shiver.

Now I understand a little, what it means to die.

∞

The locomotive gleams black and smoke coughs out of its stack, dissolving into billowing draperies of rain. The arc lamp on Albert Hollingwood's company train glares into his gritty eyes. His own workers offload pallets of lumber, steel and commodities for Darkwater Creek Station, but this pleases Hollingwood little. Since his Burlington & Missouri River Railroad platted this town at his request, it's pushed him into shady financial risks. Now it's emptied his heart.

If he'd bought her ticket seven months ago, Edith could've thanked him and told everyone on the train to Chicago how kind he was and how she loved him. There her family doctor would have safely delivered their child. But, enjoying her company and needing her warmth, he'd insisted she stay. He promised her an excellent doctor, claiming this booming Darkwater Creek, his Republican River Valley dream, was safe and no Wild West town.

Then February's influenza rippled through, weakening Edith before the three-day labor, with the only answering physician too pig-headed to intervene. Here in the smoking compartment, thrumming his fingers on his knee, Albert Hollingwood pictures his men Quoyle and Dietz settling up with that doctor. He'll sorely regret his malpractice. Vengeance flares, then gutters, as he considers the problem of his child.

Her parents will be livid not to see the baby, but they'd fight to keep him. Edith hovers in his fair hair and blue eyes, and Hollingwood covets that trace of her, yet he's not quite grateful the boy lived. He's failed to christen him, as the only name he can shape is hers, and that, unspeakable.

The train hitches, grinds and catches its rhythm, first more slowly than a heartbeat, then faster than terror as Darkwater Creek slides away. Clipping his cigar, Hollingwood scrapes fire from the match-striking pad on the sill, lights the rolled leaves and puffs. He sighs for his new son, the squalling infant who roots everywhere, even at Hollingwood's woolen pocket, for comfort he'll never find. Eyes burning, he swallows, nearly choking on the thought of Edith, that lovely girl, then blinks and stiffens himself against the speed of loss. Plummeting through rain that sheets the rail car windows, with Edith five long cars behind this one, he will settle and dissolve this account. He'll return her remains to her father and mother and settle her behind Rosehill's limestone castle gate.

That being done, perhaps she'll forgive his grievous debts and not follow him home.

Jack, some people should never have children.

My father tightens his leather grip on the Auburn's wheel when its narrow tires slip and shudder over the frozen gravel. His whole body's like one tight muscle.

I lean up from the back seat, by his wet wool shoulder, and ask, Which people, Papa?

He loops his smoldering cigar by his head. Blue smoke curls.

The ones with no money, for starters, who can't take care of their own. They're ignorant, but I'll bet dollars to doughnuts they know where babies come from.

He stops then, and glances over at Pastor beside him, then back over his shoulder at me. He gives me a cold short look that kicks away my question.

When you're older, I'll explain things to you, but know this: The best people owe it to the world to decide for the ones who don't know better. The destitute. The Coloreds, Indians and insane. The foreigners. It's our country, and we can't let them tear it all down to satisfy their base desires, consuming us in the process. It's a war, Jack. A race war. Don't ever forget it.

No, sir, I say, knowing I surely won't. I hear it often enough, but that same old song sounds off-key here on our way to the orphanage carting toys and food for the unfortunates. If the poor are undeserving, why bother? Maybe because they're only children and you can't blame them for their parents. I don't know.

But then Papa points to a white meadow with little gray tombstones poking through like teeth. It would've been better, he says, if they'd never been born. But now that they are, it might be best for everyone if they end there in Ridgewood Cemetery, instead of sending it down another generation. Poverty. Inferiority. Madness. It's in the blood, you know. They've proven it. It's the science of eugenics. Just read Davenport!

He glances over at Pastor and nods, biting his cigar.

Pastor shifts in the leather seat and nods back, but probably For the Sake of the Gospel, which is what he always says, he argues a little. Yet, our Lord did say, Blessed are the merciful. And some of the children are only victims of circumstance. Not from such bad stock. A few families in our congregation, some not even as well off as yourself, have seen fit to adopt . . .

But when Albert Dash Hollingwood, my Papa, squints at him through the blue swirl of smoke, humphs and cracks his knuckles inside one black leather glove, Pastor stops talking. His holy words melt and drip like the snowflakes down the glass windscreen.

I hold my breath for Papa to pronounce the last word, which is, The Son of God could afford to be an idealist. But even he could tell a sheep from a goat.

Hand-cut paper snowflakes dangle from threads, not getting to fall down to the white tablecloths. Three women in white blouses, dark skirts and embroidered aprons tap knives and forks like toy soldiers into formation by the plates. Red and green ribbons curl around painted glass ornaments in the middles. Man-sized chairs sit around four big tables, set with flower-painted china. Twelve stubby tables with child-sized chairs huddle together, with small tin plates and cups.

I worry I might not sit with Papa at the big table, but get stuck at a little table with the orphans.

I look in every corner of the great room for a Christmas tree, but there's not one. My tree at home scrapes the ceiling. It holds my mother's angel-faced Dresden ornaments that I try hard not to break and so much tinsel you only see a few boughs poking through.

Seeing no tree makes me think the people here don't know much about Christmas or kids. A Christmas party without a tree. I get a lump clogging my throat, afraid this won't be a real party, but a sad night with important parts missing. Maybe that's what it's like to be an orphan, to always feel what isn't there. Maybe it's like this hole I have here under my heart, where my mother is supposed to be, but isn't, because she died when I was born.

I get a thick, hard feeling in my chest wondering if that makes me an orphan—or half one. I'd ask Papa, but talking about my mother makes him angry.

I haven't seen any orphans yet, but I already feel sorrier for them than I figured on. What if they're ugly or dirty or deformed with sin? What if they're exactly like me?

I wish I'd begged off sick and stayed home with my new issue of *St. Nicholas Magazine* to finish that story about the Crofton Chums and Crofton Academy, the kind of boarding school I'll go to someday because Papa says the preparatory education here will no doubt be sub-standard when I'm that age. Yes, I should have stayed at home. Even working on next week's Sunday School lesson would be better than eating with kids who would have been better off never being born, because they have no fathers or mothers.

Does Papa ever think that about me?

I breathe in the salty sweet smells of ham, caramel and bread. The tables have straw baskets lined with napkins, with bits of brown crust poking out. Between the baskets are little silver bowls of ice with pats of yellow butter, but only on the big tables. No butter for the orphans.

We set our packages down on that table with the others when we first came in, wrapped boxes with four old toys I don't want, because of all the presents I'll get this year. I gave up two chipped wooden horses, a scuffed tin train and a top, because Papa said they'd be better than anything those children ever saw. Now I feel like I should've brought better ones to make up for no tree. My stomach turns, pinching. In the car I was hungry, but now I better not eat, or I might be sick.

It's too much like *Oliver Twist*. Children live, sleep and work here. I wonder if they pick oakum, whatever that is, the way Oliver did. Outside, this place looks like a farm. I picture kids even littler than me working in the fields, bending over, pulling weeds under the hot sun. Milking cows, maybe. Is an orphanage the same as a work house?

Later, I'll ask Papa. Not now, because he is shaking other men's hands and his laugh echoes off the high ceiling and the chalkboards on the walls. One board says, Merry Christmas. Another says, Thank You, Gentlemen and God Bless our Ben-e-fact-ors. I break the last word into pieces to sound out in my head, but I don't know what it means.

Other kids stand here with the men in suits, but no mothers, and only two old ladies in stiff black dresses with handkerchiefs pressed to their noses, as if it smells funny in here, and I guess it does. Like old clothes and strong soap, with a soft wet stink like cabbage running under the good food smells. No wonder the ladies stay away.

We look each other over to figure who's older and whose father is strongest or has the nicest clothes. I'm one of the oldest and it's easy to see Papa's the richest man in the room. When he tells a joke, the men around him laugh like dogs barking. I laugh, too, but I don't know what's funny.

That's when I notice the girl beside me, like she popped up out of the yellow-and-brown linoleum floor, making my heart beat hard. Her hair is dark and shiny, almost black, and she tips her head a little like a bird, leaning close to look at me like I'm something shiny, too. She reminds me of a black-and-white magpie, with her hair falling like feathers over her white dress.

It's pathetic, isn't it?

What?

She sighs and says, The poor orphans. To think they got nothing, nobody. Begging for Christmas presents.

I shrug and nod, then lean closer to Papa. I almost forgot to feel bad about orphans and this girl brings them

16

up. Papa's right. Girls shouldn't talk unless you talk to them first.

But look at the beautiful boxes, she says, pointing to the rickety table where red, blue and green gifts stack four and five high.

The ones Papa and I brought are in front, with the nicest star and tree paper.

She shrugs and whispers, Lots of the presents are broken, but it's nice, all the same. You know how they say, Beggars can't be choosers? I brought an old doll, but it still has most of its hair. Some unfortunate girl will be so happy.

That's nice, I say, but I'm thinking, maybe it's not. What can I say? I brought broken things, too, instead of asking Papa to shop for something nice to give. My collar feels tight, and I wiggle a finger between it and my neck. It's hot in here. I wish that girl would go find her father and stand by him. Or the women in aprons should tell us to sit down to eat, so I can scoot away from her. I pretend she's not there. I swallow, frown and study the little cracks, blobs and lines in the linoleum, listening to Papa talk about business opportunities in the wake of the daylight saloon bill. A wake is where you sit with a dead person before a funeral, but what money can you make with that? I'll never be a good businessman. I close my eyes and wish her away, but I feel her green eyes on me.

She pokes my arm and when I look up, she says, Oh, no. I made you sad. I'm sorry. Shaking her head, she reaches up to put a hand on my shoulder. She looks younger than me, shorter by a few inches, but she's playing the big sister or the boss and my face gets hot and red. Next thing somebody will say I'm sweet on her, but I don't like girls, not even pretty ones.

17

I shrug off her hand and lower my voice like Papa, looking down and asking, Sorry for what?

She bites her lip and says, I wasn't trying to be mean. I didn't know you're . . . one of them. An orphan.

I check for dirt under my nails or a stain on my shirt. I'm wearing my best jacket and knee pants, a perfectly jimmy suit like the Crofton students wear, with new stockings and shined shoes. What makes her think I'm an orphan? I figure she must see the mother-shaped hole in me, my half-orphaned heart. Maybe everybody sees it.

She smiles pity on me and I almost grab Papa's hand so we can walk away together, but it would look weak and I have to show this—what would Papa call her, this insolent girl—I'll show her how strong I am and she doesn't know anything.

I spit out the words, Stop it. Don't touch me. I'm not one of them. My father's Albert Dash Hollingwood, a rich man, I'm no dirty orphan and you're a stupid little girl to think so.

She raises one dark eyebrow and smiles like she just won. You're not an orphan?

Jesus Christ, no. I use a swear like Papa, so mad I'm not sorry right away to take the Lord's name in vain. I'm Jack Hollingwood, I tell her, looking down hard into her eyes. For a second, I do sound like my father, as rough as rust.

It tightens in my chest and scares me like falling, how I hate this girl. She sees into me, though, and that— as Papa says about people who steal from or cheat him—that, I can't abide.

I see, she says, nodding and folding her hands in front of her pinafore, polite.

Now I notice the patches on her white dress and the frayed lace on her sleeves. Her shoes are painted brown, so worn out they can't shine. The soles are thin, broken on the edges.

Well, my name is Margaret Rose and I am. I'm an orphan.

I look up at her face and her green eyes turn deeper, like grass under a shade tree, and I wonder if she will cry. I don't see any tears. She lifts her chin and, as she leaves me behind, she shrugs like she owns the room.

I huddle in the folds of my stiff woolen suit up on my man-sized wooden chair at one of those china-set tables beside Papa. I'm glad to see, in my blurry, sideways glances, the orphans are getting all the food they want, no matter how many times they ask for more. No butter, but plenty of corn, peas, potatoes, ham.

She's only another annoying girl like all the others, no more than a baby, and I need to stop thinking about her. It was a mean trick, to make me feel guilty. My stomach feels like curdled milk. I push ham, creamed peas and potatoes to cover and uncover my plate's painted roses, because I've got no appetite, after Margaret.

Margaret Rose, like the roses on my plate.

She picked me because she saw my empty mother-space. My eyes feel hot and grainy from wishing Edith Appling Hollingwood, the soft-eyed Gibson Girl with the cameo in the oval frame at home, would come here now. She'd set everything right. She'd be a mother to me and to every child here, even Margaret Rose, so full of love she was, people tell me. So kind, she would give butter to every child.

But this room is for the fathers and the pastors, the bankers and judges, the men with watches and wallets who buy and sell everything. Maybe even orphans. Papa laughs loud beside me, too loud, and I want to punch his arm and shout for him to be quiet. Can't he see these children are sad and poor and it's no easy thing to live without a Christmas tree or a mother?

Margaret is like me. And if Papa is wrong, and the sheep are like the goats, then why do some children live in this German Lutheran Orphanage that smells like carbolic, mothballs and cabbage, a stink that simmers and burns through the perfume of Christmas ham? Why, while boys like me live in rooms sweet with Jap Rose soap, wear tailored clothes and decorate Christmas trees?

What if every child is meant to be born, the same as me?

A Victrola scratches out *Stille Nacht, heilige Nacht.* The other men set down their forks to listen, while Papa explains over the table in simple terms why the government needs to leave business alone.

She was brave and not ashamed. Her eyes were so many different greens, thinking of them all makes it hard to catch my breath.

Papa passes me the little bowl of iced butter, but I say, No, thank you.

You're not ill, are you? I'll not have you making a mess in my car.

No, sir.

We fold our cloth napkins, set them by our plates and move to folding chairs for the costumed nativity program. It's like a parade with wise men and shepherds and sheep, but no goats. Joseph leads a bad-smelling donkey with long eyelashes. He jerks on its bridle, but that critter stops halfway up the aisle and won't carry Mary to the stable. Instead, it dumps a load in the aisle, making the fathers chuckle and children laugh 'til the lady directing the angel choir shushes us.

Papa checks his pocket watch three times while the holy story is read out loud and the angels sing to the blanket-headed shepherds. The glittered star dangles over the paper roof, catching the light. That rubber doll looks almost like a real savior.

Before the orphans can open their gifts, though, before the frosted sugar cookies shaped like stars and bells on those glass trays can be passed around, Albert Hollingwood announces his regrets, that we must go. When he stands up, the other men do, too, but only Pastor leaves with us.

Papa opens the door and the cold air rushes in. I can't help looking back for the girl, but she doesn't stand out from the others now.

Rattling home under a lap blanket in the Auburn, I press my warm finger against the cold window glass to melt a spot to look through. Seeing the cold blue snow slip by, I wonder whether the Crofton Academy chums ever miss their mothers. I wonder if I'll still miss mine when I turn fifteen and leave home for school. When I'm grown, like Papa.

The boys finished clipping the grass short and they're playing now. One of them runs behind, pushing the reel mower, with another one balanced on the frame for a ride. That's a bad thing waiting to happen, if he slips down into those whirling blades. My stomach gets a stab in it, picturing the pain and blood, so I look away. If one of them was my brother, I'd say something, but boys don't listen to girls, anyway. They have to learn the hard way.

The one riding, Roger, looks a little like the boy I saw at the Christmas party. I can't forget about him, maybe because he had such blue eyes. Probably because I was rotten to him, even though I saw into him, the empty, sad part. I don't know why I hurt him, except he's rich and has a father and I don't. It's my meanness again, getting the best of me. Still, I wish I'd been nicer to him. Maybe he would have come back to visit.

Three littler boys are raking up the clippings into a wheelbarrow to dump behind the privy, and five others hack away at the weeds springing up between the big house cellar and the lawn. Four big high school boys are lugging the freshly painted white tables back under the trees for the end-of-school picnic. It's for us to celebrate, but it's a chance for people to come and take a look at us orphans. To decide if they want to adopt one or two.

Beside Ida, I carry a basket out to the grove to gather wild yellow coreopsis, pink prairie phlox and purple coneflowers for the picnic tables. I pull up some wild onion with white blossoms, but Ida says they stink and throws them on the ground, grinding them under her shoe.

Ida's the bossiest girl here, and she's a year older than me. Mean as a cornered barn cat, too. To keep from socking her one for crushing my flowers, I tell myself it's better to be picking flowers with Ida than boiling potatoes in that hot kitchen. I pick some fleabane then, because we need some little white shapes with those big bright colors. She frowns, but lets me put them in the basket.

The elms swish their leaves above us, and the eastern breeze moving them smells sweet like Russian olive, even though I can't see those silvery trees from here, today. I saw them before, when I went to get cream one day from the farm over thataway, on the other side of the hill.

Mrs. Geisel made us all pray before breakfast for it not to rain on our picnic, so lots of parents will come to take a look at us. Over there, between the treetops, bright yellow-white and gray thunderheads stack up in the west. And then blows up an east wind. Everybody, even God, knows that brings rain.

So much for Mrs. Geisel being a friend of God. Thinking that, I smile, and Ida acts sweet and asks me what's funny, but I can't tell her. She'd run to the old bat and tell on me, like she told about my dancing. My backside's still sore from that licking.

When the families start to come, most in wagons and some in motor cars, we change our pinafores and shirts to clean ones. Mrs. Geisel checks our fingernails and hair, then sends us outside. Walk, don't run, she reminds us, but we're in a hurry to find families and push each other on the brick front steps. One boy falls, but he's too excited to cry. Every one of us must be thinking, This better be my last school year in the orphanage.

The men who want to be fathers carry picnic baskets or boxes, and the ladies who might be mothers have tablecloths or blankets folded over their arms. Our cooks set out fried chickens, sandwiches and cakes on a long table for everybody to eat from, so there's enough. The wind's picking up and whips the tablecloths up over the food, so we put rocks on the corners of the tables.

Mrs. Geisel told us to be friendly, but not loud. To smile and watch for the people to smile back or wave at us. I'm scared of doing the wrong thing. I can't think what the right thing is, so I stand by some flowers with what I hope isn't a stupid smile.

A woman with dark hair like mine looks at me and nods. She says something to her husband, and then crooks her finger at me. My heart thuds in my chest. I look left and right to make sure she means me, and I guess she does.

When I'm halfway to the nice people, Ida walks up to me and whispers, You have dog mess on your shoes.

When I lift up my foot between me and her to check, Ida yells like I kicked her. She holds her shin and cries, Margaret, why did you do that? You hurt me! You are so mean!

She looks at the nice people who picked me out and makes tears fall out of her eyes like the best actress there ever was. She sits down in the grass, rubbing her shin with one hand and her eyes with the other, keeping one eye on that nice lady who first wanted me.

The man and woman hurry over to Ida. They stare at me like I'm a criminal while they help her up off the grass.

The father says, Well, I never.

The mother makes sorry sounds and checks Ida's stocking, asking, Are you bleeding, dear?

Ida looks up sorrowfully into her eyes and says, I don't know. It hurts so much. And I got a grass stain on my pinafore. I do so hate getting dirty.

24

Before I think better of it, I tell them, She's not bleeding because grubbing, dirt-eating worms don't have blood.

The woman's mouth falls open, and the man frowns. They take Ida's hands and lead her off under a tree, where they spread a blanket for their picnic. Sticking her finger into some cake frosting, Ida looks back at me and grins.

Mrs. Geisel walks up behind me just as I say, Shit-fire!

She marches me inside and makes me bite down on a bar of soap and count to ten. My eyes water, so it looks like I'm crying, but she can tell I'm not sorry. She sets me in the hallway to wait for Pastor to come inside from talking with all the parents I won't meet.

Ida better hope those people take her home today.

When Pastor comes in, Mrs. Geisel's gone, so I tell him I said a bad word. He doesn't ask which one. I know better than to tell him about Ida because nobody gets a fair deal by telling on another kid. I tell him I already had to bite soap and hope that's enough to pay for my crime.

Pastor Leuthaeuser is a nice man with a soft voice and long fingers that tangle together in lots of different ways while he talks. He's long-legged as a grasshopper and has a hard time fitting in behind his desk, so today he sits out on a chair beside me in his office.

Trouble again, Margaret? He taps his chair arm and says, You're having a time of it lately, aren't you?

I nod.

You dumped pickled beets on Karl's clean britches. You gave Larry Grevins a black eye and called him—what was it?

Chickenshit, because he pushed me down and ran away.

Then you pushed Polly's face into the flour bin.

She stole my hair ribbon, I say, then ask him if I'm going to get a whipping.

He asks me if it would do any good, and I tell him, Probably not.

What do you need, Margaret?

A family. Nothing else.

He looks out the window at the other children buzzing around parents like bees to flowers and says, You're not going to get one that way, by hurting Ida.

I didn't hurt her. She stole those people away from me.

I know. I saw what she did. I mean by hurting her later, the way you're thinking of doing.

Pastor Leuthaeuser has done this before, guessing what's in my head. Maybe it's a gift from God, but it's a scary thing. I want to say Ida has it coming, but I don't because Pastor's being a good sport about my bad language.

Sorry, I say. For what I was thinking of doing.

He pours me a glass of water, and I sip from it while he pours one for himself.

Am I an idiot or insane?

Pastor sloshes some of his water on his trousers, then dabs at it with his handkerchief and asks me, What?

Well, I can't seem to get parents. Nobody wants idiots or insane children and, if I am one, I might not know it. Better you tell me the truth, so I don't keep my hopes up too high. I already have enough disappointing me.

He gets a crooked grin on his face and shakes his head. Margaret, every child is precious, loved the same.

26

Maybe by God, I think, but not by people. It surprises me to hear Pastor, who should tell the truth, say such a thing about the world, sprinkling sugar on it. And he dodged my question.

Then, what's wrong with me?

You are pretty, intelligent and perfectly sane.

Well, there is my hair. Karl said no mother would want a girl with hair that won't hold a ribbon. I could chop it off so I look like Mabel.

Mabel?

The girl in my primer. She has bangs.

Oh, Margaret, he says, fiddling with the button on his cuff, there's nothing wrong with your body or mind or hair. It's your attitude. You need to be polite, watch your language, try to get people to like you. Sometimes you have to hold your tongue, not say everything that comes into your head.

Here's the truth. When I can't sing or dance, I'm not sure how to get anybody to like me. I got people to clap and toss coins at me when I was on stage, but here the Germans forbid that. The only songs I get to sing are like *Ein' feste Burg ist unser Gott*, A Mighty Fortress is our God. You can't dance to that tune, and it has too many sticky-throated German verses to remember. I don't say any of this to Pastor. He's a nice man with too many orphans to count, and I have to figure out my own problems.

I stand and look out the window, watching the picnics.

Ida will get those people for her parents, won't she?

Pastor shrugs and sighs. If she does, he says, then they get Ida for a daughter, tantrums and all. Think about that.

I tell him I'll pray for those nice people every night.

Before he can raise his hand in front of his mouth to hide it, he grins.

Go on, little girl, he says, stretching up out of his chair. Get upstairs and iron some clothes for your punishment before Mrs. Geisel decides you deserve a whipping instead.

Looks like I'm stuck here, at least until the Fourth of July.

He nods and says, We'll have more good families coming then.

From the attic window beside the ironing board, I watch the children joining up with families down on the grass. Some men and women are standing, shaking out their blankets and leaving alone. Some orphans are looking sad, then picking up a game of baseball on the west part of the lawn, because, after all, it's the end of the school year and summer.

Sweat beads up on my face, and I breathe in the smells of hot cotton and honey. I only remember bits and pieces of my old parents. Fights. Sweat and kerosene. Papa saying, Shit-fire, when he was angry or excited or scared. Loud piano music. Silk ruffles, bright red, yellow and purple. Hotels and trains and tents, but no house to live in. Dancing, always dancing.

I miss it all.

As the sun slips lower, the elm shadows stretch over the grass. Most of the orphans are still here. Under the tree, Ida stays with that man and woman, leaning into the mother's lap while they stroke her hair. Her mouth moves like she's singing, but I can't hear her.

I dig into the laundry for the red calico dress Ida's so proud of. I'd better have it ready for her to pack, to leave for her new home.

It'll be too bad if I forget to spit on the sadiron to check its temperature or don't rub it with beeswax to make it slip smooth over the cotton. What if it gets a big scorched hole on the back, in the gathers right over her bottom, where she won't see it when she puts it on for church?

That would be an awful thing.

∞

To make sure it stayed, I touch the bow I stuck into my hair with mucilage.

Towering over me, Pastor unlocks his cracking knees and runs a finger over his moustache. You're a good girl, he says. Soon you'll be like a daughter to this new family.

Not a daughter, though, I think, only like one.

Pastor explains it as if he can hear my thoughts. Guardians, not parents, Margaret. They're looking for household help and don't mean to adopt you.

No sugar sprinkled on that, I tell myself, but I trust Pastor for telling me the truth. I ask, May I come back if they're mean to me?

Of course. You know how we treat you here. It shouldn't be much different.

Well, then. There's a usual way children are treated, except in story books, which can be better if you're a princess or worse if you're being fattened up and eaten by a witch.

But orphans always get punished, even in books. Because, like that pastor preached at the Hastings church, we are stinking maggot fodder and sinful in our hearts. That's what Luther said, and folks around here believe Luther, so we get whippings and slaps when we are bad, to scare us, and yelling and threats when we're good, to keep us that way. To keep us from going to hell, and to keep us quiet. I nod, because there's no other way.

He clears his throat and says, It won't be easy. You can't come running back for any little thing.

I never would, I promise.

Mr. Amsel is medium-sized and thin, with a nervous habit of touching his eyebrow, his chin and his cuff, one, two, three. I look him in the eye and smile. Not Mama's toothy stage smile, but a shy, quiet, good-daughter smile.

Pleased to meet you, sir.

One, two, three touches, and I almost laugh. It's a silly thing on a serious man. He's very handsome, even more than Papa was. Dark, wavy hair and deep blue eyes.

He studies me and asks, Is she healthy?

Pastor clears his throat and nods, then asks us to sit down across from his desk.

She had a mild case of influenza in October, but she's strong and intelligent. Will you see that she attends school?

Mr. Amsel balances his black felt hat on his knee and drums his fingers on the chair arm.

Pastor tells him I am good at mathematics.

Mr. Amsel pulls his pocket watch from his vest, compares it to the clock on the shelf and winds it before putting it back.

When he looks at me, I say, I like your hat.

Pastor stops talking about my spelling.

My face gets hot, for interrupting. But I keep talking, anyway, telling Mr. Amsel the red feather on his hat band is very nice. I reach out to touch it where it sticks up from the grosgrain ribbon. It's small and soft and the brightest red I've seen, redder than Christmas.

That must be some bird who lost that one, I say, and let out a little whistle before I remember girls shouldn't.

He glances at Pastor, who shrugs and smiles.

It's from a cardinal, he says. I found it on the street. And this style of hat is Italian, called a fedora.

I get a rush in my chest like a hundred wings beating. I want to say, Thank you for not being angry when I am rude, and, Thank you for telling me about your hat. But I've already blurted out enough, so I nod.

Are you a good girl, Margaret? Mr. Amsel asks. Will you work hard at our house? My wife needs a lot of help.

Yes, sir.

I wish he'd say I'm pretty, the daughter he always wanted, like a Papa in a story would say. I wish he'd promise to be kind, not to yell or hit or make me cry. Instead, he shows me tintypes of his little girl and baby boy. They have soft blond hair. When he looks down at my scuffed shoes, he must not mind, because he says, Well, fine then. Sorry to rush, but I must meet some cattle buyers. May I pick her up on Saturday?

After walking Mr. Amsel to his car, Pastor folds himself down into the chair beside me and asks, Is this what you want, child?

I want to ask if I have other choices, but I remember the red feather and say, Yes.

Pastor reaches over and touches my hair bow. He asks, Is that glue?

When I nod, Pastor shakes his head, chuckles and says, Mr. Amsel likes you, Margaret. As well he should.

Because I forget and leave the bow in my hair overnight, I have to soften the mucilage with water to untangle the matted mess. It all combs out, though, after my bath.

With only a day before my new family, I take every chance to stick my tongue out at Karl, who said a girl with hair like mine would never find a family. I'm glad he doesn't know I won't be adopted, that I'm only a hired girl.

Some of the children won't talk to me, because it's easier to pretend I'm already gone. As much as it feels warm and delicious to be chosen, it stabs not to be. I remember, but this is my turn, my happiness, and nobody gets to make me feel sorry.

I'm sweating inside my wool coat. I keep the lemon drop Pastor gave me tucked in my cheek, swallowing the sweet–sour juice, while I watch Mr. Amsel sign the guardian papers. His full name is Raeburn Elim Amsel, a storybook name if there ever was one.

Mrs. Amsel has consumption, a serious case. That's why we need your help, he explains, holding open the motor car's door. A Stoddard-Dayton Torpedo, it has fat, glossy leather seats I slide over like they're ice.

The orphans watch us from under the stone arches on the porch. Jealous. Angry. Sad. I'm terrified, but I wave at them like somebody brave and look up at the cardinal feather. Today Mr. Amsel wears a red silk to match it, in his breast pocket. That red makes me afraid and hopeful, together, it's so bloody and bright.

He tells me Mrs. Amsel's name is Florence, like the city in Italy.

Like your hat, I say.

He doesn't say what a clever girl I am, to have remembered.

Pastor told me I'll be important to this family. Important is better than unwanted, and one step closer to being loved. I have been Margaret Rose No Last Name Given since Cedric left me wrapped in a blanket under those arches I just left behind me. But when Mr. Amsel hitches the car into gear and it rolls out as smooth as butter, I decide I will be like Old Margaret in the fairy tale. I will be good enough to find and make a home of love and mercy, to be Margaret Rose Amsel.

Shivering, I wave up at the stone arches and those sad, left-behind children. With my other hand, through my coat, I feel the hard glass bottle of mucilage in my pinafore pocket.

We drive two hours to Darkwater Creek. Mr. Amsel points at the Lutheran Church and the Main Street stores. It seems like a good enough town, but no theater. He says in the summer, traveling shows and carnivals come through Red Cloud and Franklin and, if I'm good, I'll see them.

I guess from the shiny car that the Amsels have lots of money and I'm already a little proud, even though I did nothing to get it. Then, when we drive into the country to his farm and up to the house, my chest puffs up a little bigger, over a nervous stomach. I hope I know how to act in such a grand place, with its blue and rose gingerbread trim and rainbow glass windows.

Mrs. Amsel, who coughs hard into a handkerchief, talks in a high, sharp voice like a bark. She is too weak to remind me of my work, so she wrote a list for Mrs. Endicott, our English cook and housekeeper, to thumbtack on the nursery door. She says Florence told her, No exceptions.

Fourteen Rules for Margaret Rose

1. Adolph's diaper must always be dry.

2. Neither child will be left to cry.

3. Greta must not suck her thumb, or it will ruin her teeth.

4. Greta must use the toilet at 8 in the morning and every two hours after that. Adolph is to watch her, so he learns.

5. Serve meals at 8, 12, and 5 o'clock, with snacks of zwieback crackers and applesauce at 2 and 7 o'clock.

6. The children must never be spanked or yelled at.

7. Greta must always wear a clean dress and pinafore, and Adolph a clean romper.

8. Margaret will read to Greta at least twice a day.

9. Both children will nap from 2:30 until 3:30 and no longer.

10. Margaret will mop the nursery every evening, before the children go to bed at 7:30.

11. Margaret will launder the diapers and children's clothing.

12. While Margaret is at school, Mrs. Endicott will supervise feedings and naps.

13. Margaret will help Mrs. Amsel when she asks.

14. Margaret will not sass.

Margaret Will Miss One Day of School and be Whipped for Any Rule Broken!

My first day, I broke Numbers Two, Three and Eight. Then I got flustered and did a Fourteen. Mrs. Endicott whipped me four times, crying about it even when I didn't. Not getting to start school for four days hurt worse than my backside. The second week was better. I only broke Number Eleven, forgetting to iron because I was reading. One whipping and one missed day.

Since then, it's been hit and miss. One and Three vex me, and Seven is near impossible, the way those two brats spit up, dribble snot and smear their food. Adolph is cutting molars and cries over anything. Mrs. Endicott, God bless her, told me to give him ice in a rag to chew on. Greta dirties her pants on purpose, to see me whipped.

As for Fourteen, I may never get to school enough to learn my times tables.

Mrs. Endicott wipes sweat off her face, reties my pinafore and gives me a tap on my backside. The Mister is home, she says, And the Mistress told him about you yelling at Miss Greta and taking away Master Adolph's crackers. Now I suppose I'll be told to whip you again. For both our sakes, little girl, would you mind your Ps and Qs? She pooches out her lower lip like she's the one with welts under her stockings, but points to a gingersnap, steaming hot on the cookie sheet.

I pick it off, toss it hand to hand, blowing, then crunch into it. Sweet, spicy and so hot I burn my tongue. I never can wait long enough.

The bell on the kitchen wall rings from Florence's room, and my mouth goes dry around the gingery crumbs.

Mrs. Endicott sighs and waves me upstairs. Go take your medicine, she says.

I count slow, one-one-thousand for each step going up.

Mr. Amsel stands by her bed in his overcoat, his fedora in his hands. He turns and gives me a little smile and nod his wife can't see.

Florence's face is all snot and tears, red and swollen. She's pitching a real fit, today. She drives me to distraction, Florence says, waving her handkerchief at me.

Calm down, dearest, he says, reaching for her hand, but she pulls away.

Send her back. She's worse than useless, no matter how I whip her.

I clamp my teeth together to keep bad words in. Useless? I just bathed her and both children, scrubbing feet and powdering all their cracks. I hope they do send me back to the orphanage. Almost, except I like school here, when I get there. It's harder, and the teacher gives me extra work when I'm bored.

Margaret? Mr. Amsel tilts his head, not smiling now. Little girl, he says, I work hard all week and come home to chaos. What's this I hear about your bad language?

I can't tell him Florence calls me trash, not in front of her. And I did say Hell and Shit-fire, but I won't make the mistake of saying them again now. Seeing his face sag that way, because I only want to make him happy, I tell Mr. Amsel I'm sorry.

The Rules, Florence says, She has no regard for them. She despises me, too.

Mr. Amsel puts his hand on my shoulder and steers me out the door. In the hallway, where Florence can't see, he squats down in front of me, his knees cracking under his trouser creases. He sighs and swallows, rubs his fingers through his hair and turns his hat in his hands.

I was ready for a scolding, some fire and brimstone, but when he says nothing, the wind goes out of me. I apologize again.

Mr. Amsel nods and reaches into his overcoat pocket. He brings out a red, paper-wrapped candy and holds it up. I understand, he says, looking back at the doorway.

Back there where we can't see her, Florence sobs and says, Nobody cares.

Mr. Amsel gives me the candy and a sad smile, saying, Do your best, Margaret Rose, and no more bad words.

I nod, swallow the lump in my throat and unwrap the candy to eat it before Greta or Adolph can find and steal it.

The taste of cherries fills my mouth. I promise, I tell him, the hard candy clicking on my teeth.

He goes back into her room. I should go downstairs, but I stay to listen, sliding my back down the wall to sit on the floor.

Make her go, Florence cries.

The bed springs creak as Mr. Amsel sits by her and he says, Shhh.

Her sobs muffle in his shoulder as he calms her down.

You know I love only you, he says in a voice so tender, he's almost singing it.

Just go to her, Florence says. She's not using her mad, spoiled voice, though. It's deep and sad and it unlocks a door in me to things I can't remember in a shape or a sound.

I understand now. Florence is afraid. I'd be afraid, too, if I coughed up blood, but she's feeling something worse.

Go to her? Florence doesn't mean me. She must think her husband loves somebody else.

I put my head in my hands and close my eyes. I knew this feeling, before, when I was too little to know what it was. A fearsome suffering, a jealous fire in my mother, one burning so hot it could make ashes of everybody. Florence being like my mother mixes me up. What I remember and what I feel now, these chew up my belly like poison. I've got a new family, all right, not much different from my first one.

A whipping would have been better than what I understand now.

Careful not to let my shoes tap on the hardwood, I leave behind Mr. Amsel sweet-talking Florence. I should see if Greta and Adolph are awake in the nursery, but I go up the attic stairs instead.

I'm glad for my own place up here. I've got no stove, but a feather mattress on the floor, good sheets and three blankets, so if I take a flannel-wrapped brick off the coal stove, I'm warm in bed. It's quiet, though, with only rafters creaking, wind whistling and pigeons cooing in the window nooks. I do miss the orphanage girls and their sounds in the dark.

I keep my books and homework on an old chair beside my bed, like a bureau, and there's a cord with electricity, so I have a little bulb to study and read by. My three dresses hang on nails on the wall. I even have a little lock at the top of the attic stairs I can click to keep the children out. I never had my own place and it's a fine thing.

In one carton of books up here, I found *Fowles' New Easy Latin Primer*. It teaches a funny language nobody speaks, but it's a mother to other languages. It has no letter W. Latin is confusing, so I asked my teacher about declensions. She said it's not a usual question for an eight-year-old girl, but she explained well.

Trying to forget about Florence, I sit on my mattress to look at the Latin book. My teacher says I'm lucky to have a special talent to remember everything I read and with Latin, I have my own secret language. Maybe for a diary, or if I have a friend someday, we can use it for secrets. To help me feel better, I also found some little swears nobody will understand, but nothing bad enough to send me to hell. Like *puter anus*, which means rotten old woman but sounds worse. And *verres* and *clunis,* hog and buttock.

Remembering Florence's red, crying face distracts me from the Latin on the pages. I'm sorry for her and want to forgive the whippings and missed school. The Latin swears help a little, like letting steam out of my hot kettle, but I can only say them in the closet or up here. It doesn't help that Florence's little pointy teeth and long nose remind me of a fox, *vulpes*. If she looked softer, more like a rabbit, *lepus*, I'd feel more like petting her, and less like trapping her and pelting her out.

The hardest thing to forgive is as clear as the windows I wash every Saturday: Florence will never want me for her child. Her jealous heart is shut. Even for her son and daughter, she only cracks it like a window in winter, to air out the stinking loneliness. Being Mrs. Amsel's child is a sad lot in life, nothing for me to be jealous about.

Someday the whippings I take for Adolph and Greta will pass over to them, with Florence's disappointment. Like

Mrs. Endicott says about many things, That will be a rude awakening. I hate to think of it.

For now, those little children's welts and aches are mine, like in last Sunday's Bible lesson. Jesus bore the stripes of the whip for us, even when He could have said, No. Then He had to die and go to hell and get raised up again, before He got lilies and colored eggs.

I'm not sure Easter's coming soon for me. Pretty soon Adolph, who's not even two years old, will be breaking windows and stealing candy, and I'll catch heck for it. A little *vulpes* like her mother, Greta's only three, but she knows how to use the Rules against me.

It's a terrible thing, getting punished for other people's sins. Shit-fire. If I wasn't so tired, I'd make some trouble, have some fun of my own and make these welts mean something.

∞

My first train ride to Omaha was swell. With Papa all but owning the railroad, the porters Yes Sirred and No Sirred, fetching corned beef sandwiches, potato salad and my first two bottles of Dr. Pepper, the King of Beverages, ice cold.

Now for a week I been following Papa, who wants me to call him Father in front of important people, through stockyards, breweries and the Union and Burlington stations and rail yards. Men in overalls, dungarees and expensive suits treat Albert Hollingwood like an important businessman, even in Omaha.

He seems glad to have me along, but I watch myself. Father suffers no fools, and I must be quiet and smart. If I'm good on this trip, he might ask me again, so I keep a list in my head of the things I do wrong, to change.

Don't interrupt.

Don't slouch.

Don't stammer.

Don't pick at myself.

Don't burp or break wind.

Never scratch my private parts.

Father taught me some other useful lessons. For one, instead of Hello, say, Pleased to meet you, when he introduces me to somebody. Wipe off my sweaty palms before I shake hands and make my grip firm. Smile, but not like an idiot, and nod when important men speak. Even if I'm not sure what they're talking about, try to look agreeable. Figure out who controls the room and watch that person, how he does it. Smile at ladies and tip my hat, but don't gawk at their pretty parts.

Father corrects me for my own good. He also showed me how to touch, take off and hold my cap. How and when to look somebody in the eye. He tells me when it's appropriate to excuse myself for the lavatory. A few times he got angry, but he hasn't yelled at me because just being here, making money, makes him happy.

I feel nervous as if sparks crackle over my skin and tongs twist my gut, but I only vomit in private, so he doesn't hear and think I'm weak. Nothing matters more than proving to Albert Dash Hollingwood he can like and trust me. This trip will decide us. I feel it. Like he says, Nothing in life is free. I guess even a father must be earned.

The Easter Sunday gala today at Gottlieb Storz's mansion is my first big party. It started at one in the afternoon with drinks in the living rooms, around the mirrored fireplaces laid with logs nobody lights because the weather is fine. I drink bright green, fizzy punch, but the grownups all drink Storz beer. The dining room tables are heavy with platters of ham, prime rib and roasted birds, tureens brimming with soup, crocks loaded with potatoes and vegetables, and crystal bowls with fruit compotes and gelatins the colors of jewels.

After dinner, the men puff smoke rings off their cigars and sip brandy by the cold fireplaces, while the ladies disappear. I miss their gay Easter gowns and perfumes like flowers, with their flitting and coos and chirps making them seem more like birds than people. Some even had pink or blue or white feathers on their dresses, something I've never seen before. Wishing it was proper to loosen a trouser button over my bulging belly, I listen to the men mumble about brewing, banking and breeding quarter horses. I drift off to sleep on the davenport, startling awake with a drop of drool at the corner of my mouth. I brush it away with my coat sleeve, though, before Father notices.

When we thank Mr. and Mrs. Storz for a fine Easter celebration, they offer us a guest room for our last two nights in Omaha. Father accepts, and Storz sends a man to The Rome to fetch our bags.

Father is pleased, so he can talk with Mr. Storz about being partners in a brewery south of Darkwater.

By five o'clock, the Storz children, who are older than me, go off with their friends, so I'm left fiddling with my coat buttons and counting fleurs-de-lis on the fuzzy gold wallpaper. Father and Mr. Storz talk in dread tones about whether the Drys and the Suffragists will soon win prohibition. I browse the library shelves, but most of the books are in German or about philosophy, and I have ants in my pants. When I ask Father if I can play outside, he waves me away and I am free.

It's been so warm today, most of the blankety snow thawed, except for rags of it left in the buildings' shadows. Mud and little pools of water fill wherever there's no grass. I take off my wool jacket and the sweat chills on my back where my shirt's soaked through. Instead of taking my jacket back inside, where Father might keep me, I drape it over my arm and loosen my collar. The breeze ruffles my hair, and I feel like a nine-year-old boy, not a small businessman. I don't have a plan and nobody's watching me, so I follow the sidewalk west to where the sun is low, streaming rays under a thick line of clouds.

Counting a few blocks to mark my way back, I turn north, gawking at the great houses, each one topping its own proud hill above the street. Wrap-around porches, tiled gables and round, cone-roofed towers pull me along to see the next building. Some houses, like ours and the Storzes's, have two-story carriage houses. Others have glass greenhouses or conservatories tucked behind and their walls glint in the falling sunlight. Even the smaller homes, finished with siding and brick, sit high on well-groomed lawns.

I breathe in the scent of the warm earth, a soup of mud and worms and roots waking up after the winter, with chimney smoke and burned gasoline like salt. Timing my chance, I dash through traffic across Dodge Street, the oo-gah of a car horn and a driver's shout making my heart pound. Maybe one day Father will tire of Darkwater Creek. We could live in Omaha, where people move with noise and purpose, always set on the next thing and hell-bent to make it better than the last. I could bring it up in a grown-up way, suggesting he could make more money here. For now, though, this is my adventure, one hour in the city for myself. A voice in my head tells me I'll be punished for leaving the Storzes' property, but I shrug it away.

Scott Joplin's Swipesy Cakewalk ragtime melody spills out of a red stone house. It's a jolly tune I've been trying to teach myself on our piano, and hearing it, I feel at home.

Beside me, a stiff, cooler wind from the east rattles tree branches like drumsticks, then doubles back, spinning some sun-dried, half-rotted leaves off the lawn to circle like a playground game. Chilled, I pull on my jacket and walk faster. Up ahead, one house looks like a castle, its pale stone walls topped with those toothy crenellations and a tower with eight sides. I picture knights and horses just as a flock of sparrows panic-flutters up in front of me. The wind shifts hard, tossing those birds like grain from a shovel and lifting me in my shoes.

Silence, like a long deep breath going in, makes the hair stand up on my neck. Then a grinding roar as the sky shifts its center, the earth cringes and hell cuts loose.

I turn to face the noise. Clouds have been sneaking up behind me, boiling out of the southwest, fast and black, spilling onto the ground in a wide, hungry ink stain that blots out the low sun. My coat whips back around me and I shield my eyes. I can't name it. It's bigger than words. Flecks swirl

44

around the dark center, pulled in and tossed out, only to get sucked in again.

That voice, the one that warned me before, gets louder, like from outside my head, but I don't see anybody near enough to shout over the wind. Like a braking locomotive, it shrieks, Jack, it's because of you!

My hot piss dribbles down my leg. Terror tells me to run but I squat down on the sidewalk. The wind lifts a kid's wooden wagon from a lawn and rolls it end over end, like a matchbox. A motor car speeds north. I wave to hail it, but the driver leans toward the windshield, determined and blind. A gardener's shed roof lifts off, hovers and spins like a platter to crash into the side of that motor car, making it snake back and forth like the crazy one in the silent picture Father took me to, 'til the car spills over and the driver sprawls out like a stuffed monkey toy.

Under the howling, no single thing outside my head keeps a sound of its own, but everything's swallowed whole into a force so loud, it seems a magnificent silence. Tree trunks break off or come up by the roots and skid across the street. Houses, motor cars, junk I can't name—pieces of everything fly.

I duck and cover my head and that voice—not a man's and not a woman's, but maybe the devil's own—howls that this is the end of me. That I'm so bad, I had this coming for a long time.

Out of all the terrible things, the voice scares me most and shakes me loose.

I get up off the sidewalk and run for the castle, dashing across its soggy lawn. I break through rose hedges as branches snap off trees and bits of metal slice my sleeves like knives. A brick slams into my ribs. A cat falls from the sky and I feel it give, sickeningly soft under my shoe.

As a bent metal chair spins past my head, I throw myself on the ground. The sky charcoals, then greens into an eerie night and the tempest rolls me like a tumbleweed against the castle's foundation. I dig my left-hand fingers into the ground, then scrape them raw over the limestone wall, but my right arm is twisted at a crazy angle and won't mind.

Mud fills my mouth and that voice says, Why won't you just die?

I choke, and the storm sucks my breath into the pitch of its own scream.

I wake with the sun streaming, bitter medicine in my mouth and a waterfall of piano music from downstairs. Not a happy ragtime melody, but something like Chopin or Bach. The piano tones bring the storm back to me, and I bolt from the bed before noticing my shoulder's in a sling. My head's pounding and I see spots. A big, wide woman opens the bedroom door and gasps, almost dropping her tray.

You should be in bed, she scolds, right before I faint.

The Omaha Easter Tornado of March 23, 1913 was only one of the twisters that broke eastern Nebraska that night. It cut a half-mile-wide path through Omaha and killed about 150 people. The *Omaha Bee* front page says 240 people were injured. I don't know if they counted me, but I got a hard knock on my head, a dislocated, tore-up shoulder and a busted arm. Thousands of people are homeless. Eleven churches and eight schools are wrecked. The storm they call

The Devil Cloud blew a week-old baby out of her bedridden mother's arms into thin air, smashed a convent, flipped a streetcar and collapsed a pool hall on fourteen Colored folks who were only having fun. I guess nobody was safe.

All because of wind and rain.

That house the twister threw me up against, Joslyn Castle, has much worse damage than Mr. Storz's house. A policeman found me next to a broken stone wall, but it took Father a day to find me at Methodist Hospital. He checked me out of there and ever since, Mr. Storz's doctor is caring for me. He said with a head injury like mine, I may not be thinking right for a while, but he says I'm still better at math than he is. I can go back to school in a few weeks. As long as the kids get to see my cast.

Father and I stay in the Storz mansion another week, 'til I can travel.

Every minute I'm awake, I feel guilty and afraid. The voice tells me I brought this disaster on everybody. It warns and curses and blames me—for killing my mother, disobeying my father and smooshing that cat in the storm. For thinking I was smart enough to go walking in Omaha on my own, then not running to save the man in the storm-crashed motor car. For delaying Father's return to Darkwater Creek, and—worst of all—ruining his partnership with Mr. Storz, because we went from being delightful houseguests to burdens who won't leave. That one I know isn't true, because those two men are almost best friends by now, with Father spending whole days at the Storz Brewery. But I can't win arguing with the voice, and it never tires of accusing me.

I don't tell anyone about it, not even the doctor when he asks if I see, hear or think anything strange since the

47

bump on my head. I know it's crazy, to hear a voice with no person behind it, and I don't want to end up in a madhouse.

So I tell Father I'm better every day. It makes him smile.

My legs dangle out the window. I must be some six feet off the ground but I let go of the windowsill. My feet hit the packed dirt with a whump that shoots pain up my shinbones. Over me hangs a full moon but shredded clouds filter the light, a good thing. I have enough light to see by and enough shadow to hide in, running away.

It's a short dash to the apple grove. If the Genoa school wanted to keep me, they shoulda built a fence. Oklahoma didn't hold me, and this one can't neither, even by telling me they shoot bad little Indians who run away. I'm Kuruk, the Medicine Bear, the name my Grandfather Burnt Wolf gave me, and bullets will pass through me. Burnt Wolf would know how to get me a vision but sickness in his chest took him last year, while I was in that Oklahoma prison they call a school. When I was home, he taught me the meanings of some things—my name, the Ghost Dance, medicine bundles and hand games. Stories, too. I hope he taught me enough to keep me a real Pawnee.

This time I'm not gonna run home. The Indian agent or maybe even Crooked Walk would send me back or to some other White-run school. After my mother died, he hardly talked to me but I don't hate him, because his spirit broke before I was born. Burnt Wolf said so, that his son has breath going in and out but isn't living because the Whites made him like a rock in the ground. They tried to make me one by giving me the name Peter. I'll always be Kuruk Sky Seeing, the Medicine Bear.

They took my bear claw, the one on a leather thong that Grandfather gave me but I stole it back from where they hid it in a teacher's desk. It thumps up and down on my chest now, keeping time with my feet while I run.

A breeze tickles my bald head where they shaved it so I scratch my healing louse bites. I never had lice before this school and now I got no hair. A few drops of rain tap my scalp and make me shiver. Remembering Burnt Wolf's voice, I sing,

> *The wise man taught me songs,*
> *Five songs for making it rain.*
> *The first calls down cloud or mist,*
> *The second snow.*
> *The third inspires a shower and*
> *The fourth a lightning storm.*
> *But the fifth, when the wise man sings it, clears the sky.*
> *The fifth one clears the sky.*

The words are in Burnt Wolf's voice, from a Ghost Dance ceremony but the tune is mine, coming out of me like that moonlight through the smudgy clouds. Careful to leave no tracks, I jump over bare ground and only set my feet on brown grass or weeds. After an hour or so, the pattering rain slows and stops and the clouds thin to let moonlight spill down the sky, across the broken-stalk cornfields and dry-weed pastures. It lights a road ahead where there was none before but I still stumble, weak from my heart racing and feet flying over the ground. I didn't sleep last night. This day was a long one, too, climbing trees to harvest apples and carrying bushels to the storehouse. Juice from the apples clings to my fingers, sticky and sweet.

I'm walking half-asleep but I tell my feet to keep going. I stop when the moon and stars mirror off the Loup River. It's more beautiful against the dark land than the school girls' ribbons around their shining black hair and on its bank there's the log I need to hide me from travelers on the road.

Behind that log in the honey-smelling grass, watching the moon fall, I remember Grandfather telling me about the Sioux attacking his own Pawnee grandfather, killing him in a raid on the Loup Fork of the Platte. Is my great-great grandfather, dead by a Sioux arrow, watching me now? I'm not sure the dead can see anybody from where they are. It might only trouble them, if they can.

Then I remember a story my grandfather heard from White-Sun about Coyote and the Rolling Skull. Because it's dark, I try not to think about the skull on the ground and how when Coyote made it angry, it chased him. Because I'm hungry, though, Coyote's song sings in me,

What a fine place this is;
I wish I could run the buffalo around;
Thus I might get something to eat.
The song makes me hungrier so I count stars.

I only wanted to sleep for an hour but the sun don't wake me until dawn. Feeling morning on my face, I startle, feeling guilty until I remember why I ran away, to keep my name. Scooping up river water into my hand to drink, I decide to wait to eat the hard bread in my jacket pocket. My stomach might sleep a while longer, if I start walking.

The boys in the school, the ones who ran away before and got caught, told me if I angle about two and a half miles east after the Loup and fully eight miles south from Genoa, I'll come to the Platte. At the Silver Creek Station on the Union Pacific line, I can hop a freight car headed southwest to Grand Island, then hightail it as far as Denver but they said I better watch out because the dicks, bulls and brakemen at Silver Creek and Grand Island are wise to Indian runaways. Some will rough you up pretty bad. I figure it's worth the risk to jump a train even with the stories of kids getting crushed between the iron wheels and rails, because winter is coming and it's too far to walk to anywhere from Genoa. I decided on Grand Island, to save the mountains for later. I saw that city on my way to Genoa and it seems big enough to get lost in. I don't expect to blend in easy, in a White town. If I don't keep my head down, I'll be back at school, locked up in that apple storehouse until I learn some lesson or other.

My growling stomach nearly does me in. My second day off the boxcar in Grand Island, I pinch some crackers from a barrel in a general store and a policeman chases me for three blocks before puffing to a stop, yelling, Confounded Injun.

That same afternoon, I beg a ride on a trapper's wagon going south, out of the city. Joe Chapman turns out to be Cherokee. When I say I'm Pawnee, he scratches his head up under his hat and says, Close enough.

Darkwater Creek, a village south of Hastings, is where he's going. His cousin makes a living there digging privies and ditches for sewer pipes.

White men don't mind what color of man takes care of their shit, Joe explains. But if an Indian goes near their food, they get touchy.

From what happened when I put my hand in that cracker barrel, I take Joe at his word.

Traveling with Joe, I find even though the only thing the same between us is our skin color, Whites figure we're related. This is a good thing for me, looking like I belong to somebody older. And even though a White woulda asked everything about me the first mile, Joe don't ask me nothing.

He tells me stories. One is about a dog and a flood. Another is about a Cherokee who got run down in the Georgia forest by some U.S. Army soldiers on horseback. They tried to take his scalp but they were so clumsy, they only got part of it. They left him for dead but he crawled home, ten miles. His wife screamed and wouldn't let him in their log cabin because he looked terrible, with his head bleeding and brains running out.

I tell Joe that's a great story. He swears it's true.

Joe shares his bread and cheese and I use my slingshot to kill a squirrel or rabbits for our suppers. Joe shows me a better way to skin them, then trades some of last season's raccoon and rabbit pelts off his wagon for coffee and eggs. I get so I'm not looking back over my shoulder much. By the time we get to Darkwater Creek, I'm not afraid of Genoa coming after me.

Joe's cousin isn't glad to see him. With winter coming, he's got no work and his wife is pregnant with their fifth child. He feeds us because you don't say no to family but even I can see they don't got much to share. Joe don't mind. You don't want to dig holes for your bread, anyway, he says. It'll make your back crooked and you'll be poor like my cousin.

When his cousin points us to a hunting shanty by the Republican River, Joe decides to set up house there for the winter, to trap beaver. He tells me to ask around town. You're a strong boy, he says. Somebody might put you to work, if you're eager.

Remembering what Joe said about White men and their food, I pass by the hotel, cafés and grocer and ask for work first at a sawmill where they say No, then with a blacksmith named Frank Burgess. The blacksmith says I'm scrawny but he'll give me a try and if I keep the fire hot, I'll get me one meal and twenty-five cents a day.

Hauling coal and manning a bellows make me strong and the blacksmith's wife is a good cook so I'm happy. I can picture being a blacksmith, myself. I buy me some oats and bacon each week and cook them over the fire. Without anybody asking, I start mucking out stalls and feeding and grooming the horses in the back and Burgess offers me a place to sleep in the stable. He gives me ten more cents a day when he's got more than five horses in the stalls.

I visit Joe for a few weeks and he tells me stories but he paces the room, restless under a roof. One night, he shows me what's under his bandanna and cowboy hat, a long scar and a white spot of his skull showing through his hair. He lets me touch the bone.

I figure it wasn't some story Joe made up after all.

He gives me a cowboy hat like his, only mine is fancy with a red leather band that holds a chunk of turquoise. He says a wise man keeps his head covered. The hat's too big, falling down over my eyebrows but Joe says I'll grow into it.

The most beautiful thing anybody ever gave me and it's from a Cherokee.

But one day I find the shanty cleaned out. Seems he couldn't stand the walls another day. He left me bad dreams about scalps and bone and missing him is like the wind blowing through me. He didn't owe me anything but I wish he'da said goodbye. I didn't say goodbye to anybody at Genoa neither. Maybe that's why I don't remember a single face.

Leaving the shanty, I cross the river bridge to a thicket on the south bank. The trees lost their leaves and up about twenty feet, in one of the older cottonwoods, I spy a box, maybe a hunter's blind. But there's no ladder, no obvious way to get up there. I come back every few weeks during the winter but never see no tracks in the snow but mine. If I could build me a ladder, I'd see what's in there. I'll wait until spring, maybe bind one together with saplings and strips of cloth.

It's a warm winter by Frank's forge, eating Mrs. Burgess's good stew and bread at noon in my stable. She don't like me sitting by their fire but she don't begrudge me the food neither, even if I ask for seconds. She's grumpy the same to everybody and it don't seem she specially minds me being Indian, maybe because the forge done burned her husband almost as dark as me.

That policeman chasing me through Grand Island made an honest man out of me so I only go into shops when I'm gonna buy. I don't touch, just point and show my money. I been growing out of my clothes and it takes all I can save for new trousers and shirts. Shoes are the most dear—more than a dollar a pair—so I eat more oats and less bacon for breakfast for a while. It wears through shoes faster and takes a warmer coat but I love tracking and trapping beaver, foxes and rabbits the way old Joe taught me. I trade the furs for more bacon and from a traveling salesman I also got me a yellow stereoscope card with two pictures of a Head Chief of the Pawnee, Peter La Cherre. I tacked it up on the wall by my blankets to put me in mind of my grandfather. Knowing there was a chief the name of Peter makes me feel not as bad about the name but I know I'm Kuruk. I'll fight any man says I'm not.

By snow melt in April, I'm so changed none of the teachers at Genoa would know me by Peter or any other name. My wrists stick way out of my coat sleeves and my toes are curled, the tops hammering their way through my boots, so sore I got to rub them at night. I'm not eleven yet but I'm growing into myself, now I got no Whites telling me how to talk or read. At night, I sing the horses to sleep with my grandfather's songs and tell myself his stories, and Joe's, too, to never forget my truth. When I get lonesome, I go back to that minute when I found Joe's shanty cleaned out. I got no call to feel sorry and I don't need anybody.

Leaning down to reset a sprung trap, I hear a thump and clatter. Who got so close without snapping twigs or breaking through the brush? Then I see there's somebody up in that box I been watching all winter. One square window's opened and a shadow-face looks out that side.

I shift the dead rabbits up over my shoulder and turn to leave. It could be a hunter or somebody who owns this land. I duck behind a white-blooming chokecherry.

Wait!

It's a kid's voice but I pretend not to hear until I feel something tap my shoulder. He musta throwed an acorn down at me. Looking through the branches, I see the shadow in the window brighten up into a boy's grin.

Hey! You a real Indian?

I step into the sunlight, scowl and pull out the skinning knife from my belt. I been caught off guard, got beat up plenty of times by White boys trying to prove how tough they are. It's not gonna happen today.

His smile goes flat and he bites his lip. You been hunting, he says.

I nod, not sure why I don't walk away. The blood dripping off my rabbits taps the half-rotted leaves behind my boots.

You want something?

He shrugs. I'm Jack, he says, leaning out the window.

I don't say it, but I don't care what his name is. He's got a good haircut and a new blue shirt and, for sure, supper waiting on the table at home.

I saw you before, he says. You bought a half pound of bacon and a pound of cheese at Green's.

I sigh and tuck my knife away. This one's not dangerous. He could give me a headache with all his talking, though.

Yeah, I been known to eat when I can.

He studies me. You hungry now?

You got no call to pity me.

Pity? You're the fiercest fellow I've ever seen. I'm hoping you don't decide to skin me. He laughs, then, and I gotta smile. He don't seem like those other boys at all.

What's your name?

Kuruk.

Damn, a real Indian name.

I shrug.

Well, I'm a real White boy, so we've got ourselves a standoff. Terms of peace?

I shake my head. Treaties don't work out for us.

You got a point. Come on up. I'll take my chances.

He ducks inside, a trap door opens in the floor and a rope ladder drops through.

I sling my bloody rabbits over a low branch and climb.

Nicer than the corner of the stable where I live, the tree fort has an old rug on the floor, packing-crate furniture and bookshelves nailed to the wall. With shuttered windows open to the breeze, it's dry and cool. Jack points to a crate and I sit down.

This is nice, I tell him. I saw it last fall but couldn't tell how to get up here.

I shimmy up the near tree and cross over on a branch to climb in that hinged window there. The rope ladder's for guests, and you're the first one.

It's strange, a White boy with no friends in your fort. Most of you travel in packs.

He shrugs and drags over another crate to sit on.

You built this yourself? How'd you get all the wood up here?

Ropes and pulleys. It took me all last summer, but she's solid. Jack stomps on the floorboards to prove it, and nothing shakes.

I could live in a place like this.

I thought about it, he says, but it gets cold in winter. I got a little gas burner to heat up water and food, but enough flame to keep it warm could burn the place down.

You live in Darkwater?

He nods, thrusts out his hand and says, Jack Hollingwood.

I heard that name before. His father's a big man in town. Kuruk Sky Seeing, I tell him and we shake.

That's the best name I ever heard, Jack says, whistling. Did you make it up?

My grandfather gave it to me.

My grandfather's in Chicago. He only ever gave me a bicycle. You Cherokee?

Pawnee.

Why aren't you on a reservation?

I shrug and say, You ask a lot of questions.

Because I'm a scientist. These are my weather, chemistry and geology books.

I nod like I could read them, then look away to show I don't want to.

I never saw you in school.

Don't you know? They don't let Indians in White schools.

Jack's eyebrows squish down and his lips twist off to the side while he's thinking.

I sometimes wish I didn't have to go, he says. My teacher's an old bat, hounding me all the time. You sure have lots of red marks on your hands. Burns?

I work at the blacksmith's. The sparks get me.

I don't tell him when I forget things, Frank presses the glowing heel of a horseshoe on my back, where my shirt covers it.

You look strong. You get to pound any hot iron?

I work some horseshoe nails and barrel straps.

He nods and says, I wish I could do something useful like that. He reaches over for a tin of meat and an opener and asks, You hungry?

I tasted tinned meat before so I offer my rabbits instead.

We roast meat under that box in the tree, frying his potatoes in lard and boiling coffee over an open fire. When the sun starts to set, I roll up the pelt and Jack makes me promise to come back. Strange as it seems, looks like I got me a White boy for a friend.

Our one-room Country School Number 5 lights up like a torch the first week in April, shooting sparks at the moon. Folks say Gypsies, driven up from the Republican by the rain and high water, left a cooking fire smoldering in there. I suspect one of the eighth-grade bad boys, Eddie Reynolds, who failed his mathematics exam and swore at the teacher, set it out of spite. *Malignitas.* By the time the brigade arrives, the fire's burned up any proof along with desks, books and chalk, like sinners in hell.

For one sweet night, forty children dream of early summer recess, but to our dismay, the Darkwater Creek Town Council and School Board rise to do their duty. The next day, they divide us like sheep and goats among the town schools. Hopes float away, as light as the ashes of our primers over charcoal.

I find reason to be glad for the smarter teachers, newer books and big maps in the town schools. Those kids at Darkwater Creek School Number 1 are mean to country kids, but I learned how to fight when I was an orphan with the Germans, and Florence toughened me some more. On Main Street, Wednesday night, the town kids told us country brats to keep our cowshitty shoes and bean-fed farts out of Number 1. Three boys got into a tussle, but nothing came of it but a bloody nose.

We kids will have a little trouble. Our parents shun the ones they don't like, but we carry what they say and believe into one little schoolroom. It takes some teasing, tough talk, shoving and rolling in the dirt for us to sort out friends and enemies, but it should settle down soon.

Darkwater has maybe five hundred souls, with each one falling on one side of the line or the other, town or country. Even money, with its power, only smudges that line. My guardian, Raeburn Amsel, is wealthy, but lives outside the town limits, so his wife is not welcome with the town ladies for tea and whist. This, and Greta starting first grade this fall, keeps Mrs. Amsel begging her husband to build a new house in town.

Until then, I am a country kid. What will never change is my being a charity case with no last name, a servant with no parents I can prove. An orphan, and some people even call me a bastard.

Our teachers tell us in America by right we are all free and equal, but that's a lie. In my school, we are children of farmers, cattlemen, grocers, cigar rollers, brewers, businessmen, hotel keepers and tavern owners. We get along, mostly, and if I was born an Amsel, I might fit in.

The kids born to bankers, doctors, dentists and railroad executives keep to themselves, with their money.

I am down the scale with the immigrants just off the boat—three factory-working Irish and fifteen sharecropping Poles and Czechs who struggle to learn English—even though I'm learning Latin, memorized *Luther's Small Catechism* in German and English and spell, write and read better than any kid my age. Not to mention my arithmetic and science. But each is born into her place, *status quo*.

I'm not sure what my place is, except to be alone. I tried making friends with girls in my class. They called me a Gypsy and said to stay with my own kind. Before that, seeing myself in the mirror, I felt good enough. Now I wonder if there's something in me I should fear. Anyway, I'm done with little girls. They can have their embroidery circles, tea parties and pasty-faced dolls. I'll play with the boys, sticks and hoops, and baseball. They say I have a good arm.

I think about the Coloreds who live in New Eden, kept in a separate place because they're dark. They work as porters on the trains or as maids in the rich houses. I never saw it, but I heard some have their own shops in their little village, and while they are Christian people, they are not welcome in our churches, businesses or schools. I feel sad about this. We worked with musicians and dancers with white, black and brown skins in vaudeville, and my dear Cedric was like family. I remember him still. *Memini.* He taught me to sing, dance and even print my name. The New Eden folks have their own church but no school I've heard about. They either don't know how to read and write or, like Cedric, they're too smart to let on that they do.

I overheard it in Darkwater that nothing's more dangerous than an Educated Nigger. Then somebody said the same about an Educated Woman, so there you have it, one kind of dangerous I can be.

On my first day in my fifth- and sixth-grades classroom at Number 1, from my seat in the back row I notice that boy from the orphanage Christmas party. It's been almost four years, but his back cowlick is trimmed the same. From the curve of his blonde eyebrows and the slow blink of his blue eyes, I know he's that boy, and here he's been, all along.

He pays me no mind, but seeing him lights me up and gets me through the insults and pokes in the ribs that are my lot the first week. We country kids band together to ignore our tormentors. The disappointed town kids decide to ignore us back. It's a shaky truce, but it holds, with only a few boys shoving and scuffling on the playground. After all, the country school fire was rotten luck, nobody's fault, except maybe Eddie Reynolds, who quit school anyway.

That handsome Jack Hollingwood doesn't say much to the other children either, except for one dark-haired boy named George Dakin, who's a whiz at math. Jack finishes his lessons early. He gets high marks in science, but only asks questions about the weather, sun or moon. They are the kind of questions that tell instead of ask and make the teacher smile. When he writes on the board, his multiplication and division are perfect, while his cursive Ms are exact, upside down Ws, and I practice to make mine the same. Sometimes he brings leather-bound books from home. I figure, with his father being the richest in town, he has a library bigger than our school. When I think about it, my admiring turns a little bit to hating. It seems unfair that he was born into plenty.

The Amsels, though they could afford a library, keep the only old books they have up with me in the attic, to save the shelves for china bowls, porcelain dogs and Tiffany lamps. A Bible, that Catechism and a German *Augsburg Confession* stack on the sideboard. Mr. Amsel leaves railroad, cattlemen's and agriculture magazines on the sitting room side tables, and Mrs. Amsel dog-cars the Scars and Roebuck and Montgomery Ward catalogs, wishing for whatever Green's General Store won't stock. She keeps all back issues of *Rawleigh's Almanac, CookBook and Medical Guides*, too, and I learn about medicine from these, dosing Greta and Adolph when Mrs. Amsel says, with their Cod Liver Oil and Anti-Pain Oil. I make little notes about which ones work and imagine being a doctor. Of course, as far as I know, they don't let women do that. Shit-fire, here in Nebraska they won't even let us vote, but not even ten miles from here, Kansas allows it. It gives me some hope for what I could become.

Florence's door slams behind me and I stand in the hallway with my arms held out, piss soaking my dress and the fumes burning my eyes. Mrs. Endicott mutters against Mrs. Amsel, but pulls me to the back door, like she's been told.

I'm sorry, Margaret, I am, she says. It's not right, but you're safer outside, anyway.

The old woman blinks back tears, from sympathy or because of my smell, I don't know, then pushes me out and clicks the door behind me.

A fine how-do-you-do but at least I'm out back, sheltered by the filling-in-green lilacs and honeysuckle hedges, instead of in sight of the road. I hold my dress away from my skin and gag. Mrs. Endicott has no clothes drying on the line, so I pump a bucket of water and try to rinse my skirt. It's no use. No school, stinking this way, with today's lesson about China. The Great Wall, pointy hats, rice and chopsticks and now I'll miss it because of Florence's tantrum.

Did she find out about the folded ribbon of hard candy Mr. Amsel gave me when he got back from Chicago? He forgot to bring anything for his children, and Florence cried for an hour about somebody called Her and That Other One, keeping the whole house awake. Whatever set her off, I stink like a privy. I wait for a while for Mrs. Endicott to bring me a clean dress, but Florence keeps yelling upstairs. I bet she forgot.

The sun climbs and warms my skin, softening down the goose bumps that purple my arms and legs. I head east along the road next to the cattle yard. Trees and shrubs stand in a line and I hide behind them from wagons or motor cars passing, some carrying my classmates into town. I'm not going anywhere in particular, just away from Florence.

I stand in the grass, stinking and itching. Shit-fire, now what do I do? I say it so many times it starts to sound like a song. Shit-fire, shit-fire, what do I do?

He sees me before I hear him, too late for me to step behind the elderberry. It's that Indian, the only one in town. He always wears a cowboy hat and a red bandanna tied around his head or his neck and works for the blacksmith. I've never talked to him because he doesn't go to school and runs off whenever you get close to him. Everybody knows Indian children go to special schools or stay on reservations, but he's here. What does he do all day, without lessons or a teacher telling him what to think? He's handsome with high, wide cheekbones and a straight long nose, bright black eyes, brown skin and glossy, blue-black hair. He walks with one hand in his pocket and his face tilted up to the sun. His clothes are clean, which would disagree with Florence, who can't say the word Indian without saying *dirty* first.

He smiles, and we look each other up and down. If he sees my stained clothes or smells me, he doesn't let on.

You live out that way? I ask, tipping my head to the west, even though I know he doesn't.

He shakes his head and hoists a knapsack higher on his shoulder.

The blacksmith sent me, he says, to get some broken tools from Carl Meyer. Aren't you late for school?

I shrug. Can't go today. No clean clothes.

He steps nearer and I hold up both hands.

Somebody spilled on me, and I stink to high heaven. You best stay back, or be sick.

That's a fix you're in.

I can't get a clean dress while they're angry in the house.

I feel disloyal saying that much. Florence is a little insane, I'm sure, but it's not a thing to talk about. Mr. Amsel says family secrets should stay in the family. I like to think I'm family, so I oblige him.

Walk with me into town.

You have a dress I can wear?

We'll think of something. Or you can stand behind that bush all day.

You stay on the other side of the road, where you can't smell me.

I sleep with horses. I guess I can stand you.

I wish I smelled like a horse today, I tell him and cross to the far side of the road.

Twice, when wagons roll past, I duck into the ditch. In town, the Indian boy named Kuruk walks me to the stables, where he lives.

Under the soft, cool light of the horse barn, I feel better. He shows me a stall and gives me a bucket of water, a sliver of soap and a rag.

Wash up, he tells me, and drop your dress over the edge of the stall. Change into these.

He walks out to give me privacy while I wash. The trousers feel strange, chafing my thighs, and it's odd to wear a boy's clothes. I feel like a different person. I come out and find him sitting on an overturned bucket.

You still look like a girl, he says.

While I wash out my dress and pinafore, I ask him why he's helping me.

I can't let you stink up the town, he says, reaching over to flick one of my curls. I got to live here.

When he has to take the tools to the blacksmith, I ask if he has any books for me to read while I wait for my clothes to dry.

He shakes his head and says he doesn't read.

I laugh because he must be joking, but he's not. My cheeks get red and hot.

It's okay, I tell him, You can't help it.

He sticks out his chin and says, I don't want to, either. It's a White habit, like feeling sorry for people.

He leaves then, sliding and slamming shut the stable door.

I never even got any breakfast, and already I've got two people upset with me.

After petting the four horses and snooping around Kuruk's sleeping corner, I get tired of waiting for him. I find an old jacket, tuck my hair up under a cap and look at my reflection in a water trough outside. With a little dirt rubbed on my face, I figure I'll pass for a boy.

On Main Street, I follow a family of dark-haired children and their parents into the new mercantile, as if I belong.

The store smells of fresh-cut pine. The window glass lets in the full sun to sparkle on candy jars and crystal lamps. In the back, bookshelves climb to the ceiling and, on a low shelf, I spy a picture book of children's poems. Paging through, I fall into the colorful prints. The rhymes bounce in my head like a horse trotting. I can't put it back on the shelf. It's too beautiful to leave behind, so I tuck it in a pocket.

Kuruk's hand on my arm startles me.

What are you doing? he whispers. They'll throw you in jail.

Nothing!

You're stealing.

I'm not. I only want to hold it.

I feel choky, like I might cry, but I can't let him see. Acting tough, I swear all the swears I know—English, German and Latin ones. Then I run outside, but he's close behind, grabbing at my sleeve. To get away from what he knows about me, I dash into the street without looking.

My heart pounds so loud I don't hear the motor car coming up on me, grinding and squealing its brakes. Something hits me hard, knocks me forward, then holds on and rolls me into the dirt. My head hits the ground.

Kuruk keeps his arms around me until I wiggle loose.

People gather around, picking us up, feeling for broken bones and whapping the dust out of our clothes.

Are you alright?

What a terrible thing. You boys could've been killed.

Did you see it? The Indian boy saved his life.

People poke and study me like I'm a bug with a pin through it. Before they recognize me, I break away and run, leaving Kuruk the Hero behind.

Back at the stables, I strip off the trousers and shirt and wiggle into my damp dress. I hurt from being tackled, I have a long scrape on my arm and I keep seeing that motor car bearing down on me. Rinsing my face and arms in the water trough, I try to calm down, but my head throbs and my hands shake. I remember the little book and hope I didn't lose it. It's still in the coat pocket. Sitting on a hay bale, I study its little watercolor pictures of lords and ladies, castles and fairies. Since I almost died for them, they don't seem so special.

Kuruk walks in and calls me a fool.

I turn my face away. If my knees weren't shaking, I'd get up and run home.

What if you got caught or killed? He balls his hands up in fists and glares at me.

Maybe that would be better, I say, but then hate myself more for sounding pathetic.

Keep trying. You're getting close.

Well, you're the big hero now.

Why were you stealing, anyway? You live in a big house with rich parents. You got everything.

I'm nobody's daughter. Only a servant. And the book was perfect, the shapes of the letters and the sounds of the rhymes . . .

He's quiet, glaring at me, and even though it's mean I tell him, But you can't read so you wouldn't understand.

I lose my words and cover my eyes with my hands.

He sits down beside me and puts a hand on my shoulder. It feels warm through my damp calico.

I guess I wouldn't, he says. But you coulda died.

He catches his breath in something like a sob and asks, Did you like being a boy?

It was better.

I wish I was a girl, he says. Working in the house, wearing soft clothes. Everybody loves and coddles girls, and pretty ones like you don't need to work hard. You shouldn't feel sorry for yourself.

I spread my blistered hands in front of his face. Then I reach back to unbutton my dress enough to show the welts on my back. I show him the same on my lower legs and ask, I'm coddled?

He sets his jaw, blushes and looks away.

I blush, too. I shouldn't have undone my dress in front of a boy, but he made me mad.

He rolls up his sleeves, pulls his collar away from his neck and raises his shirt tail to show me festering, blistered and scarred humps of burns.

See? I get some when I stand close to stir the coals. The others I get from Frank when he drinks too much. They get infected and I get fevers, but nobody cares.

I don't want to look at them, but I do. I'm sorry, I tell him. He reminded me of something, and I sing that song for him, about Nobody.

He smiles when I'm done and says, I guess we both got a hard time of it.

I guess so.

69

When I struggle to button up my dress, he helps me. I tell him I didn't really want the book, I only wanted that life, to be a kid in a story.

Kuruk rolls down his cuffs and buttons them. His voice gets hard again.

You got to be strong, he says, to take care of yourself. Being a child is a terrible thing. Grow up as fast as you can.

His eyes squint and he takes a deep breath, staring away from me. I thought he was a child when I first saw him, but he's like a little man, tough and mean.

Go home, little White Girl, he says, so I do.

Nobody notices when I sneak into the house, or hears when I click open the hall closet for the red-and-gold tin and some clean cloths. After raiding the pantry, I walk back to town. I feel invisible and strong.

The sun is as low as a glaring eye before Kuruk comes back to the horse stall he calls home. When he slumps down on the blanket-covered hay beside me, I take his arm and roll up his sleeve to see the new burns. He lets me. I scoop salve out of the tin and rub it over the blisters. He bites his lip and looks away until after I wrap gauze around his arm. Then I tend the other arm, his hands and his back. The ones there, even the scars, look like circles and curves, a cruel design. I blink my tears back to be tough for Kuruk.

There, I say.

He nods and puts one arm around me, so I lean on him. He strokes the calluses on my palms and fingertips. We sit that way, smelling the sweet hay and manure, and listening to the horses who nicker and stamp in their stalls as their edges seem to dissolve in the dark. When the moon silvers through the stable window, I bring out the stolen loaf of bread and break it for us.

Regal Quoyle rules Hollingwood's town from his rolling chair in clear sight of the window, thrusting his chin to egg on all comers. From the corner of his eye, he studies Elsiver Dietz, huddled on that wooden stool in the corner like a dense schoolboy under a dunce cap, whittling a stick. Regal grinds his teeth. Why that man won't sit in a regular chair is beyond him. He suspects Dietz likes to aggravate him and doesn't have the guts to do it directly, so he behaves in an ignorant and undignified fashion. Knowing, of course, how Quoyle values dignity and refinement. Elsiver Dietz is Quoyle's man, but Quoyle knows better than to altogether trust anyone, especially someone weaker than himself.

Dietz, like most common men in Darkwater, drags his knuckles in a Socratic Cave of Ignorance, blind to higher Ideals. Quoyle knows he must be tolerant, as so many are blind and so few fit to rule. Even Hollingwood, the high and mighty one, loses sight of Ideals while caught up in his run for money, and when he sees that, Quoyle pictures himself a more worthy hero, the good leader elected by the people of Darkwater Creek. Yet he remains loyal to Hollingwood for now, even as mundane duties tempt Quoyle to forget his destiny.

As now, when he wishes he were only a common man, one who might indulge himself by beating the shit out of Dietz. Simply to see the respect and panic and smell the blood.

71

Something flickers beyond his own reflection, outside the glass. That little Indian boy is on Main again, always with that hat, probably stolen, since he'd never earn that silver and turquoise on the band. Strutting along as good as a White, and it irks Quoyle. Why the hell is the little savage living off the reservation? The government put those people away for a reason, to keep their lice and filth off decent White folks. Next, he'll be staggering drunk in the street, the sort of public disorder Mr. Hollingwood can't abide, and Quoyle's duty, to nip it in the bud. He stands and stretches.

Dietz stops whittling, his knife poised in midair to look up at Quoyle, as loyal as a dog. Quoyle clears his throat. Dietz rises off the stool and sheaths his knife, wood shavings drifting to the floor.

Quoyle knows how little a person needs to say to get what he wants. He grunts at Dietz and leads him out. On the threshold, he settles his bowler and eyes the Indian boy, who stares in through Green's window glass, wanting what he doesn't deserve.

Dietz follows Quoyle's gaze to the boy and nods, then spits on the boards underfoot. Quoyle cringes, lifting his glassy-polished boot over the splattered snuff. Together they cross the street—among motor cars puttering out acrid blue smoke, and wagon wheels and horses churning puffs of dust—to the opposite boardwalk. They watch the boy slip inside, tinkling the bell above the door.

There's a way Hollingwood prefers to handle these things, to avoid confrontation on the street, so they wait to follow the child home. When he comes out, he carries a wrapped package. Maybe he paid for the merchandise this time, Quoyle reasons, but he remains a thief. It's in his blood. The little heathen works for Burgess the blacksmith, sleeping in his barns like a rat. Despicable.

They lag a stone's throw behind the child, through the alley and around the corner. When he enters the stable in back, Quoyle and Dietz wend between the buildings to the front door of the blacksmith's shop.

It's Quoyle's way, to begin with reason.

Silent, he watches the bull-shaped blacksmith grasp a chunk of red-hot iron with tongs, slam it with a mallet the size of a melon and taper it into an orange blade. Physically formidable, Quoyle observes, and belligerent by nature, but surely undermined by mental and moral weakness. Quoyle glances at Dietz, who fingers the handle of his scorpion-tipped Bowie knife. He quietly clears his throat and Dietz sighs, removing his hand from under his coat. Too eager, Dietz fails to grasp the fine points of negotiation. Quoyle once hoped to train the younger man as a partner, but even now, in his thirties, nuances elude the dolt, although his enthusiasm and lack of inhibition are useful.

The blacksmith ignores them. Quoyle, piqued, tallies this against the man's account, to be settled later. As if sensing the resentment, Dietz steps forward and asks for a moment of the working man's time.

In a minute. Iron's hot.

They wait. Quoyle filters his smile, considering how and when the oaf will pay.

Finally, after cooling the iron in a hissing bath, Burgess turns to face them, gripping the tongs and mallet.

The Indian boy, Dietz begins.

What about him? You his daddy? He glances at Quoyle and leers.

Quoyle takes a deep breath and narrows his eyes as Dietz steps into the space of his resentment to say, Because of you, the boy stays, and he's not the kind we want in town.

None of your goddamn business, the blacksmith sneers, spitting on the dirt floor.

Send him back to the reservation, or wherever he came from.

The blacksmith narrows his eyes, first at Quoyle, then at Dietz, flexing his grip on the handles of his tools. His right eye twitches.

You're Hollingwood's strongmen.

Quoyle flinches but keeps his face placid. It's a double insult, first to imply he's no more than a lackey, with all he does for this community, and second to suggest he's on the same level as Dietz. Another strike to be settled in good time.

Dietz pipes up, Mr. Hollingwood doesn't trouble himself with such small matters.

If it's so small, let it go.

Burgess turns away and grasps another hunk of iron with his tongs. The boy is my worker and you got no say here. Raising his mallet, he pivots to the forge, his face flickering with orange, reflected light.

Quoyle smolders. He touches the brim of his bowler, nods at Dietz and leads him out.

Anger surges like desire, and until Quoyle can deal with the blacksmith, someone else must do. Dietz straggles at his heels, pelting him with questions Quoyle doesn't intend to answer about the blacksmith and the Indian boy.

He raises a hand, the first part of a slap. Dietz flinches and shuts up.

At the back door of the Red Lantern tavern, he nods at Dietz, who jiggles the latch. When it fails to give, the smaller man rams it with his shoulder and the frame cracks, popping open the locked door. Ray Marlow gapes up at them from a table where he's sorting dollar bills and coins into stacks. The wind rushes in, scattering the bills, and Marlow jumps to his feet, tipping the table. Coins ping and jangle against the hardwood, then thrum, rolling.

You fellas are early, he calls out, his voice cracking with failed welcome. I'm getting Mr. Hollingwood's payment ready, now. See?

Dietz reads Quoyle's expression. Drawing his blade, he shoves Marlow against the wall, one arm at his neck. Pressing the gleaming point to the tavern owner's cheek, he ekes out one drop of blood to trickle down. Marlowe struggles to breathe. His eyes bulge from Dietz's weight on his throat.

Quoyle reaches down and rights the tipped chair, seating himself a few feet away. He glances at the scattered bills and coins, sighing, This surely isn't enough.

You said I had until tonight.

Dietz trails the blade down Marlow's cheek, etching a sliver of blood.

Easy, Mr. Dietz, Quoyle chides. He settles back and inhales as if drawing on a cigar. The blood lust throbs in his veins and his groin and he savors the moment, saying, Slowly, now.

Dietz pushes, choking Marlow up the wall until boots kick above the floor.

Please, the dangling man gasps.

Quoyle shakes his head, sorrowful. I'm sorry, Mr. Marlow, but your day of grace has ended.

Marlow sobs from where Dietz has him cornered, crying out with the snap of each finger bone. Quoyle's attention wanders, as it often does during the act. The vision, the anticipation is the better part, but the violence, when it arrives, leaves something to be desired. Like many mortal events, he reminds himself over Marlow's pleas, it pales in light of its Ideal form. A few broken bones offered up to settle a score, these effect no true Justice, which remains unattainable. One must make do with a lower, chaotic manifestation. It is the essence of human tragedy, he thinks with a sigh.

Quoyle considers how a girl, a harlot at Roquette's brothel, might resolve some of his frustration. But this usual indulgence, or even a lonely wife, is not what he craves. Watching Marlow, he remembers the tavern keeper's not-for-long virginal daughter, about sixteen. She's lately a byword, said to sneak out at night to meet her sweetheart for kisses, down by the creek pond. Quoyle plays out the seduction in his mind. He'll catch her off guard, coerce her into walking with him and lead her to a point of no return. She'll look back on it and blame herself, keeping the secret. A fine penalty for Marlow, a ruined daughter, to make up for this disappointment. It will calm Quoyle, help him reason through the situation with the blacksmith and Indian brat. He quickens with a surge of anticipation and clears his throat.

Enough.

Dietz's shoulders slump and his fists clench. He kicks the man in the groin and hollers, The money!, before backing away.

Quoyle's smile turns down. Dietz never fails to degrade their art with excess. Quoyle has urged him to read the Greek heroes, but Dietz prefers dog-eared copies of that pulp *Wild West Weekly*. There's no redeeming his gutter mind. Quoyle longs for an equal with a like mind, but despairs of Dietz.

Perhaps a son, Quoyle tells himself. Someday. But the idea of a wife ...

Marlow crawls over the floorboards, seeping blood. Scooping scattered bills in his twisted fingers, he thrusts them at Dietz.

I've got more than enough, he cries, holding up an arm to shield his face and offering rolls of dollars from the open safe.

When Dietz glares at him, he cowers and calls out, Mr. Quoyle, please.

Quoyle shrugs. The money is for Hollingwood, who already has too much, and the girl by the pond drives him now.

Dietz barks in alarm and Quoyle tracks his stare. That Indian stands beyond the doorway, peering in. Before Dietz can cross the room and grab him, he darts down the alley.

When Quoyle steps outside, Dietz is kicking up alley dust in a circle, swearing his apologies for letting the boy escape. Quoyle waves him off and gazes down the alley, smiling at the opportunities that yawn ahead. The sun is shining. It's altogether a fine day, full of promise, and it will be a memorable night for Justice.

Before ten o'clock chimes in her father's house, Sarah Marlow limps home sadder and wiser, weeping over a series of events she'll forever question and regret.

One hour before midnight, the blacksmith's shop goes up in flames. The Darkwater Creek Fire Brigade volunteers save the gasping, smoke-streaked family and the panicked horses, but the shop and stables char to ashes.

Through the milling, babbling crowd, Elsiver Dietz asks after that poor Indian child who slept in the stables, but there's no sign of him or his possessions. For weeks, people discuss the darker boy's absence from the stores where he bought his bags of oats, slabs of bacon and wedges of cheese. Most people say it's for the best, claiming he and his kind don't belong in Darkwater Creek, although—don't forget—he did save a little boy in the street.

Albert D. Hollingwood sends lumber, cash and a crew to restore the humbled smithy's buildings and fortunes. As Joe Marlow reminds his tavern clientele, the people of Darkwater Creek are blessed to have such a generous man investing in their future. With his hands gloved in plaster casts, he calls a barmaid to set up free drinks for Regal Quoyle and Elsiver Dietz. Joe Marlow, usually a somber man, forces such loud laughter from behind the bar that people raise eyebrows, then join his shrill toast, To Our Benefactors!

Two weeks after I leave Kuruk in his stables, and a week after those stables burn, there's still no sign of him. I fear he died in the blacksmith's fire. I suffer nightmares of losing everyone. I feel feverish, panicked as if I'm falling, with a desire to touch everything, even what isn't mine. Greed grips me and I shudder to think—the book of poems was only the beginning of my fall. I am, and forever will be, a thief.

After an early rain shower, a bluebird hangs behind everything and buds blur pink, white and green through the schoolroom's ripply windows. I feel trapped underwater. My mind drifts between worrying over Kuruk and bits of today's lesson on the nation of India. Starving people. Buddha. Dogs in the street. The teacher has to call on me twice and I don't know the answer, so I'm trudging up the aisle past Jack's desk to write I Will Pay Attention fifteen times on the chalkboard when I spot *The Forms of Water in Clouds and Rivers, Ice and Glaciers*, on Jack's desk. Until recess, I can think of nothing but holding that heavy, red book. Once my classmates spill into the schoolyard, I grab it up, carry it to the coat hooks by the door and stash it in my raincoat.

Jack misses it after recess, looking under his chair and accusing the boys beside him. When Mrs. Lathrop asks, he denies any trouble, but slumps over his desk and glares at his neighbors.

Just thinking about it, I'm inspired by that book in my raincoat and what I have done to get it. I'm saucy and terrified and it shocks me to feel no remorse, stealing from a boy I want to love.

I read the beautiful book cover to cover, in one night, and bring it back to school the next day, risking getting caught red-handed. All because I can't part from the gold-edged pages, its leathery scent or the cool, pebbled texture of its cover.

My eyes won't focus the next day. I'm drowsy at my desk, so back at the board writing repentance again, but amazed at the words etched in my mind, entire paragraphs and pages. I always had a fine memory, but terror and sin must sharpen my remembering because the book lives like a tintype in my head. Even the parts I can't fully understand are clear, word for word, entire.

I imagine being a book miser, gaining knowledge the way men hoard coins or land or kingdoms. Already a thief, now I covet words, the coins of true wealth, and books, their storehouses.

In class, Jack is distracted and pines over what's missing. I'm not sorry until I realize I deprived him of not only a beautiful object but worse, the words and their meanings about water, the most important thing on this earth. To do that to a smart boy like Jack is downright mean.

By the time the school bell rings, my crime weighs on me. I tell myself not to be a fool, but I love Jack's mind. I want him to know what I know about the water.

I follow him home with that heavy book banging on my hip with every step. I dread my comeuppance. He will surely hate me and may call the sheriff. I wish I could make up my mind to either be bad or good.

Instead of walking home, Jack walks south out of town. When he meets Kuruk at an abandoned sod house, I'm so relieved to see he's safe, my knees almost buckle. Yet I'm strangely sad he's secret friends with Jack, asking him for help, instead of me. When I think about my stable boy, putting salve on his burns and him putting his arm around me, my heart hurts. I can't resist following those two, tugged along by threads of guilt and love.

They cross a pasture and a bridge, south to a dense stand of elm, ash and peach-tree willow by the river. On either side, the ground falls into marshy ravines knotted with poison ivy, dogwood and wild plum, but I hide behind a bur oak at the edge.

Jack shimmies up an angled trunk and hops like a robin to the next tree's branch. From there, he drops a rope ladder for Kuruk. I creep nearer, trunk by trunk, to see what they've built.

It's the size of Greta's bedroom, with three shuttered windows the boys throw open. Settling out of sight on the windowless side, I listen to the boys discuss which girl in Jack's class is ugliest. I'd expect them to talk about something more interesting, but at least they don't name me. They talk about Custer and the Sioux, agreeing the general deserved every arrow he got, but they disagree on which is better, licorice or horehound. Of course, it's lemon drops.

I'm miserable in my loneliness. It's an evil thought only a thief would consider, but it was easier to picture Kuruk run away or even dead instead of stolen by a rich boy. Shit-fire! Maybe I'll keep his book after all.

Then Jack complains about losing the book, a gift from his father, who might whip Jack if he finds out.

Even if I don't tell him, Jack says, He'll know. He asks after my reading, to test me.

I know what it's like to get whipped for something you didn't do. I may be bound for hell, but I'm not that far gone. I holler up to one of the window sides of the tree house, Hey, up there!

A white face and a dark face gawp down at me.

Pulling the book out of my raincoat pocket, I ask, Is this yours?

Jack nods and his eyes get wide, then narrow, and he asks, How'd you get it?

I found it.

You stole it.

I shake my head. My heart beats faster, but I make myself smile and look innocent. With both of those boys looking down on me, I want to be good enough to be their friend, so I renounce the devil and all his empty promises, for today. Except for lying.

Kuruk gives me the eye. He knows I'm a thief, but he doesn't say anything. I feel mixed up and queasy in his forgiveness, so grateful my heart aches.

If you don't want it, I'll take it home, I say, looking up to make them believe me.

Jack whispers something to Kuruk, who shrugs.

Where'd you find it?

In the street. I saved it from getting run over.

Kuruk's eyebrows go up and I look down to keep from smiling.

Jack tilts his head and says, I remember you. You're that Miss Smarty Pants from the orphanage Christmas party.

Remembering how I tried to be tough, a warm flush creeps over my cheeks. Instead of walking away, though, I wait.

He says, I'll come get it.

I'm afraid he'll hit me to get even. To keep him off, I hold up the closed book and start to recite. *Rain does not come from a clear sky. It comes from clouds. But what are clouds? Is there nothing you are acquainted with which they resemble?*

You discover at once a likeness between them and the condensed steam of a locomotive.

Jack leans out the window. You memorized that?

I remember what I read, I tell him.

I flip through my mind to another chapter. *Part 7. Tropical Rains. 70. But long before the air and vapour from the equator reach the poles, precipitation occurs. Wherever a humid warm wind mixes with a cold dry one, rain falls. Indeed the heaviest rains occur at those places where the sun is vertically overhead. We must enquire a little more closely into their origin.*

He twists up his face, doubting me, and asks, How long did you have to study to remember it?

I told you. I read it once and I remember it.

He studies me with a strange expression and whispers to Kuruk. They laugh and shake their heads.

Do they think I'm stupid, that I can't remember anything because I'm a girl? I wonder. With the book closed in my hand, I keep reading it out of my head. *259. It is interesting and important that you should be able to explain the formation of an icicle; but it is far more important that you should realise* (I wonder why the word is spelled funny, but I remember it that way) *the way in which the various threads of what we call Nature are woven together. You cannot fully understand an icicle without first knowing that solar beams powerful enough to fuse the snows and blister the human skin, nay, it might be added, powerful enough, when concentrated, to burn up the human body itself, may pass through the air, and still leave it at an icy temperature.*

They lean out the window farther. Kuruk grins at me and whispers something to Jack.

Do you want your book or not?

I almost set it down on the tree root. The boys don't want me in their little club anyway, no matter how much I know, and maybe because of how much I do. Miss Smarty Pants. I forgot girls aren't supposed to be smart. If I hurry, I'll get home before Florence tells Mrs. Endicott to cut a switch from the lilac.

My shoulders sag. Then Jack hollers, Wait a second, and lowers the rope ladder.

Bring it up, he says.

They quiz me and I remember it all. The more I recite, the funnier it is, like my brain is playing some sort of trick, and we laugh until our bellies ache. Finally Jack snaps shut the book and tells me to keep it, his gift to me, that I earned it. I don't need it, because every word is burned in my mind, but I say thank you anyway. I can't remember the last time somebody other than Mr. Amsel gave me a present.

They invite me for supper, some berries and a rabbit roasted over coals. We eat it with our bare, greasy hands, wiping our juicy chins on our sleeves and tossing bones onto the fire. After a bright orange sunset, Kuruk stays to sleep in the treehouse. Jack walks me home and I promise I won't tell anybody about Kuruk. He thinks some fellows who work for Jack's father are after him, for seeing something he shouldn't have.

I take my whipping without a peep and miss three days of school with joy. I see it now. There are things in life the adults don't decide. We children keep a secret world of our own, as wide and deep and splashing-full of life as the river flowing by our tree house. We are the fish who dart and curve, free in the gold, underwater light.

Now that you've been through a tornado you know how it feels,—almost. After the funnel passes hail falls, lightning flashes through the lessening murk. Heavy rain succeeds, and if you're alive you go out and rescue the perishing.

——

Stories of any degree of incredibility crop up after each tornado, often with accompanying photographs as proof. People are plastered with mud, pianos are deposited in neighboring lots, babies are hung up unhurt by their clothes in tree-tops, and often one person is killed and another nearby escapes unhurt, Bible-fashion.

I read this in one of my books, *Reading the Weather* by T. Morris Longstreth, but I've got news for him. He never got caught in a tornado, or he'd be singing a different tune. With all that wind and hail and darkness coming down on you, throwing people in the air and dropping them, who needs to make up lies? The truth is so bad, you don't want to tell anybody. For example, you don't want to say a storm has a voice. Nobody would believe clouds and wind blaming you, screaming for you to die before they try to kill you.

Some things, a boy has to keep to himself.

I smuggle jars of food, a shirt, some socks, matches and tools out of the house in my rucksack for Kuruk, who's hiding out in the tree house or at the old sod house. I pretend I'm a trapper in the Rocky Mountains, befriending an injured redskin pursued by the U.S. Cavalry. Or I'm Leatherstocking, wise with fancy words, teaching my noble

Chingachgook the White way. Either one, I'm lucky my story is like a book or legend.

Today, I step toe-to-heel, stealthy and leaving no tracks. It's a jimmy trick and I wonder why Kuruk never walks this way, with him being Indian and that's how they're supposed to. I look back over my shoulder to make sure nobody follows and rats us out to Quoyle and Dietz.

It's tough keeping the tree house a secret from the older boys, even if they're not supposed to come on Father's land. They shove me around after school, because their fathers work for mine and they're poor. Nobody likes the rich boss's son. While they wait to beat me up, I hide in the stores, listening to old men gossip around the pickle barrel. Finally, the bullies get bored and go to pick on somebody else. It can be almost suppertime before I get to Kuruk, but it doesn't matter, because we'll eat something he trapped or Marta will keep my food warm at home. Of course, Father's in Chicago or Omaha this week, I forget which.

The June sunrise is spilling pink and orange into the sky and shadows are starting by the road. I set out early, because the voices don't like sunny mornings. I wish I knew why. There are two. The Man sounds like Father, but once He gets worked up, He rumbles like a train. The Woman sounds like a sawmill ripping pine logs. I think of Her like Jezebel, after the wicked Bible story woman whose blood the dogs lapped in the street, but I'm no fool. I never call Her that when She's around. They come and go since the Omaha tornado and I try to keep a truce with them, by not arguing and letting them having their way.

They seem to move with the weather, like on that first day. That's why I study meteorology. I believe science will save me, but I don't have enough data, and now clouds are churning in the sky. A storm sneaked up on me again, and I've got that crowded feeling of more than one person in my head.

Walking fast, I set my shoes down with the drops splatting in the dust. One spits on the back of my neck and makes me shiver, so I kick up into a trot. Wheeling around, I see nobody following. Veering off the road, I cross a field, then run down toward the marsh and trees. By the peachleaf willow, a bolt of lightning makes me flinch and my heart gallops.

In case Kuruk's up there, I cup both hands to my lips and birdcall to the treehouse. Nobody lets the ladder down, so I climb up the black walnut and cross to the cottonwood, raindrops pattering on the leaves and the wind stirring branches. Just as I'm coming through the tree house window, a crack of thunder shakes the walls.

Almost got you, He says.

Taking a deep breath, I grab down *Our Own Weather* and start reading out loud, to block the voices.

The large amount of heat and moisture in the summer keeps it at that season peculiarly well prepared for quick overturnings.

Angry clears His throat and says He won't tolerate being ignored, but I keep reading.

The descent of a body of colder air instantly sets things off.

I tell myself science can explain all things, and the voices are a change of atmosphere in my head.

The sharpness of the conflict provokes electrical discharges, made apparent in lightning and thunder, and provokes also strong dashes of wind and rain.

Listen to me!

I'll laugh about the voices once I know the science behind them. I flip a few pages and read more.

The small storms are often scattered by the irregularities of the land; but the large ones often cross high mountains without breaking up.

Angry spews indecent words, ones I don't remember hearing before, so nasty I bury my face in the book and fall down on my knees.

I won't listen, I tell Him, I'm a good fellow and I won't hear it. You're not a person and I don't believe what you say.

I practiced the brave words this morning on the quiet road when my head was still mine, but now I forget them. Rocking forward and back, I drop the book and cover my ears, but the noise is inside. Jezebel screeches in.

Stop just stop just stop just stop just stop, I say. I'm choking on snot and tears, rocking harder, ready to bang my head on the wall. I open my eyes to see how close it is.

Kuruk.

Goddamned Indian get him the hell out of here!

Kuruk surely hears Him, too.

No, he's my friend, and I hate you hate you hate you.

Kuruk backs away.

I hold out my hands and beg, No, not you, don't go. Stay, please stay.

Kuruk kneels with me.

I tell him I'm not crazy, it's voices. They're real and they come in the storms.

It makes no sense, but Kuruk nods. He puts a hand on my shoulder and the warm weight unlocks a closet door in me.

I tell him what nobody knows, about the Omaha tornado. The nights I sweat in my bed, ignoring what the voices tell me to do and the names they call me. How I don't know what they are, but the science of the pressures and wind and heat and cold will help me keep them away. How lately they come even when the weather is fine and this is the worst part, because if they're not from the weather, then what brings them? And how can I stop what I can't understand?

When all my words are spilled, He and She get quiet, too. The wind dies and the rain falls straight down, drumming on the tin roof instead of being thrown sideways, lashing the leaves. Kuruk stays in front of me 'til I stop crying. When my breaths come slower, I pick up the book and read out loud some more.

It is in thunder-storms mainly that those tremendous downpours known as 'cloud-bursts' occur. They are well named, for the spill, besides being enormous, is confined to a small area and all is accomplished in a very short time.

I close the book and tell my friend, If I study enough, someday I'll understand the science.

At first, Kuruk thinks the voices are a vision, spirits talking, and I should listen. But when I tell him the sickening things the voices say, he says, That's nothing good to listen to. Probably not any kind of medicine. He offers to go down to the reservation in Oklahoma, to ask the tribal elders. He insists there's at least one wise doctor left who'll know what to do.

But if Kuruk goes to Oklahoma, I know he'll never come back. I beg him not to. They'll cart him off to another Indian school in nothing flat.

Instead, I ask him to help me build a hygrometer, to predict storms. He lets me pluck one of his thick, dark hairs for the instrument, but he says Whites are crazy to think by measuring something, we learn what it means.

For five days after Jack's voices in the storm, I get shut up in crazy old Mrs. Linneman's house, where she calls me Charlie, bakes me sweet shortbread and dresses me in her dead boy's clothes. For an old lady, she has good hearing and catches me every time I sneak down her creaky stairs to run off. I feel safe from Quoyle and Dietz but I'm a prisoner again.

She says she's gonna save me, dresses me in wool and drags me to church. Not a good painted-up Catholic church with arches, bleeding statues and stained-glass martyrs neither but instead a square white Methodist box with clear windows and only one picture to pray to—a bearded old White man, a long-haired White Jesus and a dove. Trapped between fat White ladies in that pew, I'm desperate. I pray to them all to take away Jack's spirit voices and to get me out of the old lady's house. I pray at night to Tirawa, too, when I'm looking out Mrs. Linneman's window at the stars. Of those four gods, I bet on Tirawa and the dove.

The next day, Mrs. Linneman's face and right hand twist up in a stroke and her rose teacup shatters on the hardwood floor between us. I woulda settled for the front doorbell ringing so I could slip out the back but I got this for an answer to prayer. It seems like an ornery Coyote trick, not something a dove-god would think up. I feel grateful but sorry because the crazy lady was kind and I never meant to bring a bad thing down on her. Seeing what happens, I may not pray again soon.

After I run for the doctor, Mrs. Linneman's daughter comes on the train from Omaha but I'm long gone by then, back up in the tree house. Glad to be free but missing shortbread.

Crazy Mrs. Linneman was different from other Whites in Darkwater Creek. For most everybody, I'm invisible, a shadow boy with no bones, easy for them to look past or through when I'm walking on the road. In stores, when I hold out my money, they look away and open their hands for me to drop it in so they don't touch dark me. I guess they can't figure a living Indian outside Buffalo Bill's Wild West Show, because the schoolteachers say we got wiped out by the U.S. Army and the Whites won everything.

Some may feel a little sorry for what they did to my people. They're peculiar about it, though. Now and again, White ladies with tears gave me a coin or a piece of candy. One forced a blanket on me in the name of Jesus and I took it, because if I let Whites think they done their Christian best by me, they get soft eyes and forget me. Then I'm invisible and safe again.

The thing about Whites is you got to protect them so they don't feel pitiful, guilty or sad or any particular way about you. Let them believe they are good and any trouble you got, you brought down on yourself by not being like them. Let them look through you.

Even being noticed by somebody like Mrs. Linneman isn't any good, getting sneaked up on by her sorrowful emptiness. To her, I wasn't Kuruk the Indian to hate, not even a could-be-made-Whiter boy named Peter. I was nothing but a child-shaped sack for Charlie's spirit, even with him dead some fifty years and buried back in Illinois.

But worst are the angry ones like Quoyle and Dietz, who can't stop seeing me, especially since I saw them beating that man and know some bad truth about them. They won't rest until I'm bones underground, the same way the Army soldiers musta been with my ancestors. Those two remind me it's not always a bad thing to be a shadow with no bones or edges.

If not for Jack and Maggie, I'd never know what it's like for somebody see me instead of seeing their guilt or need. To look me in the eye and see a person. To touch my hand and feel the blood and human bones inside.

Next time Jack comes up to the tree house, he says the voices are still yelling. Which god do I blame for that unanswered prayer? That's the trouble with religion—some gods are no-account and there's no way to get after them for it.

I got my suspicions about Jack's voices but nothing for sure. One of the teachers at the White school in Darkwater Creek has some Indian bones and skulls somebody dug up from a mound near the river. Because the teacher says all Indians are dead and conquered, a lost civilization, and those bones are fine for children to study, Jack picked them up the way she told him to. He says he felt queasy about it and wishes he'd told her, No. But what's done is done.

I remember Grandfather said if our ancestor's bones are disturbed, their restless spirits will talk to the living. Or maybe Jack's hearing a lonely Scalped Man who lives underground near here. They can make many voices but not always for good. Spirit animals can talk and they're usually good to hear but can a White boy touch that Pawnee mystery? I got me more questions than answers and nobody wise to ask. I let Jack talk me out of going down to the reservation to ask a Pawnee doctor because I'm scared of getting caught and sent back to Genoa but if there is an answer, it's probably there.

From the priests and pastors at the Indian schools, I know a little about that White Jesus who walked on dirt and water and drove evil spirits into pigs. But where can I find him since he flew back to heaven to be with his father?

I keep coming back to those bones. I wake up with bad dreams some nights, feeling sick about them getting played with in the Darkwater classroom. They could be my ancestors and they deserve better than being toys.

To ask them to forgive Jack for touching them, I follow the moon to the school and jimmy open a door. While I'm walking down the hallway, the smell of lye makes my eyes water and chalk dust makes me sneeze while I look through glass-and-wood doors into classrooms.

In one, when I open the door I find a snarling stuffed Coyote mounted on a board and a big map on the wall. I get chills on the back of my neck. Those bones are close by. I look in boxes and desks until I find them in a drawer, jumbled up like they're all one person. I feel cold sweat on my face and my teeth chatter.

What kind of people stuff a sacred Coyote and play with bones?

The moonlight breaks through the window panes in hard blocks and the room is painful tight with angles. Desks, doors and tiles on the floor. The air's thick with a sick sweet smell and that stuffed Coyote posed like he's running and gritting his teeth in pain makes me want to cry. The room crackles with hate like cold lightning.

The Indian skulls got shattered holes through them and no jaws hooked on. The ribs and leg bones look hopeless, piled together. I want to warm them with my hand and put them back together but my hands won't move. Seeing them in all their colors—gray, cream, yellow, brown and black—and busted to pieces, with the marrows grainy and dry and holes where red blood used to beat through, I'm sick with sadness. The empty eyes in the skulls look up at me.

How did the people die, in their lodges or in a fight? Are they Pawnee or Lakota or another tribe? What language did they speak out of the places in their skulls where the tongues were? I feel the finger bones itching to touch something, with no tendon to bind them together and no skin left for feeling.

I could carry them out in the cloth I brought along and bury them back by the river but I don't know the ceremony or how to explain to the dead ones the good I mean to do. After my prayers went so wrong with Mrs. Linneman, I'm sudden afraid to ask the bones for a favor or even talk to them. What if they misunderstand and shout and I go insane like Jack? These bones don't know me.

I don't know how to make right what I didn't do wrong. It's all bigger than me and I'm far away from Pawnee things in this White place.

I step back, feeling younger than eleven years old. Closing that drawer, I run out of the school and cuss myself for leaving a good thing undone, for being a coward and not the Pawnee or friend I oughta be. At least I coulda stole that Coyote and buried him free. It woulda been something. But what isn't done, isn't done neither and I carry that load.

Running to the tree house where dead hands and voices can't reach me, I swear to at least stand by my friends. Already my heart is in a snare, like we are brothers and sister, my crazy rich White boy Jack and that little soft-eyed thief Maggie, the girl who makes my heart run fearful hot with love.

Hiding under my blanket, I dream of seeing them and them seeing me, our hands tied up like knots in the mirror light reflected off our river. Wading with the cool water ringing round our legs, going forever.

To teach me the power of my name, which means Medicine Bear, Grandfather gave me this story.

After Bear spared the Pawnee boy's life and made him his son, he took him to the prairie. There he showed him the medicines of roots and leaves and how to use them. He told the boy to eat the medicine so he could cure wounds and illnesses by breathing over them.

Bear tore off a claw and gave it to the boy, with a little bundle of medicine. He told the boy to wear them on a string around his neck, the claw hanging in front. He gave the boy his feelings, too. From that day on, when the boy became angry, he grunted and when angry, his teeth showed like a bear's, to frighten his enemies. Bear gave the name Ku ruks la war´ uks ti, and the powers of the animal lodges,

95

of which Bear was chief. With this power, the boy could enter animal lodges and talk with the animals.

Bear also taught him things to amaze the people, to gain their respect and provide. He showed the boy how to make plums grow on trees and make ground-cherries come out of his mouth.

The red-twig dogwoods shake in the cold nights, their green leaves bleeding and curling yellow. The sumac flashes bright red on the hills and the fleabane is like tiny daisies drying out, petals curled to gray around yellow eyes up on skinny necks. The orange butterfly milkweed's little bursts of stars are husks now. Monarchs flapping south stop anyway to visit the empty parts, then drink off the goldenrod and purple asters.

I'm not glad for the cold coming down hard. It takes three blankets and a half-growed black mongrel pup I got me from a garbage can to keep warm at night in the treehouse. Wind seeps up through the planks, freezing. While it's still dark gray morning, I can't stand it no longer. I got to boil some water for coffee. Then my dog I call Toss, for Tossed-Away, walks the prairie with me, the sun a low hot coal on the east ground. All round us, the dew and melted frost sparkle. Toss snaps at grasshoppers and chases mice but always comes back to me.

The late September prairie is a drier, dirtier green than it was in May but I like kicking through the clumps of little bluestem, finding the last pink wild roses hidden from the frost down in the buffalo grass. Toss hops, dives, shakes his head and brings me back a limp gopher. A meadowlark sings before he flaps up stiff, beating the air like a quail and fanning his tail feathers.

The days get shorter but feel longer with Maggie and Jack in school. They learn so much there I don't know, I feel left behind so I been thinking about teaching them a hand game, hiding and guessing for counters in ceremony.

I want to share it so I remember but it might be wrong to show a sacred thing to Whites. Is it better to forget it by not doing or remember by spilling secrets? A hand game is nothing with one person. If I had a Pawnee doctor or even my father to remind me of the truth, I could do right. Alone I can only do my best and hope it counts for something.

I start to teach them on a Friday after they get out of school. They're rambunctious from being quiet all day and interrupt me with questions. The ceremony blurs between my head and my hands. Getting everything wrong, I'm ashamed, like I spilled something holy on the ground or showed my nakedness. Then they laugh and jump up and down when they guess which hand holds the counter, like it's a joke. I yell at them for having no respect.

I'm sorry, I tell them. I can't face them now so I tuck the counter in my pocket. I slip on the last knot of the ladder on my way down and cuss at my rope-burned fingers.

Crackling through the brush and weeds with Toss beside me, I cry since nobody can see. I never felt this lonesome, even tied up in the wagon on my way to Genoa.

It pains me Jack and Maggie can't understand what is holy to me. They can't share the color of my skin or hear Grandfather's voice, filling in the words when I stammer out the ceremony. They can't feel the drums or hear the songs I remember but they save and hide and treat me like I'm good as a White. I love them so deep and painful it turns me inside out but it's not enough to make us the same.

I lean over, hands on my knees and choke on a sob. A good dog, Toss licks my face and that's not enough neither so I sing from my grandfather's mind, heartsick for a place I never saw.

The place whence you come,
Now I am longing for.
The place whence you come,
Now I am ever-mindful of.

A riverbank like this one. Earth lodges with poles standing straight at the right directions. A door that faces morning. Or maybe even the house in Oklahoma, where my father couldn't keep me. A Pawnee home.

Toss barks and a stick cracks behind me but I'm too slow. My hat falls and fingers knot in my long hair, jerking me up straight. Dietz laughs and stuffs a rag in my mouth. Quoyle rubs his hands together.

I break every branch I can grab along the way they drag me, crashing like a buck so Maggie and Jack will hear but it's a short way to the road through a swampy patch. The two men tie my hands and legs together and shove me in the back of a wood-paneled truck. Dietz holds me while Quoyle drives. They unload me in a warehouse by the railroad tracks where I pick up Frank Burgess's iron from the train.

They only mean to scare me. These men won't hurt me, I'm just a boy. I sing the words silent, along with my heart-drum beating, as if I can make it so.

For two hours they sit me in the dark and scare me good with fists, a blade, ugly names and silence. Dietz yells I got to leave Darkwater before the sun sets. Quoyle sits looking at the floor, shaking his head like my pain bothers him but he licks his lips for more. I stare at the dirt and nod to everything.

98

If I don't go back to the reservation where I belong, they promise to hurt my friends. I know they won't touch Jack but Maggie's got nobody to take up for her. Thinking what they'd do to a nice girl like her, I shake my head and Dietz punches me in the mouth.

I mean yes, I nod, tasting blood. Yes and yes.

What seems like days later, the heavy warehouse door rolls open on its track. The sudden light makes me squint and blink the one eye I can open enough to see with. Mr. Albert Hollingwood steps in with Jack and that rich man starts in yelling. Dietz unties my hands and feet. I stand but my knees give out and Jack rushes to lift my arm over his shoulders. He holds me up and walks me out to the railroad street. The sun is too bright and my eyes water. A train whistles loud and I jump, my arms and legs shaking.

Inside, Hollingwood curses and threatens them for harming a child, even if I am Indian, and within town limits to boot, where anybody could see or hear their malfeasance. He asks if they're fools or insane. He asks if they'd like to seek employment elsewhere, then says nobody would take on such imbeciles as a liability. He uses the word whoresons, which is a fine new swear I tuck in back of my mind for later.

When I grin at Mr. Hollingwood's command of the English language, my lips crack open and bleed more. Jack gives me his handkerchief to hold there while we watch through knotholes. Dietz almost bends in half and Quoyle bites his lip, stiff as a lodge pole and pale as ice, his round hat in his hands. It's a fine thing, hearing Mr. Hollingwood dress down those two scoundrels. The words he's using!

What the heck is a clotpole?

Jack shrugs. He reads Shakespeare for the swears. He likes to curse elegant, to make people feel stupid.

Damn, I say, and try to whistle but my lip's swollen up. I got to remember that one.

We listen some more.

Fustilarian! Hollingwood shouts, and I think there may be some good in learning to read after all.

I thought I was dead, I whisper.

They'll leave you be, now.

I oughta go anyway. They won't let this sit and all they gotta do is make it look like an accident.

Father's on your side. I said Quoyle was after you for spite, and you no more than ten years old.

Eleven.

Ten sounds more helpless. You can stay at our house and work for Father, safe.

Well, do I want to work for a man who can swear like that? He might unleash on me but I could learn some new words. I won't be ungrateful anyway, not with my eye swollen shut and cuts bleeding fresh. And rich Jack, like the chief's son, is being a brother to poor me like that Pawnee story, taking me to his home.

Jack told his father people in town like me because I saved that boy who ran in front of the motor car.

By the way, Jack asks, who was that kid?

I moan and touch my eye like it hurts too much to answer.

Jack says, We'll get some ice on it. I told Father, People will ask why you let Quoyle and Dietz hurt a hero. That got his back up.

Good thing some people don't watch where they're going, I say, thinking of Maggie.

He nods. Good thing Father hates people criticizing the way he runs his town.

That's it. I get to live because Albert Hollingwood's fearful of something he can't buy.

Not such a good thing is Quoyle and Dietz now got reason to hate me more.

Jack's father storms out of the warehouse, huffing and talking down in my direction without looking in my eyes.

Son, this was a sad misunderstanding that will not be repeated, by God, and those two scoundrels were definitely not working under my orders. I'll see to them, but that's not your concern.

He asks about my parents.

They're dead and if you send me back to the reservation, I'll run away.

His chest gets bigger in his suit vest and he says, Boy, you're not making the decisions here. He gives me a sharp look to shut me up.

Blood in my mouth reminds me I'm only a kid and better act like one so I nod.

He asks my name and when I say, Kuruk, he shakes his head. What name did they give you at the reservation?

I look at the ground and shake my head but he grabs my ear and twists it. I say, Peter.

He nods. You'll answer to your Christian name.

He brushes his fingers against his trouser leg to wipe off me, then pulls a handkerchief whiter than snow out of his inside pocket. He dabs the corners of his thin lips where he's been spitting mad, then folds that cloth two times and tucks it back like it matters. He smells good, like horses and pine, and the muscles inside his sleeves pull the suit cloth tight over his arms. His eyes stay narrow and critical when he points them around, sizing up everything. I see why Jack's nervous with him.

Get your things, he says, raising his hand like a little salute, and Jack will bring you to the house. He walks off, talking to the man who drives his car, forgetting me.

I live upstairs in their carriage house. Somebody lived up here before, with a little coal stove for cooking and for heat. I got me a bed, a table and two chairs and pegs and shelves on the wall. I even warm my toes on a flowered rug over the plank floor. Like at the tree house, branches, leaves and birds grow outside the window. I sleep on the floor the first night, then get used to the bed.

I got my doubts when a White says, Here, I'm giving you this. What they give, they take away so for a few weeks I stay out of sight. Jack comes up to my room and we play poker, first with acorns, then pennies.

After two days, the gardener starts me driving a horse-drawn delivery wagon. I go to and from that new brewery Hollingwood set up with that German south of town, turning sweet artesian well water into beer. It's hard work, loading and unloading barley and hops and driving horses over muddy, rutted roads. I'm not complaining. At least they're not mules and nobody burns me for fun. Maybe when my legs get longer, Mr. Hollingwood will let me drive that truck Quoyle and Dietz threw me into. I got stranger things happened to me.

The Indian boy should serve him well. He's smart, if uneducated, but what good would books do him? Raised properly and treated well, he may prove loyal to the man who teaches him how to live. It's in the red man's nature to submit and follow, after all, Hollingwood muses. Steady work will keep the lad from running wild or becoming a drunk.

Hollingwood glances at the child, who sits on the leather seat with his eyes closed, the breeze from the car window drying his sweaty face. The businessman grunts, pleased with himself, and checks his pocket watch.

The Lozier 6 cruises past the last lines of Darkwater's young, gold-leafed trees and platted dirt streets tailored to Hollingwood's design, into pastureland and beige rows of dry corn waiting for harvest. The river valley rolls and dips ahead, south of town, its clustered trees a calico of yellows, oranges and reds. Clouds of dust billow behind the motor car like fat ropes and the tires *ka-whump* a rhythm across the Republican River's plank bridge.

The quiet boy beside him sends Hollingwood elsewhere in memory, to heat-shimmered summers with his brothers—chasing, war-whooping, wrestling and sweating in fierce mock soldier-and-Indian wars. Lashing tomahawks together with sticks and triangular stones, roasting squirrels over campfires and firing popguns with blue, tangy gunpowder smoke: He misses the best of his days. Instead of choosing to represent the good guys, the U.S. Army, Hollingwood always chose to play-fight as

Sioux or Comanche, owning the red savages who terrorized his dreams. Too many of his father's bedtime stories and Frank Starr's dime novels, with scalpings, kidnapped pioneer girls and brutal massacres, Hollingwood realizes now. His father, who served in the 1st Nebraska Infantry under U.S. Grant, swore he was glad to fight Confederates at Shiloh, instead of wild Indians in the territories. Godless savages, Rutherford Hollingwood called them, shaking his head at their fearlessness in battle.

Yet, studying double-pictured cards of Indian chiefs with his stereoscope, young Albert noted nobility in their high, dark brows and steady gazes. Their bone and feather adornments quickened something in him, a longing for freedom, a nomadic life on the plains beyond his father's hard authority and Grand Island's dust, traffic, steel rails and commerce. James Fenimore Cooper's novels sealed his impressions.

In April of 1886, his father took the Hollingwood boys by train to Denver to see Buffalo Bill's Wild West Show. In hindsight, Hollingwood recognizes the choreography, but back then, what an authentic ruckus it appeared to be, a free-wheeling extravaganza with a cast of hundreds: buffalo, cattle, sharpshooters, cowboys, soldiers and breech-clouted braves and chiefs thundering on horseback, bright feather headdresses trailing behind, lances pointed and bow-shot arrows arcing high. Gunfire, shouts and ululations over drums and hoofbeats pounding the hard ground. The cavalry, pioneers and rugged mountain men in beaver hats, all tangled in delicious violence. Even now, almost thirty years later, Hollingwood's heart beats faster. He swallows and smiles to himself.

Now he has his own Indian. How strange life is.

Whenever he's home between business trips, Hollingwood reads Cooper novels aloud to Jack. He wants to inspire his son with noble ideals, to be proud of his role in Western expansion, here in Nebraska. The boy must understand, too, why Destiny favors his Christian kind over lesser races. This unfortunate child, Peter, can be for Jack an example of the power of civilization. He glances warily at the boy, wondering if he harbors in his blood any remnant of savagery, then dismisses the idea. He's a child, and half-civilized already.

But the West. Hollingwood still dreams about it, and while the frontier may be closed, it fires his imagination. An Eden reclaimed with bloodshed, the West remains a spiritual proving ground for heroes. Once a desperate, lawless place, thanks to men like himself, it's now safe for White women and children, a veritable garden profitable for savvy businessmen. The conquest of the Indian was a regrettable necessity, and as he ponders the orphan beside him, Hollingwood shifts in his seat, ill at ease. He takes a deep breath, exhales and repeats what he believes .. . had the Indians known when they were conquered and promptly surrendered, many more may have survived. And doesn't the government, like a good father, provide for the survivors? Those allotments, reservations and Indian schools, all at considerable taxpayer expense. Once our enemies, now the red men are embraced with paternal care.

He shudders to think of this boy back in that warehouse, black-eyed, bruised and bleeding. What if some gossip blamed him for that atrocity? Damned Quoyle and Dietz—necessary, yet impossible to control. Given their cruel indiscretion, the only way to quash rumors was to take the boy in, to raise him up like a White.

It's a rule Hollingwood lives by: The unfortunate events, people and circumstances we cannot prevent, we must administer justly.

With the boy riding beside him, already less gaunt from his improved diet, dressed in new dungarees and cotton shirt and smelling fresh with Pears soap, Hollingwood feels the spiritual lightness, the peace of the benefactor.

Glimpsing that German's brewery up the lane ahead, over his driver's shoulder, Hollingwood tenses, leans forward and squares his shoulders. The immigrant is proving to be a problem. With Hollingwood and Storz's investment, he's overseen rapid growth in the brewery, but has the gall to challenge transferring property ownership, the last stage of their verbal agreement. The terms should have been set down in writing, but the man's English is abysmal and he couldn't read a contract, so it seemed beside the point. Nonetheless, Hollingwood faults himself for not forcing the issue into print, even if all the man could do was mark an X on every page. That, at least, would stand up in court.

One oversight, and he suffers this nonsense of the hard-headed German stalling, claiming the three-story house is his life's work, too valuable to sell, and where will his wife and children live? Sentimental bullshit, Hollingwood knows, while the crafty Kraut simply wants more money. Well, by God, he won't be some foreigner's fool.

You keep quiet, he warns Peter. Watch and learn how business is done.

In the yard, he points out the farm's most valuable asset, its artesian wells that spurt the finest water around. Purer than rainwater, filtered through the underlying aquifer's clay, sand and gravel to a pristine state, it flows faster than they can brew it, rushing its excess into the Republican River to the north.

Peter nods as if he understands, pleasing his new guardian, who wishes his son would take the same interest. But Jack's been strange for some time now, most likely taking after his mother. Too sensitive. No grit.

Hollingwood explains to Peter how Klaus Voegel, a builder in Germany, isn't much of a farmer. His skills are evident in his three-story house. Dovetailed joints, hand-carved newels, posts and rails on the long staircases and lovingly crafted door frames rival the European craftsmanship in Hollingwood's own home. Probably the German had a hard time finding jobs, due to his greed and poor English.

Luckily for the German, Hollingwood's workaday Model T broke down for the last time near the Voegel farm four years ago, and Klaus offered his guest a glass of home-brewed Altbier. Seizing an opportunity and promising the immigrant a fortune in brewing, Hollingwood began what he'd hoped would be a beneficial relationship. The German leaped at the chance, but he's been a problem from their first handshake.

Prophesying a statewide, even national, prohibition of alcohol, Hollingwood decided on low-key brewery structures disguised as typical farm outbuildings, barns and sheds. The farmer, coveting his neighbors' envy, argued for large warehouses. He haggled with Hollingwood over the recipe, the quality of the barley and hops, even the keg and bottle shapes. And the prices, always the prices and his own percentage of the profits. Nothing's ever enough for the man.

It wouldn't be so bad, Hollingwood explains to Peter, but for his hodgepodge German and English. It's all growls and spit. He should talk like an American.

When the driver opens the car door, Klaus meets them in too-large gray overalls that shift around his thin frame. He's in high spirits, mopping his bald forehead with a blue handkerchief and calling out, *Willkommen*. Hollingwood and Peter follow the man into his kitchen, where his wife serves cherry strudel. She narrows her eyes at Peter, then sets a plate in front of him.

Klaus shrugs. *Meine Frau* never saw red Indians before. Me, neither. You hunt *Büffel?* Live in vigvam?

Peter glances at Hollingwood and shakes his head.

Hollingwood laughs and chucks Peter under the chin. He's an orphan, my ward now.

You *ein guter Mann*, Klaus says, smiling. He speaks German to his wife, who pours coffee in their cups, steaming, fragrant and black.

Asking after the farmer's five sons, Hollingwood then swerves to business, saying he can't wait for Voegel to decide where to live. The family must vacate this month for the brewery overseers to move in. It's a matter of security and was our original agreement, he insists, leaning forward and smiling with his teeth.

Nein, the farmer says, scowling and sipping his coffee. Our home and not going. I built. *Mein Schweiß und Blut*, you say . . . sveat and blood. Voegel's wife interrupts and when he cuts her off with a wave, she slams the coffeepot on the cast-iron stove. Coffee sloshes, hissing into burnt-smelling steam.

I took you as a man of your word, Hollingwood says, looking sorry. He dabs his mouth, compliments the cook and folds his napkin before tucking it alongside his half-finished strudel. Gesturing to Peter and scooting back his hand-carved chair, he settles his hat on his head.

Klaus Voegel protests, but the important man is leaving and all he can do is follow and plead.

Peter double-steps to keep up with Hollingwood to the car, where the driver tends the shining blue-black Lozier's yawning door and purring motor.

Voegel tries to stop them, his hand nearly catching in the slamming iron door. He grips the window frame as the car backs out, begging, Ve can talk more. Don't go. You need to unterstand.

Hollingwood avoids his eyes, waves a hand and says, I'm done talking.

A mile down the road, he sees Peter staring. He asks, Any questions?

Peter blinks. What will you do?

Whatever it takes.

After I catch him in a string-snare under the tree house cottonwood, Kuruk says I'm ornery as Coyote the Trickster in his Pawnee legends. It's not the first time I've surprised him and it won't be the last. I have some exploding powder from my chemistry kit that'll make him jump. I'm waiting for the ideal time. Kuruk's so serious, it's like I win a prize whenever I make him laugh.

Coyote can look like a person when he wants to and loves nothing better than causing trouble, but Kuruk says, Don't feel too proud of yourself, being a Coyote, because he's not as smart as he thinks he is. He never does anything the right way.

I like my new nickname. Kuruk says the word like *ky-oat*, and here I thought it was *ky-oat-ee*. I like his way better. Coyote sounds like a good friend to Medicine Bear.

July is hot as my exothermic experiment where I add calcium chloride to water. To cool off, Kuruk and I swim where Darkwater Creek feeds into the Republican. Maggie comes, too, but she's too shy to go naked and keeps her underclothes on. She sneaks a look at us now and then and things look interesting under her wet cotton, but we try to look away, with her almost like our sister. Girls are mysterious and we say we've seen naked ladies, but we haven't.

The river's great fun. We splash each other, pull up rocks from the bottom and race. I'm surprised how Maggie can swim, with her just learning and that thing she calls her chemise tangled round her legs. She's as fast as us and not afraid of leeches or the blood that drips out after you pull them off. She doesn't mind crawdad pinches, either.

Once our hands and feet turn to white prunes, we get out. Stretched out on the grassy bank to dry in the sun, smelling sweet clover and the fishy water, we talk about other adventures and then Kuruk says, We oughta hop a train.

He's done it before and it's not dangerous if you get on and off when the train's stopped. The trick is to not get caught and the best time is after dark, so we plan to do it after the Fourth of July fireworks. If we catch an opposite train back by morning, nobody'll notice we're gone. Kids stay up late that night, running wild. Grownups don't worry because the whole town's out and everybody's watching everybody else, hoping to see people's secrets lit up by the falling, colored sparks.

I love fireworks for the chemistry. Strontium and lithium salts make reds, calcium salts burn orange and barium-chloride compounds fire green. Copper and chlorine make turquoise. Copper acetoarsenite, called Paris Green, turns bright blue, and it's magnesium or aluminum for bright whites.

Last year I stood around with the firemen who set off the fireworks, and Ted Ellis said if I'd run like the dickens after, he'd let me light a fuse. I did and almost soiled my drawers. I got bored after that, though, and I'm glad to have other plans for this year.

Train hopping will keep me awake to observe if fireworks bring rain. I hypothesize they will not, that Edward Powers and R.G. Dyrenforth were incorrect to believe concussions cause clouds to burst. Most serious scientists believe it false, but if it rains after the fireworks, I might reconsider. If the barometer in our front hallway says the pressure is rising and then it rains after the fireworks, fireworks may be the reason. If it's falling, then rain is probably already on the way and the fireworks will make little difference.

I'm teaching myself to live by scientific method and rational thought to help with the voices in my head. I don't argue with them because they're belligerent, but if I focus on a scientific problem or read something difficult, they talk to each other in the background and don't tell me as often to kill myself or run away from home. I study hard to find the science behind the voices. They tire me out and sometimes I think I should kill myself—and I would—if there wasn't so much to learn. Besides, I'm only twelve and I never heard of a suicide so young. To tell the truth, I wish some days I could die by accident, but I don't tell anybody.

A low blue curtain of smoke hangs over the park like fog, smelling like a war. My heart's racing and ears ringing from setting off the fireworks, this year five ignitions by myself. The firemen said I can run faster than they can, so they handed me the punk and said, Go to it, young man.

I told them, Next year, add on longer fuses, but they laughed and called me a smart aleck.

Every time I set the punk by a fuse, the voices told me to stay and blow up with the rocket, but I got the heck out of there, never mind their swears.

The bully part nobody will forget about this Fourth of July was the seventh rocket got knocked off-kilter by the fellow who lit it, then skewed off to the south instead of shooting straight up, arching a red-and-white streak into a pasture. The dry grass flared up like kerosene. The firemen had to quick hitch horses to the red, white and blue bunting-draped tanker and then slap that team out over the river bridge, air siren wailing and wagon careening like in the Charlie Chaplin flicker show we had in town, up and down pasture ruts with the men bouncing, dangling off the sides. The cattle that didn't run from the fire stampeded off when they heard the ruckus rolling in. It took half an hour to put it out, but they flooded the ground and came back muddy to finish the show to the Veterans' Band playing The Stars and Stripes Forever. And forever those fellows will get ribbed, starting tonight, with folks calling it the Great Charlie Chaplin Fire of 1916.

Kuruk, Maggie and I grab up fried chicken, sweet rolls and cakes, any food the farmers' wives don't want to take back home, 'til we may never eat again. A boy from our class, George Dakin, gives us his mother's tart cherry pie, and I never ate any as good. George walks around with us for a while 'til his father yells he's got to go home.

Another woman feeding us is Mrs. Voegel from the farm where Father brews beer, and her son Rolf pals around with us after George goes. He speaks English better than his parents and shows us some Mutt and Jeff and Katzenjammer Kids comic clippings he keeps in his back pocket for a laugh. Using a long stick for a cane and a stubby one for a cigar, then swiping a top hat off a picnic table, he plays W.C. Fields bumping into people and pretending to be drunk and sorry. Because he's funny and strong enough to help us out of a jam, we ask him to come with us on the train.

All the hullabaloo makes it easy for us four to disappear into the dark and smoke, like we're spirits beyond the veil. It's a short hike to the rail yard, where we pick a boxcar with a low step and a firm ladder on the back. Maggie's game, tucking the back of her skirt up between her legs and into her belt, as good as wearing trousers. She calls out, Ladies first, then climbs up lickety-split like no lady would, making her the first one up top. We lie whispering up there 'til the depot lights glow on and the warehouse workers straggle over for their midnight shifts to load the cars with marked cases of beer, bricks and cigars, the ones hand-rolled over at Tooney's.

By one in the morning with the bright stars over us, we're speeding east, clackety-clacking, rails rattling our bones with coal smoke and steam blowing over us on the boxcar roof. We hang on 'til we're sure we won't roll off, passing through Red Cloud, then Guide Rock and Superior.

I tell everybody, We may not be home by morning. I never checked the schedules, figuring freight trains stop at every town, but when the old engine speeds past Pawnee, I swear we're bound for Missouri.

It gets cold up there in the wind we're making, so I put my arm around Maggie and she lets me. I tell her she's pretty as a magpie.

She punches me on the arm and says, That's no decent compliment. Magpies are noisy birds that eat dead things.

Magpies are beautiful little thieves, like you. They swipe anything shiny that catches their eye.

That's not fair, I only ever stole books. Maggie bats my hand away and says, You better come up with something sweeter than that for a girl to like you.

Who says I want you to like me? I let go of her, but when I call her Magpie again, she smiles.

All the while, the four of us sing and tell jokes, yelling over the train's *chuck-a-chuck-a-roar* and pretending not to be scared where we'll end up. Kuruk tells us Indian stories about the stars, and those lights look low enough to pick like cherries.

When I spot Rolf holding on to Maggie, the voices say, Shove that bastard off the train before he steals your girl, but I grit my teeth and tell them, You to go to hell. To shut them out, I picture Mendeleev's periodic table I have tacked on my bedroom wall and list the elements from left to right by atomic weight.

Finally, the train slows down and pulls to a stop in Table Rock. While men offload the beer, brick and cigars to ship northwest to Lincoln, we climb down the far side of the boxcar, our muscles sore from hanging on. We cross to another track with an engine pointed west and hope it'll take us back to Darkwater Creek Station. We're so tired, Rolf has to boost every one of us, making us glad we brought him and not only for the dirty songs he taught us. I forgive him for latching on to Maggie the way he did. I only wish it was me.

Heading west, those other three huddle together, falling asleep. When they get quiet, my voices get loud and I'm feeling lonesome with only them. They say, Throw yourself off the train, and, The world would be a better place without you.

I sit up on the boxcar and once I get used to the wind and lean into it, I like how it pushes and how strong I am, pushing back. I try up on my knees, and then I stand. Spreading my arms like wings, I feel like flying. Peaceful. Free. The wind is a mother's fingers in my hair, and my shirt billows out like a sail with the cloth snapping, stinging along my ribs. The train thump-rocking under my feet is all that ties me to the ground.

I close my eyes and picture flying in the Lafayette Escadrille in Verdun, killing Germans from my airplane. If I was older, I'd run off to be a pilot in the war and Maggie would fall in love with me, because that's what girls do.

The wind in my ears drowns the voices. The whole time I'm dream-flying against the cool black wind, it's quiet in my head, and I decide when I'm grown I will train to be a pilot, to fly free, up with Kuruk's gods in the stars. Up where the voices can't rain or roar down on me from their clouds.

When the others stir around, waking, I squat low to keep my flying secret. Darkwater Creek Station's lights glitter ahead of us, and the train shoots down a straightaway along the river valley so fast I hope we'll fly through to the Colorado mountains to pan for gold. The whistle shrieks and we cover our ears. When the brakeman pulls up hard, we grab the top rails and each other to keep from sliding forward, coming to a screeching halt.

With the locomotive rumbling and coughing soot, Rolf climbs down and gives us the high sign, but Dietz pops from behind the caboose swinging the billy club he keeps for drifters and hobos. Maggie's halfway down the ladder and jumps, slicing her hands on the shale siding, then I drop down with Kuruk to help her. Dietz isn't as fast on his feet as he is with his fists and we get away.

Back of the hardware store, we rip some rags off our shirttails to wrap Maggie's bleeding hands, while she blinks hard to keep from crying, all the time saying, Shit-fire, Shit-fire, and, Now I'll catch hell for sure. She lets us walk her to Amsels' new house in town, watching for Dietz on the side streets. Rolf hightails it home, down Main.

Sure enough, Father bawls me out for running with riffraff, a one-trunk-inheriting Kraut immigrant and a rampallian servant girl. Don't I care about my future? He says I need friends with money and good breeding. I bite my tongue to keep from blurting out, Maggie's the girl I love for my wife.

Up in the tree house after school, those boys only talk about the war and how America should get into it for them to enlist, fly aeroplanes and shoot down Germans. They only hush about it when Rolf is with us, because his family came from Bavaria. Rolf's a nice boy, but nothing like Jack was before he went aeroplane crazy.

Jack still studies the weather and taught me the elements of rain—hydrogen and oxygen, the same as water of course, but also bonded with dust for the condensation nuclei. Nitrogen oxide, from lightning and coal fires, makes rain good for plants. He wants to conduct aerial experiments with rainmaking, burning coal or dropping dust and nitrogen into clouds. I told him, Burning anything in an aeroplane is the Once Upon a Time to a story with a bad ending, but like any boy, he figures nothing can hurt him. He laughed at me, flapped his arms and buzzed his lips like a motor.

I'm not a skittish little ninny. I don't mind snakes, bugs or blood, and I slice off my own knuckle warts. I'm the first to jump off a barn crossbeam down to a haystack or swing over the river on a rope. When the next hot air balloon demonstration comes to town, I'll buy a ride and if I have enough nickels, I'll take Jack up, too. Maybe he'll kiss me in the sky, where the rain is born. Probably he'll only spit off the side and joke about being a rainmaker.

Mrs. Endicott says it's a long, frustrating process for a boy to become a man, but a girl becomes a woman overnight. I believe her, and my first kiss may be a long time coming. Jack did hold my hand on the boxcar. That's something, but come to think of it, I may take the bull by the horns and kiss him. For as they say, *Fortis fortuna adiuvat*. Fortune favors the bold.

On that subject, Mrs. Endicott pulled me aside for a talk in the pantry, turning my ears bright as those Mason jars of pickled beets about that overnight situation. She says don't be scared when I start bleeding. She gave me some rags and told me how to wear and wash them. Most alarming is I'll be able to have a baby. With Adolph and Greta rubbing snot on my skirt, last thing I need is a baby of my own, so I asked how to keep from having one and she said, Just be a good girl.

Heavens, I'll soon be in the family way, because being good is not, as the French say, my *forté*. Mrs. Endicott was kind to warn me, though, and I will do my best. I have some idea how babies come, from seeing dogs and cattle climbing on each other at the farm. I can't picture it with people, though, without a giggle fit. And do you think I can find anything about it in a book?

Even so, it's no laughing matter to soon experience the many female complaints women whisper about. At least I have Mrs. Endicott to play the mother's part. She's kind and may love me a little in spite of her pooched-out disappointed lips, slaps upside my head and grumbling. Lately, when Florence tells her to whip me, the old woman says, Let's not cut a switch and say we did, then hands me a cookie or slice of warm bread with butter melting in a puddle. She doesn't say Florence is insane, but she raises her eyebrows and sighs when our lady-in-waiting hollers or throws things.

I harbor serious doubts—not only about Florence's sanity, but also her consumption. Mrs. Endicott says, There's a stone better left unturned. But I never found anything under a rock to take my breath away or make me sorry I looked.

When a Darkwater girl's mother died of consumption, she gagged up a gob of blood and choked on her last breath. Some kids said, No, she wound down with a wheeze and turned blue. Maybe it was one right after the other. I can't argue the point because I never witnessed a death. We figure, though, consumption must kill a person in ten years. A seventh grader has an uncle doctor at a New York hospital, so we trust that boy's opinion and he concurs, the way doctors concur when they agree. His uncle told him bright red blood coughed up in a handkerchief means tuberculosis.

Grownups say Mrs. Parker was from childhood a pale, skinny thing, so how long Caroline's mother suffered her disease remains a mystery. But if Mrs. Amsel was sick since 1906, she should by rights be six feet under, yet she's hale and hearty with a few rust-colored smears on her embroidered hankies, like from chapped lips. It's a poor showing for somebody at death's door. Then I take note, Florence only coughs when her husband upsets her or she tires of children jumping on her mattress and wants to read *Harper's Bazar*.

From *The Principles and Practice of Medicine* by Osler, a book Jack gave me after teasing I'd steal it, anyway, if he didn't, I learn tuberculosis can affect other parts of a person, not only the lungs. Perhaps Florence has a bad case elsewhere.

The book suggests high altitudes and dry climates improve chances for recovery, and it cheers me to think of Florence on a long excursion to Utah or Montana, which could do us both a great deal of good, if she were to leave me behind. When I asked if she'd consider a sanitarium in a better climate, she swore she's too weak to travel. My eye. Anybody with that strong a backhand could bear up for a month in Mr. Amsel's new Pierce-Arrow.

To fortify her, I offer doses of cod liver oil, listed in *Rawleigh's Good Health Guide* for tuberculosis, but she pulls a face and calls me a pest. Because Osler recommends a healthy diet, I set extra vegetables and meat on her plate, but she refuses them and picks over the French chocolates Mr. Amsel brings from New York, biting into every one for her favorite fillings. Probably also to keep me from taking any.

While Mr. Amsel is away, I watch her flutter downstairs to the parlor chair with a blanket over her knees, ready to receive afternoon callers. She takes her meals in the dining room, makes up her face for visitors and has me hot-iron fifty curls in her hair. Once her husband returns, she picks at her food tray in bed and insists he eat from a spider-legged bedside table. She doesn't touch up her lips or cheeks and lets her hair go flat from her pillows.

As Jack would say, I gathered the evidence and now pose my hypothesis: The woman's a malingerer who pretends to die for attention. The more pathetic she appears, the more her husband speaks love and tenderness to her. I feel a little sorry for her, but he might like her better if she didn't throw tantrums, pout and cough loud.

But what do I know about love? *Mysterium gloriosum et doloris.*

Late afternoon on this October Saturday, Florence hooks Mr. Amsel into working a jigsaw puzzle, and I spring free of the house.

The three boys and I follow a dirt road under milkweed-flossy clouds. Roadside sand dropseed sticks up high as my chest, with green leaves and pink-and-white stems tracing up and out, graceful as ballet dancers' wrists curved over their heads. Hackberry leaves are spotted and yellow-green, their dark purple berries dangling for the winter birds.

The river is where we are going, across a pasture where one roan and one black horse gather grass with their dark velvet lips, their skin rippling at fly bites and their tails flicking. One whinnies when I pass.

Today, in this place, I never felt so much like I belong anywhere, rooting in the ground under my feet and floating in the crystal blue-white air with these boys I love. They jostle and shove and scuff, puffing up the powdery light dirt until I laugh. I love even the little beads of sweat on their skin from play-fighting and their white teeth shining in their suntanned faces. The rips in their gray-striped overalls and blue jeans, the threadbare red bandanna knotted around Kuruk's neck and the dust on Jack's new shoes. I love it all.

We stomp on the shaded plank bridge and spit off the side. The river smells both fresh and dank, as birth and death happen together in the rippling brown. No light bounces on the river here, no reflection because of all the trees arching over. It runs slow and shallow, crisscrossed by fallen gray trunks.

On the south bank, evening primrose's long silver leaves and dried husks are coated with dust like Mrs. Endicott's powdered sugar biscuits, but I remember their wide yellow spring flowers. I break off a husk and roll it between my fingers and thumb, for the breeze to carry off the tiny curled seeds.

I filter the low sun with my eyelashes, bringing the things ahead and those behind me into focus. I find something more than father and mother here, with the pods and husks and seed-bearing wind and in the sound of water. I feel the season swinging down into chill, ice and whiteness, scratching with sharp fingers at the bright surface of summer and I'm sorry, but not afraid.

We walk around a clump of elderberry to look down where the Republican shines, reflecting a glory of blue sky and clouds, curving and splitting around sand bars and running, running east. I hurry down along the limestone outcroppings and shale, where lemon-tan grasses stand like uncombed hair and sumac flares crimson and blood. The boys pick up chunks of stone to toss at each other, joshing and dodging. I close my eyes and listen. Rolf's voice is deep and thick as river mud, while Jack's is bright and sure, echoing off the water. Kuruk's is low and gentle. I feel more than hear it, as if he's the sun warming my hair. My sense of Kuruk seeps inside me, disturbing and comforting.

Seeing me stand still as church, the boys come over. On my right, Jack and Rolf keep poking each other with elbows, snorting, but Kuruk quiets, and on my left side, where the other two can't see, he laces his dark fingers with mine, a surprise as gentle and natural as a pheasant rising from switchgrass.

We stand together on a crumble of limestone above the water. Wild geese practice pilot formations over us, slanting their Vs to the south and honking goodbye. The sparrows, who stay through the winter, fluff and huddle in the red cedar, rustling and *chirrup-cheeping*. Magpies clatter, roosting on naked branches near the water. I already miss the rhythm and music that will fly south. Thank goodness the cardinal stays to sing *purty-purty-purty-purty, sweet-sweet-sweet-sweet* over the snow.

Kuruk's so near, my breaths fall into rhythm with his, even as those other two rascals, bored, break away. So they don't notice our touching hands, I unweave myself from my Pawnee boy, who gives me much to think about, even after I open my eyes.

We four walk to the Voegel farm, where George Dakin joins us and Rolf leads to his favorite spot on the river. It bends and widens, shallow and slow, perfect for wading, but the water's too cold now. Rolf explains in the mornings how frost crusts those cattail spikes in the shade and lacy ice gets trapped in oxbows. His father read in an almanac it'll be a hard winter, and a dry summer next.

George says Rolf's lucky to have those artesian wells on his place, to never worry about drought.

Rolf says, Having something other people want ain't always good luck.

Those fellas keep on twisting your Pa's arm about the land?

Rolf turns away. It'll be alright, he says. Pa can handle Hollingwood. He ducks his head at Jack, a kind of apology.

Jack grins and whacks Rolf's arm with his cap to show it's okay.

A breeze curls down my neck, under my sweater. I smell smoke and shiver. Winter's coming too soon, I say.

Rolf nods, breaks a stick and tosses it in the water.

We talk about winter, how the tree house leaks wind like a sieve and we'd put a stove in, if it wouldn't likely burn down. Rolf says we need a padlock on the trap door to keep out trespassers. George says he has a spare one in their shop.

The boys plan setting traps for fox and mink, stomping in the snow while I'm trapped another way, in Florence's new Frank Lloyd Wright house. I'll be filling hot water bottles and carrying pots of hot tea all hours. That woman always has a chill. No fireplaces, either, in the new Amsel house, only clanking, hissing radiators drying out the air so your fingers pop sparks on everything until they're sore. I do miss a good crackling fire.

After we toss Rolf's baseball back and forth and skip flat stones across the river, George points out the magpie under a willow. One wing's cocked at a peculiar angle, with feathers spread like fingers. It can't have been dead long, because no flies buzz over it and no critter got at it last night.

More magpies crowd in the tree over it, and one swoops down to stand beside. With magpies being carrion birds, I guess what comes next. But this one didn't come to eat.

He cocks his head and turns a bright eye on the dead one, then grabs hold of that spread wing and tugs the body onto a flat rock. He stays like a statue beside it, then spreads his own wings and lets out, *Ack-ack-ack-ack*, his beak cupping the sky. He calls out until another one, then ten other magpies gather around the rock.

The sun angles in between half-naked willow branches, lighting up the magpie feathers, shimmering on the iridescent blue and flashing off the white. The bird who started it preaches while the others strut and take turns standing over the body to holler.

This is a funeral. The dead magpie is more than carrion to his friends and they're grieving.

A young one nudges the fallen bird to help him up, then cries out when he fails. Another pokes him and lifts a wing feather. All the while, more magpies come. Another hops circles around the body, *Ack-ack-ack-ack*, telling what a fine magpie this friend was, how he built the biggest nest and flew the fastest and gathered more seeds off the ground than anybody. Another bird brings a tuft of seedy grass and lays it by the body, a funeral bouquet.

For ten minutes the noise is like an alarm, raising hair on my neck and tingling down my arms. I'm afraid and don't know why.

Then they fall quiet.

Those magpies stand for a while, black and still. Then one by one they flap away, leaving their brother on the rock.

Jack and Kuruk wipe their noses on their sleeves and I dry my eyes. George blinks fast, clears his throat and whispers, Well, if that don't beat all.

Rolf suggests we dig a hole and we lay the magpie down softly there by the rock, where his friends can find his grave.

Brushing dirt off his hands, George says he has chores, so he walks west on the dirt road. A few feet away, he turns and says, I'll come over later, once I got everything buttoned up at home. Save me some beer.

Kuruk and Jack wave. Rolf crooks a smile and says, I ain't promising anything.

Jack and Rolf walk ahead on our way to Rolf's. Kuruk puts his arm around me and I rest my head on his shoulder, not caring who sees. I breathe him in, spicy and warm. We don't talk, because those magpies said everything.

Rolf's house is as big as a church, but smells of cinnamon and bacon, even with Mrs. Voegel away on a trip with Rolf's brothers. He takes us up to the boys' room in the attic, warm and dry with three soft, clean beds. His little brothers share, but being the oldest, he gets his own. From under his bed, he shows us his treasures, glass marbles and skeleton keys in a cigar box with a rainbow-colored butterfly on top.

With his father out working in the brewery, Rolf sneaks us into his parents' room. He pulls back a braided rag rug to show us a hole built under a floorboard, a secret compartment. His mother put a purple silk lavender sachet in there, too, as musty-sweet as the cedar is sharp. Rolf reaches in and pulls out a pocket knife. Hey, this is mine, he says, holding it up. Pa took it away for a week and forgot to give it back.

You shouldn't be showing us your father's secret, Jack says. It's like a safe in a bank.

Rolf pushes the hair back out of his eyes and says, But you guys are my friends. I can trust you, right? Pinkie swear not to tell anybody.

We look at each other, nod and lock our little fingers together like barbed wire to say,

Pinky, pinky bell
Whoever lies or tells
Will sink down deep to hell
And never rise.

Rolf nods and leads us downstairs to the kitchen for bread and cheese to take to the barn, away from Rolf's father. If he finds us in the house, he'll put Rolf to work.

The milk cows and draft horses keep the barn warm, so we climb up the ladder to where Rolf hid some beer from the storehouse. The loft is packed near bursting with bales, and we huddle down in a corner.

I don't like beer, but the boys drink two bottles each, and Kuruk and Jack fall into first-grader giggle fits. Rolf brags that Germans take beer like water from the time they're babies, so it doesn't affect him the same. We watch Kuruk and Jack spinning and falling in the hay, punching each other on the arms and laughing.

Rolf scoots closer on the bale beside me and puts his hand on my leg. I get ready to jump up if I need to. He's two years older than the other boys, three older than me, and he has my head mixed up about which boy to like, with his arm muscles and voice deep like a man's. I've been in love with Jack, so wishing Rolf would kiss me is confusing. Kuruk watches Rolf with a scowl, but Jack doesn't care what Rolf does, or he's too drunk to see.

Jack and Kuruk go to pee out the hay mow door, but call Rolf over and point down at the yard. I stand up and get closer.

Kuruk buttons his pants and whispers, Quoyle and Dietz are down there with your Pa.

Rolf shushes us and Quoyle drones on. That man uses more words to be cruel than anybody, fancying up his threats. Instead of saying, Go home, I've heard him say to a child on the street, You are a pestilence, and fortune frowned the day your father begat you. He thinks it makes him sound intelligent, but he's what Mrs. Endicott calls a Pompous So-and-So.

Down below, Mr. Voegel throws a long soft shadow that dissolves behind him on the front porch. He points a pistol first at Dietz, then at Quoyle, back and forth like he can't decide. The dusk is thick purple but his face shines the color of apricots in the last setting sunlight.

Es ist mir, Gott im Himmel, meine Farm!

Quoyle raises his voice, clear as the school bell to say, You have a verbal contract with Mr. Hollingwood.

I never sign!

A man of honor . . .

Honor? Voegel breaks in. Is it honor to take land I farm with my boys? We homestead here and prove the claim.

As sheriff, I serve this eviction notice. Quoyle holds out a paper, but Mr. Voegel knocks it to the ground.

Damn, Rolf mutters, brushing past me to climb down the ladder.

Jack holds himself up on the loft doorframe, watching with Kuruk. I step back.

Maybe we should go down there, Kuruk says.

Maybe we're drunk as skunks and best not, Jack answers, burying a giggle in his sleeve. He reaches out and bats Kuruk's cowboy hat off his head. Before Kuruk can grab it, it tumbles out the open loft door, sailing into the yard to land not thirty feet from the men below. We draw back, afraid they'll notice and see us up here, but the argument continues, unbroken.

Jack slumps down on a bale beside me and whispers, I'm gonna be sick. I push his face the other way and say, Not on me, you won't.

Kuruk stumbles over Jack's legs to go after Rolf, but I catch hold of his shirt sleeve.

Quoyle and Dietz need only one more reason to hurt you, I remind him. He shrugs and gives me a sad smile before he pulls free.

I'm as sick as I guess I'd be if I drank four beers, breaking out in a cold sweat. Chilled and angry to see Kuruk go, I decide if I must, I'll sit on Jack to keep him in the loft.

It happens fast.

Rolf storms up to the three men hollering, I'm here, *Vatter*, with his fists balled up tight and pumping at his sides, ready to fight.

Rolf, go in the house! His father takes a step back from Quoyle and Dietz, but keeps his eyes on them.

You get out of here! Rolf yells.

Quoyle shakes his head and raises his hands, acting reasonable. Dietz touches the knife sheathed on his belt and lunges at Voegel to startle him. Voegel swings from Quoyle to Dietz, shaking so hard the gun bobs like a duck.

Sohn, go inside!

Rolf charges Quoyle. Dietz pulls his knife and dives at Rolf as Quoyle sidesteps, grabs and twists Voegel's hands, pointing the gun at Rolf.

The gunshot cracks and echoes back off the hard-packed ground, the side of the house and the barn, like three shots instead of one.

Rolf falls, holds his head and tries to crawl.

Oh, shit. Jack sways toward the open loft door, but I pull him back before he can fall.

Quoyle lets go of the gun, raises his hands and steps back. Dietz looks around, but not up at us, and wipes his blade on his trouser leg.

Voegel's mouth falls open and he drops the gun, yelling, *Mein Gott, mein Gott!* On his knees beside Rolf, Voegel rolls him face up, pushing the dark hair off his face and spreading his hand on the boy's chest.

I don't know what I saw. Was it a bullet or the knife that got him?

Kuruk darts out from the shadow below us, but he must think better of it. Seeing him step back, I sigh and hope he didn't catch those scoundrels' attention.

Jack starts to howl, but I cover his mouth and whisper, Be quiet or you're next. He focuses on me, confused, but nods. We huddle, holding on to each other, watching Quoyle and Dietz back away into the dark. Then their truck starts up and they leave the poor man in the dirt, cradling his son.

Kuruk's clinging to the top of the ladder, waving for us to follow him out the side door.

We need to get a doctor, I say.

Jack nods, but he can't walk fast or straight. Kuruk's doing better, but he'd be hard pressed to run. I offer to get Dr. Reed.

That old doctor has his hand on his doorknob, just getting home when I trudge up on his porch, panting. He crank-starts his motor car and says, Get in, I'll need a nurse.

I don't want Quoyle and Dietz to know I saw them. I don't want to see Rolf that way.

Dr. Reed glares and reaches over to swing open the car door. I climb in, thinking, I can stay hidden in the car, but if Quoyle and Dietz have gone, maybe I can help Rolf.

Damn this town. Who shot the boy? Shut the door, girl.

I tell him I only heard the sound and found Rolf lying there.

He stomps down, kicking the car forward and mutters, This bullshit again. It's always about the money or the land. Will it never end?

Running into town, I decided there's no point being honest. And what would the truth be? Voegel shot his son, but it was Quoyle and Dietz pushed him to it. Or maybe it was Dietz and the knife, or Quoyle pointing the gun and pulling the trigger while they wrestled for it?

Until I know Jack and Kuruk are safe, I'm keeping mum.

Voegels' farmyard is like a silent, dark underwater world, except for headlights beaming blurry tubes of light on the house, brewery buildings and barn.

Be careful or you'll drive over him. He's here in the yard. I swing my finger in an arc, and Dr. Reed shoves down on the brake.

My friend's body sprawls on the ground, with his father nowhere to be seen. It's easy to imagine Quoyle and Dietz hurt him, too, but I push the thought out of my mind.

Dr. Reed angles the car for the gas lamps to light up Rolf. We go together into the bright white glow that makes his face like chalk. Dark blood wets the dirt under Rolf's head. The doctor checks him for breath and heartbeat and mutters, Dammit.

Help me get him in the back seat, he orders, and I do, then crawl in to hold Rolf's bloody head in my lap. I make myself look. Part of his scalp is torn away, with bits of white bone in gray brains and blood. He's breathing a long snore once every minute or so, and I tell the doctor and ask, Isn't that good? He shakes his head.

Dr. Reed drives fast on high, smooth grades, but slows to a crawl over gravel washboards. Once or twice he scares the bejabbers out of me, swinging his head around to yell, You didn't see anybody?

When I answer, No, what feels like half a dozen times, I'm sure he knows I'm lying.

He bangs his hand on the steering wheel and says, Damn this corrupt, godforsaken town.

Gusting out a big breath, he tells me, If you're afraid, you say so and I'll protect you. He swears on his life, but his trembly voice tells me he can't keep his word.

Rolf's face is wet, my tears slipping flat and silvery down his pale, moonlit cheeks. I want to believe his chest will rise high with a living breath. I want to believe Quoyle and Dietz didn't do this for Jack's father with all his money, that he isn't the reason this beautiful boy, who wanted to kiss me not an hour ago, now is dead.

So it isn't anything Mrs. Endicott warned me about that makes me a woman tonight.

When Mrs. Voegel comes home from Lincoln the next morning, her youngest boy finds his father swinging from a rafter in their barn. Sheriff Quoyle, who is there at ten o'clock to notify her about her dead son, rules the old man a suicide.

Jack, Kuruk and I sit on barrels outside Green's, listening. Carrying paper-wrapped parcels that stink of cheese and drip from bloody meat, Main Street shoppers gossip.

What a tragedy, and, Who would have thought?

They breathe fast and widen their eyes, telling how the widow screamed and tore out her hair. They say, Bless her soul, as if they're sorry and not delighted for the scandal, not giddy believing they're too righteous for evil to touch them.

One red-haired woman says, The boy's face was shot off. No wonder the father went crazy.

Well, another says, Foreigners don't think the way we do, but suicides go to hell in any language.

I climb down off the barrel, cussing, but Jack holds my arm and says, Let it pass.

They act like they knew the Voegels and saw what happened, I say. It's not right.

Well, the ones who did see are keeping mum, Jack whispers, so the story's theirs to tell. That's how it works.

I chew hard on my lip and it starts to bleed. The taste of iron is a peculiar comfort.

We're too glum for penny candy or Coca-Cola, hanging our heads. The bag of popcorn we bought from the red-and-gold cart tastes like dust, and we're dropping pieces to Toss, who crunches them and stands on his hind legs to lick the oil and salt off our fingers.

I'm feeling Toss's rough tongue, how it scratches and tickles, when Quoyle's shining boots clunk over the boardwalk. Kuruk stiffens beside me and tucks his hands under his thighs. Jack draws a deep breath and looks up against the sun at the shape and shadow.

Sir? Jack asks, squinting to look that monster in the eye.

Are you children consoling one another?

We're managing fine, I answer, trying to sound brave but my voice comes out high and squeaky. I study his hands and wonder if those fat fingers tossed the hanging rope over the crossbeam, or if they only waved to show Dietz how. They are the soft hands of a man who gives orders.

With his boot, he crunches a skittering beetle. You must be beside yourselves with guilt.

We take a deep breath, all together.

Maybe you boys learned your lesson, that if you imbibe demon alcohol, terrible things happen. He stares at Kuruk and adds, Although, you weren't in your right mind when you shot the boy, you are responsible.

Kuruk looks sidelong at me, his face twisted in misery.

I squint up and whisper, You're saying Kuruk killed Rolf?

Quoyle sighs and lays a hand on my shoulder, sending quivers through my neck and face. He keeps his voice low, so only we can hear him.

You didn't see it, my dear, but I stand as witness to the crime that occurred as I served official papers to Mr. Voegel. By rights his death is also laid to your Indian friend's account. Morally, if not legally speaking, for the poor father was overwrought, seeing his son shot dead.

Quoyle releases my shoulder and strokes one of my long curls before sighing and scratching his chin.

However, as I see it, there's no bringing back the dead, and your Indian friend is but a child. It was unfortunate, carelessness with no premeditation, and the law is unwieldy if not yoked with compassion.

Jack whispers to me, What the hell is he saying?

I shrug and shake my head.

Kuruk understands before we do. He asks, Mr. Quoyle, will you spread this lie or will you hold it over me?

Jack's eyes widen and he nudges Kuruk. My chest swells with love for my brave Indian brother, even as I shudder to think how he'll pay for the truth.

A wide, uneven smile slithers across Quoyle's face.

Peter, he says, the sun is unseasonably strong today. How unfortunate that you've misplaced your hat.

Kuruk looks down at the ground, then at me.

Jack probably doesn't remember knocking it off, for Quoyle to find it at Voegels'.

Shit-fire, I blurt out, and Quoyle glances at me, surprised.

My word, he mutters, then says to Kuruk, Mr. Hollingwood is blind to what you are, boy. He's plagued by tenderheartedness and thinks of you as a son.

Quoyle's eyes flick to Jack and he nods, pursing his lips in sympathy. How difficult, he says, for you to watch your father squander his affection on a savage. Mark my word, this conniving red child will wrestle away your inheritance as well.

Jack blinks and his dry lips part, but no words come out.

Quoyle kneels to pet Toss, who cringes against Kuruk's dangling leg.

As if he's telling us a bedtime story, Quoyle says, I once spied a three-legged dog in the street. He was a disturbing sight, hideously deformed, and although he ambled fairly well, I believe he felt great pain from his missing limb. Better, I suppose, if he'd died from his injury, but life can be cruel.

Toss slinks behind the barrel and peers out, sharp puppy teeth bared. Kuruk narrows his eyes and takes a deep breath.

Quoyle stands, brushes his hands as if they could get clean and touches the brim of his hat. Clearing his throat, he speaks now for the passersby.

My condolences, children, for your loss. Mrs. Voegel requests that you boys, with others from your school, serve as pallbearers. As for you, Miss . . . what is your last name?

He knows good and well I haven't a real one. He might as well call me a bastard.

My name is Margaret Rose.

His eyes glitter at me. That's neither here nor there, he says, smiling as if he meant no harm. Dear girl, I hope you have the self-control to mind your language as you walk in the funeral procession attired as an angel. Mr. Hollingwood plans an elaborate funeral for the destitute family, with the finest mourning costumes from Chicago and fresh flowers, priced exorbitantly in this waning season.

Quoyle pauses in his speech and clears his throat to add, For the son, only. Mr. Hollingwood argued with the pastor, to no avail. The father will molder in the potter's field. A cautionary tale, a byword. Children, take note.

He breathes in and exhales the word, both a breath and a hiss, Alas.

He peers at Kuruk and continues for any and all to hear, saying, As for the matter of justice, the record stands that Mr. Voegel shot his son before taking his own life. as there's no testimony to refute it, and no evidence . . .

Kuruk reaches up out of habit to adjust his missing hat, then spits on the walkway by Quoyle's boot.

My heart hammers in my chest. We'll honor Rolf like you say, I whisper, covering Kuruk's hands with mine.

Quoyle nods, fondles his bowler brim and steps off the boardwalk to cross the street, chest out and thumbs tucked in his belt.

Today I play Quoyle's and Hollingwood's song and dance in their dark vaudeville show in this crowded church. Our only protest is not to show how it moves us. Jack and Kuruk stare at the floor. Stone-faced, I take it all in and swear never to forget the drape of the green altar cloth. The sweaty stink. The honey perfume of those infernal beeswax candles lined up everywhere. If we move, we'll topple one with an elbow and set somebody on fire. I even memorize the sparrow trapped up in the vaults. Is that the one His eye is on while it flutters and cheeps, exhausted, beating the rafters for an open window with nowhere to rest, shooting out little white flashes of shit? Bumping against the stained glass, desperate. Unless somebody leaves a door open, he will die in here. Maybe even then.

Graveside, the pastor drones like a bee in love with a blossom, spreading yellow words. Innocence. Sorrow. Justice. Glory.

The sky is too blue, too bright with no clouds to interfere and the air tangs with manure. Freshly turned dirt smells damp, half rotted as a secret. In the near pasture, milk cows gather to watch and scratch their loose necks on the barbed wire fence. Dead leaves crunch under our new shoes. The boys tug on their collars.

When Whites found our Kitkehahki band in earth lodges on these river banks, because we were free, happy and peaceful, they figured we had a republic government like theirs. To make sense of us, they called us the Republican band and this water, the Republican River—just like that, as if we and the river waited for them to decide, with no names or meanings of our own.

But my people called this river Kiraruta, It is Filthy, because so many buffalo grazed and drank here the water ran brown, no good to drink but spreading manure to make the valley fertile for corn and squash. The Whites got rid of the buffalo, the manure and the names and then sent my people to Oklahoma.

But here the river runs and I'm standing in it.

My ancestors, the ones the Whites didn't dig up yet for their schools and museums, are buried around this river valley, hiding from the Whites in the mounds and bluffs. Little broken bits of their bones and spirits must wash downhill when it rains, laughing and glinting in this water, touching and blessing me here.

I take back this river. I name it for an ancestor whose name is sacred, a woman my grandfather loved to remember from when he was young, to tell me her stories. My mother's mother's mother.

I cup my hands and call her name over the water to the birds and animals who remember her, too. I say her name four times, a ceremony.

She Who Holds You.
She Who Holds You.
She Who Holds You.
She Who Holds You.

He scuffles fast out of the bushes and bowls me over onto the frozen road, his weight hard and sudden down on me. Air whuffs out and pain jabs my lung. Toss circles us, barking. Squirming and clutching, I can't keep ahold of the man for his big wool coat that slips like a dog's loose skin under my numb hands while we roll over each other, back and forth.

He breaks away, backs off and stands where I can get my first good look at him. He's not full-grown but tall and thick like a coffee can, with brown hair that tangles down alongside his eyes and red-spotted skin. He squinches down his eyes and pulls his lips back off his brown teeth to look mean but he's breathing fast and shallow like he's scared. He glances back into the bushes. I figure it's a trick so I don't look.

What the hell, I pant, getting up as fast as I can but that stabbing in my lung makes it hard to raise my left arm. The son of a bitch musta broke my rib.

I gotta finish what he started so I charge him. Damn, he's solid. I all but bounce off him and he don't raise a hand. Darting in from the side, I hook a leg around back of his knee and bring him down on his backside. I can't get a full breath but I raise my right fist and use my left arm to guard that hot iron burning in my side. Get up! I groan down at him, nudging him with my boot. You started this, now get up and let me finish it.

I hate these White boy ambushes. I shoulda been watching but I was daydreaming about Maggie. How many men died in the middle of remembering a girl's shining hair or feeling sick about how she moons over another fellow? More than died in wars, for sure.

The boy takes his time getting up, like he has to instead of wanting to. I put no scratch or bruise on him yet but his palms are bleeding and little bits of gravel stick in them. He picks and rubs them off on his trousers and slow, like he's got all day, raises his fists to come at me.

I don't wait for him to hit first but rush in solid and tight as I can, my elbows to my body and when he guards his face, thinking I'll punch up there, I thud my right fist into his belly. He hasn't even braced for it so he folds, groans and sinks down on his knees. He says, No, no.

What kind of fight is this? I back away and wait for him to get up or give up. I'm hoping for the second because moving in fast that way hurts like hell. Toss rushes in and grabs his collar, tearing the brown wool with his long yellow-white teeth. The boy cringes and rolls like a pill-bug, covering his head.

Toss, get off! Enough. I ease my arms down.

Toss backs away, growling, then comes to sit by me.

The fellow's breathing hard. He coughs and drags himself up but won't look at me. I don't want to know why or who, I just want to go home and see the bruise I feel growing on my side but he starts talking. For such a big fellow, he has a high, thin voice almost like a girl's. I took him to be older than me but even if he is beyond my years, I hear it now in the way he talks, he's simple.

I'm sorry. I got no problem with you, he says, and a sob catches in his throat. I got me no problem with Indians atall.

I roll my shoulder to loosen my neck and study how his eyes droop and his wet lips pooch out sad.

This wasn't your idea? Somebody told you to come after me?

He bites his lip and takes a deep breath. I ain't supposed to talk, just beat the hell outa you first thing.

What's your name?

I can't say nothing. Sorry, sorry. He shrugs. Now I figure I get the hell beat outa me. They will.

The ice-wind feels like needles on my face and makes my eyes water, blurring until I blink. My heart slows down and all my strength runs out my arms.

You got you a nice dog, the boy says, picking at his face with his thick fingers. He gotta name?

You come after me again and I'll let him kill you. As soon as I say it, I feel bad because the boy looks afraid, real deep afraid of everything and with him being feeble-minded, I got no call to threaten him. I spit on the ground. Shit.

Shit? The boy wrinkles his forehead.

Listen, I say, You tell whoever sent you he's a coward and I'm ready for him. Tell him to come on any time.

I didn't want to hurt the dog, neither, the boy-man says, so low I almost don't hear him. Just don't let him bite me, okay?

He told you to hurt my dog.

He digs in his pocket for a fold-up knife and shows it to me. After I knock you out, I'm supposed to saw off one of his legs with this here blade. But he's a fine dog and I never woulda.

What's your name?

He looks me in the eye this time and whispers, Carson Dietz. A tear runs down his pimply cheek and he tucks his knife back in his front pocket.

You his son?

He shakes his shaggy head. No, he's my uncle. Crouching down, he rubs his fingers and thumb together, snaps them and whistles out a feather of frost, calling my dog to pet him.

I click to Toss and say, Go on, dog. Be friends.

Good Shit, Carson says and runs his hands through my dog's ruff, muttering, No sir, I got me no problem with Indians.

When it comes to running, all a fellow needs is what he can carry. I got my bear claw round my neck, my double picture of Peter La Cherre and all the warm clothes I can wear and still move in. I pick an old knapsack from somebody's garbage and stuff it with half a ham, some dried beef, bread and corn meal, along with a copper pot, a cup and a spoon. Matches. Salt. An old Civil War canteen full of water.

Christmas always brings me low, anyway, sitting up in the carriage house with no family or presents except what coin Hollingwood thinks to toss me, last minute. I never grew up with any tree or special songs but Whites coming together, singing and getting charitable and wet-eyed about their religion—well, it unsettles me. Takes me back to Mrs. Linneman and what can happen to somebody looking as poor as I am, especially this time of year. Some do-good's likely to try to change my life. But it's thinking about Toss that decides it. If Dietz has it in for me so bad he'd send his half-wit nephew to hurt Toss, then I best get moving. Hollingwood may find me useful, worth protecting but he's got no love for my dog, to protect him.

I never hopped a train since Rolf died. Sneaking around to the dark side of the boxcars, away from the station lights, I get a lump in my throat remembering that hot sweet July night with all four of us hanging on to the train and each other so tight.

The wind beats at me here on the north side, spraying ice crystals in my face and I get a bad feeling like I shoulda stayed by my little coal fire. Toss trots beside me, his head turned a little away from the blasting north wind, squinting, his fur standing out thick and tail curved down.

I find the one, packed almost full with the door still open a foot or so. I got a time talking Toss into putting his front paws up on the boxcar floor but he won't go until I shove his rear end in. Then I climb up beside him. The boxcar door's hard to slide, half-frozen but I get it. Then we bed down under some straw and burlap. I feel scared like a kid in a story, only numb and empty. I try to picture where I'm going but there's a big difference between running to something you want and running from what's after you. I only ever done that second kind.

I tell myself this is what I always wanted, anyway, from the day I climbed out Genoa's window. I meant to go to Denver and climb me some mountains. If I hadn't stuck my hand in that cracker barrel and got chased by that policeman in Grand Island, I'd be in Denver already. There never woulda been Joe or Maggie or Jack. No Hollingwood, Quoyle or Dietz. No tree house or seeing Rolf killed. No scars on my hands or back. So I tell myself I'm running to something better, not just away from what might kill me. I tell Toss we got a better life ahead of us.

Even with Toss curled up beside me, I'm half-froze before the train car jerks and bucks ahead out of Darkwater Creek.

When I wake up, the sun's slitting cold little beams between the slats on the back and top of the boxcar. I got warm finally but when the train grinds to a stop, I knock the straw off of us and press my eye to a side wall hole to look

143

out. There's less snow here than there was in Darkwater, the rangeland smudged with grays like coal and slate and the fields stubbled with glistening yellow cornstalks. But that don't mean it's warmer.

We climb down from the boxcar, slipping on a shining bed of ice gotta be two inches deep, and then down the siding into a grove not far from the tracks. It's just a little town without even a name posted on the station so I see I found my way to nowhere special. There's no mountains to the west. We're not anywhere near Denver but the whole place seems higher, flatter and drier than Darkwater. I know from listening to Hollingwood that the Burlington line follows the Republican as far as it goes into Colorado and then past it so maybe the river is still close. I'm afraid I left it behind, though, with Margaret Rose and Jack.

My eyes hurt from the wide open brightness. I squint against the glare of the sun off the iced grass and twigs over my head. Some of those globs and lines of ice split the light, breaking colors out of the white clear day. I could go blind from those reds, yellows and blues that needle my sight.

Toss whines, nudges me and pants so I pour some water into my tin cup for him to lap up. I feel sick and dizzy like I just dropped off a cloud. I scratch my dog's ears and then whittle off a sliver of ham for him. While he licks the salt off my fingers I ask, Toss, what've I gone and done to us?

I lean against a tree, blink and hunt for a horizon but the ground and the sky freeze together far as I can see. Behind the short train I see the empty white town. Somebody tied sparkling silver and gold ropes of Christmas tinsel on the signposts, like it wasn't already icy and shiny enough outside. Those ropes flap and curl in the wind, twinkling back sunlight like strings of stars. With that boxcar door still open how I left it, the black locomotive idles, guzzling water from the station tank, choking out little gray clouds of steam.

My heart beats so fast I can't catch my breath and when I look back east, I know. I got me a bad case of homesickness and it's bigger, sharper and stronger than the fear that got me on that train. It cuts deeper than the wind. My chest throbs with heart roots tore out of the only ground, the only place I ever had. God help me, that place is Darkwater Creek and I got nowhere else. My blood pulls, calling me home to my friends.

But what about Quoyle and Dietz and what they mean to do to me? What about my dog? I got some fight left in me, maybe enough to survive and maybe I'm smart enough to stay in Hollingwood's good graces. Should I leave Toss here, get back on that train without him? He could find somebody in that town to feed him. He could live a long, four-legged life by somebody's crackling fire, get fat and father some pups. Or he might freeze here in this grove, nothing but another stray but one thing's sure. I can't take him back to be crippled or killed.

I order him to sit and stay. Like he knows what I'm up to, he tilts his head and stands so I yell it. He drops his tail and looks to the side like I got bad manners.

When I walk south, I don't look back. Blinking hard, I break into a run for the train, where a fellow's climbing up to move the water tank siphon away. The puffs are coming faster out of the stack. When I get to the siding and scramble up, I picture Toss shivering out there under that exploding light. One boot slips on the crushed rock and I fall, slicing my hand when I reach down to catch myself. Worse, my busted rib from where that Dietz kid slammed me to the ground takes my breath away and I lay there, rocks poking sharp through my coat. I close my eyes and say, Kuruk the Medicine Bear, get up. It's the best thing for that dog to stay here. Get up and go.

I hear rocks slide and clatter and think that rail yard fellow musta seen me from up on that tank. I look to see big yellow eyes looking down and a wet black nose by mine. I grab his thick ice-powdered fur and he licks my face.

Good dog, Toss. Don't ever listen to me.

The east-bound train pulls into Darkwater Christmas Eve. Even the fellows usually working nights at the station are celebrating tonight. I hear folks singing when I walk by two churches with Toss. Silent Night. Holy Night.

It feels holy to me but empty too, like I got no other people in my story. Did anybody notice I was gone? Jack and Maggie woulda thought of me soon enough though, missing me because once people got no use for them, they're like me, alone.

Instead of walking straight to the carriage house and my dead-cold little stove, I walk through town and across the river bridge to George's. I wait on their porch swing with snow falling like a ripped-up feather bed, my breath puffing out of me in a spirit and then falling to freeze on my chest. No moon, full dark.

In about an hour they come home from church. His beautiful little sisters brush around me in their stiff cold dresses, smelling like lavender and cinnamon and fussing over me because I'm George's friend. The littlest one presses into my hand the orange she got after her Sunday School

146

program. They ask me to stay for some egg nog or hot buttered rum.

I go inside and let them warm me for a while but not too long because where I'm going next, nobody's there to make it a holiday. I don't want to come to expect this good feeling of family. Before I go, I take George aside and ask him a favor.

For a while I need you to keep Toss here. Like he's your dog, to keep him safe.

George asks me who's set out to hurt him but I shrug and say, Just do this for me. A Christmas present.

It's Quoyle and Dietz, he guesses and I keep my face stiff not to agree. He smacks his fist into his palm. If you need me, I'll help. George swears like holding a Bible to protect me and I know he means it.

This is what I need tonight. This is all.

I walk down the steps. This time Toss stays when I tell him, maybe because one of those sisters is petting him. George calls out he'd be glad to give me a ride home but I wave back, No. Walking down their lane, I miss the feeling of Toss beside me but I know I done right by my dog. I couldn't stand him getting hurt because of me.

I almost don't look up while I'm crossing the bridge. Feeling that snow-coated iron like skeleton ribs on both sides makes me colder so I tuck my head down in my jacket, turn the collar up by my ears and push my hat down. The wind wails through the girders but I hear singing, too.

If the river was booze
And I was a duck,
I'd dive to the bottom
And never come up!

147

There's a man or boy in a heavy coat standing up on the top girder, five feet over my head. Looking down at the frozen river, he sings and I know him.

Oh when I die,
Don't you bury me at all
Just soak my bones
In alcohol.

Jack? What the hell?

He sways and looks between his legs back and down at me. Kuruk! Come on up!

How did you get up there?

It's a fine view. Over there's the town. The church steeple with the clock, you could see it from here, except it's the new moon. I heard it chime a while ago so I know nobody's moved it in the night, ha ha. And the streetlights are lined up like football players. Once your eyes get used to the starlight, you can see snow settled on the ice, right down there. I bet that water's dark and cold.

He musta been in his father's Heilbrau again.

I figured your father woulda dragged you to church tonight.

Jack waves an arm. Nah. He's off somewhere. Milwaukee, I think. The busy businessman. Busy, busy businessman.

Looking for the places where snow's been knocked off, I figure out how Jack climbed up there. The iron's coated with ice under the snow so it's a Christmas miracle he's not dead on that river ice.

Come down, Jack. We'll get into your father's liquor cabinet.

Nope. I'm giving up the stuff, he says. Ethanol can kill your liver. Did you know that?

I sure did. But you had plenty tonight.

Jack squats on the beam, almost falling again. Maybe I'm a little drunk.

The bottoms of my boots are slick so I untie them, kick them off and climb up in my socks. They melt the snow and stick some to the icy iron but that's better than slipping off. Up by Jack, the wind's stronger.

Good to see you, Jack says. Sit for a while.

Shit, Jack. This is crazy. You got to come down.

I got both arms wrapped around the girder but Jack squats like he's shooting marbles.

Oh, I will come down, he says. Newton told the truth. He stands again and inches away from me. Taking off his cap, he turns it in his hand and stares at the ice. They're telling me to jump, he says, teetering.

Damned voices. Don't listen to them. I'm your friend and I'm telling you to stay with me.

Why? What good am I?

The wind's driving a nail in my forehead so I take a deep breath and close my eyes to think. Because I ran off two nights ago and hopped a train with Toss. I got halfway to Denver and I thought, You know, I got a good friend Jack who'll be sore if I leave him behind. I'm gonna go back for him.

You went all the way to Denver?

Halfway or so. And you never missed me.

Sure I did. I figured you were being a busy businessman with my father. Jack drops his cap into the wind where it catches like a sail and tumbles down. He fiddles with a loose button on his coat and pops it off. Holding out his hand, he lets the button go and the dark swallows it. He

149

waves down into the space and says, Goodbye, Jack's hat and button. I didn't hear them land, did you?

They fell on the snow. But if you fall, you'll go through, break the ice, maybe even your neck and freeze to death in that shallow water.

He bends his knees, closes his eyes and laughs.

Hey! I was almost to Denver for the adventure of my life, climbing mountains and panning gold but I came back for you. We're gonna make the trip together. That's how much I think of our friendship and here you won't even come down off this bridge for me.

Jack turns, scratches his head, opens his eyes wide and grins at me, devilish. Don't shit me, Kuruk. You came back because you're in love with Maggie.

I'd bang my head on the girder from frustration but I'm sweating and my face would freeze to the metal. The pain in my rib is flared up hard from hanging on and I can't catch a good deep breath. Bright spots burn like Christmas candles in my vision. This keeping Jack alive is hard work and I'm exhausted. I better just agree with anything he says. There's no arguing or conniving him down and he's right anyway, even if I don't like what he's on to.

Well, sure. I'm back for her, too. We're all friends.

Nope. You're in love with Magpie. You're not fooling me.

That's enough. I'm about to climb down and leave him here. But I keep after him because he's all I got and this is no summertime tree he's climbed himself into.

She loves you, Jack. She might lose her mind if you break your neck and drown. And then she'll chase you to hell just to make you sorry.

Hah! Jack looks at me and barks it again. Hah!

I can't feel my feet. I look down and they're still on a beam but my arms are trembling weak. Every breath comes in and out with a wheeze.

That's it, Jack. I'm done. Climb down or I'll go get Maggie. She'll fetch you and wallop you good and you'll never hear the end of it.

Jack sighs. Hell hath no fury, that's for damn sure. He takes one last longing look at the river snow. Then he says quieter, You believe she loves me?

You're the only man for her. Saying it, I get a bitter taste in my mouth.

Jack sighs and his shoulders slump. Well, then, he says, taking a deep breath, I'd better not disappoint my girl.

∞

I tell Pastor I need to write a story in German for school, but I don't know enough words.

Ach, he says, stroking his gray beard and thickening up his old accent. This wouldn't be a problem if your father had kept funding the parochial school here at the church. You'd be fluent in German. He glances at me, then leans over his desk and bites his lip. I mean to say, if the congregation hadn't decided to embrace English, and send their children to the public schools instead.

I nod as if I'm sorry I'm not still a little German-speaker like the kids who get pelted with rocks at school. Like our enemies in the War.

He hands me a smudged German Sunday School paper with a drawing of Jesus holding a lamb and lots of blocky letters that mean nothing to me.

I thought maybe you'd show me some lines in the German Bible, to start me on the right track.

He raises an eyebrow, but nods. The Word of God is the best origin for any endeavor.

Sure is.

He rolls his chair over beside me. When he cracks opens a black leather book, I take the pencil and paper out of my jacket.

How about that part in the Bible when Judas got sorry he sold Jesus for silver and hanged himself?

I was thinking we'd start with Psalm 23, but, if you wish. Pastor sighs and opens to *Matthäus 27* to read for a while. I pay attention but it's only throat-clearing and spit to me. When he finishes, I ask as politely as I can, So which sentence says he hanged himself?

That's not the spiritual value in this passage, Jack.

But it's the part I need for the story. The words, He hanged himself.

He traces his finger under *erhängte sich selbst* while I write it down.

So, I ask, what if Judas didn't hang himself? What if somebody else did it to him? I need to understand the grammar here, what my teacher calls the reflexive. The difference between when you do something to yourself and somebody else does it to you. For example, how Judas would say, They hanged me.

Pastor studies me. I put on an innocent and studious face.

Judas hanged himself, Pastor says. Scripture leaves no doubt. But if you were talking of someone hanged by others, that person might say, *Sie hängte mich.* Except the dead don't speak until they answer God at the Final Judgment. Is your story about Judas?

No, Judas is just an example. And here, where it says he threw the coins on the ground, what if he hid them under the floor, instead?

Pastor taps his finger on the wooden arm of his chair. Who's in your story?

A pirate. He hides his treasure before he dies. And he's in love with a girl he'll never see again, so he writes her a note.

Pastor blows out a harder sigh and looks up at the cross on his wall. This line of thinking could lead you down the wrong path, Jack. You should set your mind on righteousness.

Well, sure I do. All the time. But the teacher said the story has to be an adventure, so I figured, nothing beats pirates.

Indeed. *Der Seeräuber* means pirate. He spells it out for me, then one by one, the rest of the words and phrases I'll need, along with some I won't.

That should be some tale, he says, folding his hands on his belly. He smiles then, and I guess maybe he was a boy once, maybe even liked pirate stories, too.

Thank you, I tell him. I ask if I can keep the Sunday School paper with Jesus and the lamb, to study. He slides a small German dictionary off the shelf, gives it to me and smiles.

Jack, have you ever given thought to the ministry? You're such a bright, inquisitive boy.

No, sir. You think I should?

He nods and I thank him again for his help. The Almighty might frown on me tricking a man of God, but He'll see soon enough it's for a good cause.

Back when I was ten, I watched Father open the safe behind Mother's picture, so I already know the combination. I try it three times before it works, but then it clicks open.

The harder part is deciding how much to take, enough to be generous and not so much he'll notice. From up on that chair, once I can see into that black hole, I have no worries Father will miss what I take. Bundles of hundred-dollar notes stack up like loaves of bread on a bakery rack. I take one bundle from the front and replace it with one from behind, so there's no gap. I flutter through it, counting up to a thousand dollars. Not enough, because no amount could be, but if I get away with this, it might do some good. Some kid told me once, thieves get caught because they're either careless or greedy. I won't be greedy.

As for being careful, since I read about the New York police using fingerprints to catch bad guys, I use my shirt tail to wipe off where I touched the safe. Sheriff Quoyle maybe read that same news story last summer. I swing Mother's picture back on its hinges and wipe off the frame, then put Father's chair back the way he leaves it. I straighten the rug where I tripped on it coming in and close his study door. I'm almost disappointed, it was so easy.

I see George riding his horse up from the south when I'm crossing over the river bridge and he says, Hey. When he asks me where I'm going, I tell him I've got to study for our algebra test, that my book's up in the tree house.

I'd sure be glad to help you study.

No, you go on. If you help me too much, I'll freeze up on the test. I need to get the habit of the problems for myself.

He nods and says, My Ma wants me to buy her some baking soda, anyway. Biscuits tonight.

I no sooner get rid of George, then comes a farmer who just finished planting and wants to chew the fat with me. The sun's slipped down to the trees before he's done bragging how he loves his new Heider Model C friction drive tractor with seven different speeds, how he finished planting before all his neighbors. He spits on the ground, clicks to his horses and I wave him goodbye. Before another comes along, I cut down the bridge slope and follow the river east past the treehouse, to the Voegel farm.

I've stayed away since that night. It gives me the willies to be here again with the sun setting like it was that night, only farther south, even though I don't remember much except drinking, gunshots, running and being sick in the bushes by the road. I'm afraid Maggie and Kuruk remember it better than I do. I see how it pains them. George is lucky he never finished his chores in time to meet us, the way he wanted to.

Most of the brewery workers have gone home, so I hide in the barn until I see the last ones lock the mash tun and copper sheds and, finally, the warehouse doors. After the road dust settles behind them, it's getting dark, but I know my way around the back. I know where the loose boards are, to pry them off.

The swan-neck valves on the lauter tun stick out, just asking for trouble. Next to the lauter, I find a wrench nearly as big as my arm and shimmy up to break off the tubes and valves. I like the rotten sweet smell that comes out. It won't take them long to fix the lauter tomorrow and it won't spoil the beer, but it makes me feel better. Then I go to the copper building where the brewing kettles boil the wort with hops to make it bitter. Those tall kettles shine like new pennies and I bash my reflection in the bright copper all the way around, 'til I look as bent as I feel inside. The hum of the machinery is so loud, I don't worry about the noise I'm making. Or maybe I want to get caught.

The wrench is heavy and I'm sweating, my arms rubbery and tired when I set it down and go back outside. If my damage frustrates Father a little bit, I'll be happy. He's hard to touch, though, and I never yet figured out a way to hurt him as bad as I'd like to sometimes. Mad as I get, even when I get in trouble, I'm never more than a fly buzzing round his head.

I heard what's left of the Voegel boys went to Lincoln to stay with family, while Mrs. Voegel came home yesterday to pack up her last things. I heard she bought a ticket to take the train east tomorrow noon. I wonder that she's not afraid, being here alone, but maybe she figures the worst already happened to her.

Standing in her yard behind an oak, scuffing my feet in the loose dirt, I watch for that high front light to go out, the one up in the attic where Rolf used to sleep. It glows yellow a long time, and I picture that mother sitting on his bed, maybe looking through his cigar box of treasures, rolling those cool glass marbles between her fingers. When that light finally goes, I circle around to the side, back of the lilacs, and watch her bedroom window. She must be using a little candle or kerosene lamp or maybe she's in the dark, it's hard to tell, but I see the moonlight shiver on the curtains when she pulls them back to look through the glass. I duck down behind the stick-brush and wonder if she's crying. From down here, I can't tell.

I watch the moon until it rises a few finger-widths higher, figuring maybe an hour has gone. Any time I go in, I'll be taking a chance, so I might as well go ahead, around to the front porch. Maybe by now she's cried herself to sleep.

I thought I'd have to jimmy the lock, but the brass knob turns and clicks open in my hand, like an invitation. Moonlight streams through the lace curtains, spreading black curls and flowers on the hardwood floor. Either she means to leave most everything here or she's not packed yet, except for two crates on the kitchen worktable with excelsior spilling out like tangled hair. I brush up against something in the dark, and it's Rolf's old corduroy jacket on a coat tree, smelling like oats and hay. Remembering my friend, I slip it on over my light cotton jacket. It slides onto my arms with plenty of room and, when I shrug it over my shoulders, I feel how big it is on me. How big he was. Wearing it, I feel strong and brave, like Rolf agrees with what I'm doing. Come on with me, then, I tell him, in case he can hear.

Mr. Voegel dovetailed those stairs tight and not a one squeaks under my weight. I don't know what's wrong with me that I'm not scared of getting caught, but why should I be? This may be the only true, good thing I ever do. When I get to the second floor, I have to pause to get my bearings. Moonlight falls through a round window at an angle that shows me Mrs. Voegel's bedroom must be that one on the left. The door hangs open, unlatched.

I don't know why I didn't leave it on the kitchen table, but the giving seems more sincere, up close. And that hiding place in the floor is where Mr. Voegel would leave his hopes and dreams for her. Surely she's checked it by now and knows there wasn't much in there when he died. But that's partly what the note is for, to send her back to look.

The door glides open when I push it. I see her lying on the stripped mattress with nothing but a loose sheet over her and a naked pillow under her head. The moon lights up her bare arm like ivory and her hair like the copper kettles I just beat to thunder. I never saw her with her hair down. It makes her seem not like the old lady I thought she was, but young like Maggie. I think how she didn't deserve any of this to happen to her.

She takes a deep breath and rolls to face me and the door, with her back to where I need to be. The sheet drags around her like the wind is blowing it back and she's trying to run against it. I hold my breath and stay still in the doorway until her breathing settles.

I look at my feet and realize I forgot to take off my shoes, but thank goodness there's still a rug on the floor. I take a step and watch her. She doesn't wake.

Between steps, I count to eight because that's about how long it is between her rising breaths. When she breathes in, I step down, shift my weight and then watch and listen for the next one. It's not a big room, so in a few minutes I've stepped around the bed's cast-iron frame and Mr. Voegel's hiding place is at my feet.

When I kneel, my knees crack and I duck low in case she rolls back over, but she doesn't move. I'm not sure how to remove the board without making any noise, but this is no time for second thoughts. I unfold my pocket knife and pry out the plank with a little scraping sound softer than the sound of my swallowing. Cedar rises up in my nose, fresh and sharp, along with something like flowers.

After I set the bundle of money down in there, I replace the plank. Then I take the little note I wrote and unfold it in the moonlight. I follow the letters with my eyes, remembering which word is which from what Pastor showed me. I copied out these strange foreign shapes with my own hand, even knowing Mr. Voegel didn't know how to write. I can only hope his wife's need to believe will convince her when she reads it.

Rolf? *Mein* Rolf? She sits up on squeaking springs and gathers the sheet around her.

I tuck my face down away from the moon behind me. My heart leaps and bounds, rushing in my ears like a river broken through a dam. I should run, but I don't. Instead, I stand up between her and the window so all she can see is an outline and shadow.

Rolf. Her voice cracks and she sobs, clutching the sheet to her lips. *Mein Sohn.*

What made me think this was a good idea? I pull myself up bigger inside Rolf's coat to seem like him. Too quick for her to touch me, I lean over and drop the note on the bed, then step back to watch her. She has to believe. For her to believe, I have to first.

Rolf, I tell myself. Be Rolf. I puff out my chest, roll one shoulder down and tip my head the way he always did, thinking how my outline needs to look from where she sits.

She picks up the paper and flattens it on her sheet. Tears shine on her face. Her lips move and she keeps glancing back at my shadow as if I'm a dream. She reads German to me, her son, from the meaning I patched together, the mercy I stole from a Lutheran pastor and puzzled from a German dictionary.

159

Meine Frau Gerte,
My wife Gerte,
Sie töteten unser Sohn.
They killed our son.
Sie hängte mich.
They hanged me.
Ich versteckte das Papiergeld unter dem Boden.
I hid the money under the floor.
Mit Liebe, Klaus
With love, Klaus

When she looks back at me, puzzled, I think I went too far with that last line. I never saw him even peck her on the cheek, but she smiles and I know I did just fine.

She starts to get up out of the bed, arms reaching to grab and hold me, but I step fast to put the end of the bed between us, all the time pointing at the floor. Keeping my face out of the light, I run out of the room and thunder down the stairs, the way Rolf did when we came down from the attic, the last day I saw him alive.

Kuruk has friends he wants me to meet at New Eden on Lovely Creek, some Colored, Indian and even some Whites. Father doesn't ask where we're going. If he did, I'd lie to his face. He won't get the truth out of me anymore. Especially not about the voices because he'd cart me to Ingleside in nothing flat.

George meets us at the bridge. His Irish mother's brother married a Colored seamstress back East, and they were the first to settle in New Eden. With people in Darkwater all-out hateful about mixing races, George's mother wishes her brother had found a White woman to love but he didn't. She goes to New Eden after dark to see her little Mulatto niece and nephew, her brother and his wife. She wishes the world could be a different place, where she wouldn't have to hide, where people could get along.

We kids walk down Honeysuckle Lane in broad daylight and folks wave us up to their porches, pour lemonade and say, It will sure get warm today, and, What kind of trouble you looking for? I expected since some White people treat them mean, New Eden folks might treat me the same but Kuruk says, No, cruelty taught them to be kind.

George takes us to see his Aunt Sadie, who's just wiping off oilcloth-covered table clean after breakfast. She sets out cornbread and side pork for us, anyway. Her house could fit into my father's library, but it feels more of a home than ours, even with no fine upholstery or oil paintings in gold frames. Lots of old books line the wood shelves and a clean rug spreads over the plank floor. The furniture smells like lemons and glows in the sun filtering in.

Aunt Sadie beams down at me, messes my hair and pats my back and says, Eat up, your shoulder blade's so sharp I nearly cut myself on it, and Boy, don't you have a cook at your house?

George winks at me and frowns. Auntie, it's unkind to tease him that way. His mother died when he was born.

Instead of blushing or saying, I'm sorry, she waves at me with her dishrag and makes a little *puh* sound with her lips. Why, my mother died when I was two and no stiff wind could carry me off, she says. You got no excuse.

I like how she doesn't think I'm pitiful.

If I could eat your food every day, I'd be as fat as— and I almost say, You, but I catch myself.

She pulls her eyebrows together, but then rolls out a laugh like a bell.

George says, You almost stepped in it.

Kuruk's too busy shoveling in food to talk or laugh.

The African Methodist Episcopal Church is a whitewashed building at the end of Honeysuckle Lane. They've no pastor of their own, but the Reverend from Hastings comes down to preach. Six plank benches split the inside, and up front of them, Kuruk, George and I look at a painting of a Colored man in a white robe. Maybe a child did it, but the eyes are good and the colors are bright and I like it. When I ask Kuruk who's that fellow in the painting, he starts to laugh.

George elbows me and says, Why, Jackie-boy, that's Jesus Christ. Don't you recognize your Lord and God?

I laugh, thinking he's joshing me, but he means it.

Well, if that doesn't beat all, I say. I study the painting and once I get used to his skin being dark, his nose being flatter and wider, and his lips not as thin as they are in the Lutheran Church, I start to see Jesus in that African face.

I ask, Is that a broken chain he's carrying?

Kuruk steps up beside me, nods and crosses his arms. He studies the painting with me and says, He'd look better with a Pawnee scalp lock, combed up and back, like so. He moves his hands over his own head to show me. Or a cowboy hat, he sighs. I sure miss mine.

That could look fine, too. I guess no matter what, Jesus is a good-looking fellow.

George argues, Jesus wasn't supposed to be handsome. The Bible says, *He has no comeliness, no beauty that we would desire him.*

You're lying, Kuruk says. White Jesus is always the best-looking man in church, with light skin and blue eyes.

Sure, so you could invite him for Sunday dinner, George says and smirks.

Well, that explains why they never paint him Pawnee, Kuruk says, whacking me on the arm and heading out the door, but I get caught in the deep brown eyes of Colored Jesus. Seeing him that way disturbs and settles me, both. As a scientist, I wonder if there's any evidence for what color Jesus was.

Of the twelve New Eden families, three are Irish and Colored mixed, while seven are Colored through and through. The other two are Oglala Sioux and Cherokee. I ask Kuruk how they got mixed up with the other lot.

He says, It's the sort of place to let in anybody who works hard. If you drink or play cards too much, they don't run you out, but the women will pray over you loud and whack you with brooms when you got too much of a hangover to defend yourself. The preacher will come and visit you and give you a personal sermon until you wish you never done wrong.

Sounds like they don't need a sheriff.

Kuruk says the men usually play cards in a barn four miles north.

You play with them?

They taught me everything I know, and I got proof. Kuruk pulls out his pockets.

The only thing in his pockets was an old watch Kuruk found in somebody's garbage. Since it won't wind, we take it to a watchmaker named Carl who lives two doors down from Colored Jesus's church. He sits out on his porch in the sun, where the light is good, and uses a little lathe and staking tools from a wooden box to fix old clocks and watches. Two doors from him, we visit a woodworker,

James. He builds, carves and polishes furniture in a shed behind his house. He tried to sell his tables and sideboards in Darkwater Creek, but he gets a better price in Lincoln, he says, where nobody knows who built it.

Most of the other men in New Eden farm plots along Lovely Creek or work as porters for the railroad line. One runs a little store in his house with flour, sugar, corn meal and sundries. Some of the women keep house for ladies in Darkwater. George's aunt sews dresses, and her best friend is a nurse who drives a mule wagon back and forth to a clinic for Negroes in Lincoln.

While we buy some horehound drops in the store, two men talk about something called Kincaid. One argues they should pick up their whole town, plank and nail, and move up to Cherry County, where a hundred Negro families already filed claims on bigger farms and ranches than they can get here.

At the Cherokee house, two women in calico dresses and one old man take care of three little children. They don't have much, but the children look happy and fat. When Kuruk asks if he can taste what they're cooking in a pot over a fire in the side yard, the older woman answers loud and waves him away.

She called me a dirty Pawnee, he says, but she mends my clothes and sneaks me molasses candy when her sister's not watching.

We don't visit the Oglala family. There's some old uneasiness there, since that massacre in '73. It happened not far west of here, Kuruk says, and some things are hard to forget.

That night, we go to the barn to play cards with the men, and Kuruk loses three dollars. I always wondered where his money went, but he claims it's like paying for lessons, in case he has to make his way as a gambler.

The poker players offer us sips of their whiskey and I take some, but since Rolf died, Kuruk's lost his thirst for alcohol. Three of the men, the Oglala and two of the Negroes, drink beer from my father's Heilbrau brewery. When they drain their bottles, they shatter the brown glass against the inside barn wall.

Some night soon, I whisper to Kuruk, let's steal a case from the brewery and leave it here at the barn, like Robin Hood.

While the men are still betting and cussing, we three boys fall asleep in the hay, and I dream about Colored Jesus walking into the barn, carrying those broken chains. His eyes are big, brown and lit up gold with anger. His voice isn't cruel, though, like the ones I'm used to in my head, but strong and wide and fast like running water.

Get up, get up, he tells me, you have better things to do than playing cards. The world is about to dry up like a bone.

Jesus nudges me with his bare brown foot, and I look down to see it's bleeding from nails and broken glass. He asks me sorrowful, Boy, will you bring the rain?

I wake up with my heart pounding and Kuruk asleep beside me. George and the men are gone. Stumbling outside the barn, I feel a dry wind sift my hair and hear crickets, but no angry voices.

The sudden silence in my mind scares me so I count stars, starting with Polaris, as if those broken lights will add up to enough to fill my head. I don't look, but I feel Colored Jesus behind me, tallying with his finger in the dust.

∽

This linen is woven so fine, it's slippery as silk. The blouse pleats are sharp as blades down to the wide waistband, then pick up on the skirt front and travel down to my high-buttoned shoes. No lace or gewgaws, simply elegant. A woman's dress.

Mr. Amsel bought it in Omaha at Brandeis. Florence's eyes bulge at the shiny box and tissue paper, resentful he'd spend this much on me. When I hold it up to myself, she says the ivory makes my skin look muddy, like I need to wash. You take more care with the sun this summer, she warns, and wear a hat or people will think you're Indian or Gypsy.

Mr. Amsel stands in the doorway and says, Florence, that's enough. Margaret, you're lovely.

She'll get me for that.

His compliment makes me blush. Like a father, he bought me the nicest dress I've ever had and I love him for it.

In my room now, I try it on, smoothing down its flat collar and turning, holding up my hair to see how the fabric falls in back. In the old mirror with the only light filtered through the curtains, my edges are blurred, but I glimpse the woman I could be.

Letting my hair down, I turn back to face myself and think about Jack. It's something special for us to be graduating eighth grade together, with him a year older. I studied hard to skip a grade, to get through high school to college, maybe, if I get a scholarship. Hard work won't keep me with Jack, though, because this August, he's off to boarding school with better teachers and books than I'll ever see. I get angry hearing him so cavalier, swearing he won't go away, just to spite his father. I wish he'd mean he wants to stay because he's sweet on me, but he's never even kissed me. Mrs. Endicott says, The problem with a boy his age is he hears the bells a-ringing, but don't know where they're hanging.

Kissing aside, what I wouldn't give for an education like the one promised to Jack. Make the most of it, I tell him. *Fugit inreparabile tempus.* It escapes, irretrievable time.

He answers back like a smart aleck, saying he doesn't give a shit, except to ruin Albert Hollingwood's plans and reputation.

But when I ask, What about science?, he still cares about that.

I always thought, what I wouldn't give to be a rich beloved son, with every good thing served on a platter. But Albert Hollingwood is not what we reckoned him to be, and I'm better off with no real father than one like him. While I am bereaved, Jack is enraged, feeling guilt for what his father does, so he steals and drinks his father's beer at all hours, even before school, to punish and shame the man. Nothing comes of it, though. Nobody will hold Jack to account in this town.

Not one of us—George, Kuruk, Jack or me—has been the same since Rolf. After the funeral, we watched Mrs.

Voegel and her sons lose their land and Mr. Voegel's hand-carved house to Jack's father. It wrung out our hope to see him win. The truth of Albert Hollingwood, Regal Quoyle and Elsiver Dietz opened our eyes to connections like tight, thin roots running underground, from those three to the Amsels and other families in town, feeding them while starving others. And seeing people just take it, that was worse.

Even Mr. Amsel, the father I hoped for and now love, walks through a tilted world he helped to set wrong, acting like the ground is level. This white dress probably comes from dirty money, but what else can I wear? Should I refuse the food he gives me, knowing some other child goes hungry? I depend on Raeburn's Amsel's spi 'ly root of care, whatever love he can feel for me, for an end to my shame, an education and a way out of here.

For my high marks, Mr. Amsel overruled Florence and I'm to continue with high school. She will find a way to punish me for it, but I'm tough from these years under her hands. Her vengeance is sharp like a needle, fast in and out, not long like a dagger that slices and leaves a scar. It catches in my throat, though, that I've been a child in her house for six years, unloved. It seems motherly love is a particular taste, not easily acquired.

Jack, Kuruk and I, three orphans more or less, expect no love but what we give each other. We huddle together in the tree house in summer and barns in winter, imagining and fearing how we might grow into the world. We say anything is possible, even our own happiness. We swear, when we inherit this broken earth, we will right it somehow into a safe haven, a home of mercy.

But we are children yet. From Rolf, we learned that, rich or poor, children pay when their fathers' sins fall down the generations. The truth of life is like that horrid lace funeral veil Quoyle and Hollingwood made me wear. I still feel it brushing my face and its thin white net blurs my future. Not yet thirteen years old, I am unprepared for whatever life will require of me, but this exempts me from nothing. I can only harden myself for the speeding shock of a world where rich men decide who will eat, who will die and which girls must carry the funeral flowers.

For the vaudeville show tonight, I hang up the ivory linen and slip on my cornflower blue. It's a little tight over my breasts, but it serves as well as any of my everydays. To distract from its frayed collar and cuffs, I slip on the filigreed silver bracelet Jack gave me for Christmas. I hope when he sees it, he'll remember how he felt about me then.

My hair tumbles wild over my shoulders, so I wet and smooth it into three parts, twist it with a ribbon and knot it in a bun. It gets blacker every year, almost like Kuruk's, only his is straight. He says I could pass for Pawnee, if my skin were darker. I don't ask him how much, because it might be too many shades and I like imagining he's my brother.

But of course, I have no living family. Dressing for tonight's show tightens my nerves and makes my palms sweat because memories fluff and swirl in me like ashes in a cold stove, bringing back the feelings and sounds of people I lost. Gritty boards under my tapping, sliding shoes. Fiddle trills and piano chords. The smoke and stench of kerosene footlights. The spinning, laughing and falling without getting hurt, as if somebody tossed and then caught me. A woman, my mother? Bright red lips and slashes of rouge, dark hair somehow piled high and yet falling down, and rustling dresses—purple, scarlet and goldenrod yellow. A stick-man father holding up a black hat, a pipe stem clenched in his white teeth and blue smoke curling up, sweet as burned sugar.

Last and best, like a bookend on the shelf of memories, Cedric carrying me through a clear cold night, a sense of floating over snow and at the orphanage door, his whisper, You forget everything, except your name is Margaret Rose and I love you.

Why did he want me to forget? The colorful bits I kept, I hold as tight as religion—the music, colors, lights and smells—and all these years, *credo*, I believe. I am Maggie Rose and Cedric loves me.

I didn't know what show people were, to know I was one, until I was eight. Before that, I thought everybody loved to sing and dance, or at least clap along. Dancing for the orphan girls I felt Cedric, like seeing through the brown curves of an empty bottle.

I pat my hair down and practice a smile. Jack asked me to go with the boys to this show tonight, or I wouldn't dare. I stayed away from years of shows in Red Cloud, Franklin and Alma, even when the Amsels offered to take me along. But now Darkwater's bringing in its first troupe in seven years, and I'm ready to swing open memory's door. Not much frightens me since Rolf, with the world being a painted-over, broken thing and everyone acting a part. At least in a show, what's false is painted up to make you smile.

Folks are filling in up front during the dumb act, terriers in tutus dancing on their hind legs. The brown canvas drapes and puffs in and out behind us like cheeks.

George, Jack and I could move up front after paying our nickels, but we won't leave Kuruk alone under the sign, Coloreds and Penny Standing Room Here. Kuruk says he's not sure the other three of us are allowed, that these are reserved spots, after all, and his Colored friends from New Eden join in scowling and waving us forward like we're in the way, before laughing and making room.

For the second act, two scarecrows sing lovesick longing to each other from up on their frames until a buxom fairy bewitches them down to waltz among the papier-mâché pumpkins. Jack, George and Kuruk jostle each other and joke about the fairy's fat bottom.

For the third, a pigeon-chested one-man band bangs and wails and crashes and flutes while squeezing an accordion through When Johnny Comes Marching Home.

The troupe manager in a red coat interrupts to read a tear-jerker poem about mothers and soldier sons, begging us to buy Liberty Bonds for America in the new war.

But the fourth stirs everyone with a name, the Negro blackface act from the show bill. Easter and Elroy wear tuxedos and shuffle soft shoe on sandy planks and their dancing is swell, with people half-standing at their chairs to watch their feet, but when Easter barrels out his bass the crowd holds its breath, as if to trap that voice the way you press a leaf into everlasting green between dictionary pages. To keep and ponder it in the night like a scripture or a hymn.

No more rain fall for wet you,
Hallelu, hallelu,
No more rain fall for wet you,
Hallelujah.

Hair prickles on my neck because the sound thrums into my bones.

No more parting in de kingdom.
Hallelu, hallelu,
No more parting in de kingdom,
Hallelujah.

I stand too far back to make out his jaw, cheekbones or nose under the shiny cork and greasepaint. The footlights flicker strange shadows over his face, bringing doubt. But my arms and hands, legs and feet, head and hips anticipate the pivots, shuffles and taps I felt in his arms before I could walk. Strong and loose in the joints but fluid, like he holds his own gravity, giving barely an ounce to the ground.

He sounds the same, throaty as a thrush and cooling-deep as river mud on a hot August afternoon. Cedric comes back as a flush and catch in my chest and the taste of lemon drops. His hair is gray tonight, maybe powdered or maybe he is old, by now.

I am persuaded. My hands tremble and sweat trickles down my face in spite of the breeze puffing in behind me. I want to run onto the gaslit stage and out through the canvas, both at once, to touch and escape him because he is the past that spit me out and the home I thirst for still. He is the one who held me, the one who gave me away. He alone knows who I am.

I grab Jack's arm to steady myself and close my eyes to keep them dry. I press my toes hard through the soles of my shoes to keep from following, shuffle tap step slide spring.

After the dance, the ventriloquist doesn't make me laugh and the dying mother melodrama can't make me cry. The child balanced up on nine stacked chairs who pretends to fall doesn't make me gasp. I'm looking through them at the purple velvet curtain.

Jack notices and squeezes my hand, or maybe I squeeze his, but I don't care for his noticing. I've set my heart on that backstage man. I will talk to him tonight.

Fugit inreparabile tempus.

He glances at the mahogany grandfather clock, then back out through the long and low-slung window. She's late. He counted on Jack Hollingwood to escort Margaret to and from the vaudeville show, but now he pictures Jack's hand on Maggie's arm, her hip, her breast. Amsel's heart races remembering being thirteen, when feelings easily boil over. The fascination with French postcards, frustration and furtive sessions in his room, his back against the door to keep his brothers from barging in. He was a fool to trust Jack with Maggie. The two were like brother and sister, but that time is past, the safety of childhood fallen away.

Amsel sighs to think of Greta's oncoming adolescence and his role to bar the door until her wedding night. He can teach Adolph about manhood, but girls need a mother and Florence, from Margaret's first day here, has written off the girl as trash, beneath her concern. Florence is at odds with most people, though, and it exhausts him.

Florence is too perceptive about him and the girl. From the day Amsel chose Margaret, he's loved her differently and somehow more than he loves Adolph and Greta, as if he is her sole savior and protector. She inspires him with her fiery spirit, hearty laugh, unruly hair and those singular green eyes.

Little more than a child, already she draws him in and, confound her, she surely knows the effect she has on him. Yet he knows his own fault, that old devil burning, tapping the veneer of his self-control to test for weakness. Since Annabelle, he senses the pulse, the radiant passion of every young girl's womanhood, long before it raises its veil.

At five thirty each morning, Raeburn Amsel rises to the jingling trill of his Junghans alarm clock. For ten minutes, he soaks in a steaming tub. While other men might make do with the previous day's shirt and rumpled suit, replacing only the grungy collar, Amsel dons the clean pressed shirt, brushed suit and mirror-shined shoes Mrs. Endicott supplies to his cedar wardrobe.

By six twenty, he parks his automobile and settles into Grayson's barber chair for his shave, manicure and, if needed, a trim. Leaving the shop, he settles his fedora with confidence and takes his seat by the window at the China Cup Cafe for coffee, toast and plum jam.

Six mornings a week, he arrives well-rested, cleansed, polished and fed, unlocking his office door by seven thirty. The motto framed above his desk declares, A Working Man's Day for a Wealthy Man's Life.

So he orders himself from cuticle to shoestring and from whisker to button, presenting himself for the citizens' trust. He garners their wealth in his Cattleman's Bank and trades their livestock and grain through his stockyard and elevator. He is a man of means, if not power. His alliance with Albert Hollingwood secures his funds while undermining his sense of being his own man.

A deacon of the Augsburg Lutheran Church on State Street, Amsel organizes meetings, confesses his faith and sustains the choir with his baritone. He loathes his own sin and prays for grace, with hell's near fires warming his soul into conviction.

Amsel means well, but knows better. Beneath his fine-spun linen and wool, hair pomade and talc huddles a crustacean in its shell. He shudders to ponder his true nature, sluggish and base, all tongue and tentacle, consumption and filth. He barely contains himself by cleanliness and self-regulation, rising and working and sleeping by the clock. He forebears his dying, difficult wife and, to keep from hating her, gives her everything. So they might cherish him when he grows helpless with age, he dandles and indulges his children. He travels often to keep a pious distance from Margaret Rose, all the while burning for her. He resolves to win that battle. There will never be another Annabelle.

The window glass fogs with his breath as he peers down the gaslit street. The clock chimes from the back wall, eleven times. Where is she? He hears her voice before he sees her. Amsel pulls down his vest, shoots his cuffs and prepares to confront Jack Hollingwood.

Margaret breezes in, color high in her cheeks and her dress carrying the scent of lilacs.

You're late, he charges her. Where's Jack?

He walked on.

It's not proper to be out with him this late. People will talk.

It was the seventh act, she explains, a musical drama that pushed everything late, but it was superb. You should have seen the heroine. Lovely, and her voice was like—

175

Margaret pauses and reaches into the air for the word—those caramel creams you brought from Chicago. She smiles at him and his anger vaporizes.

Forget the boy, he thinks. Scolding him would only rile Hollingwood. Patting Margaret's shoulder, Amsel says, Get some sleep, Margaret dear.

For an instant, he pictures her dress slipping off her shoulders, how her skin must be smooth as caramel cream, but he takes a deep breath and touches his brow, his chin, his wrist, whispering his ritual, Pure in mind, in word, in deed.

Listening for her heels clicking on the slate stairs, he closes himself in his study. There are those grain elevator accounts he must review by morning.

From his carved desk, the one his wife considers too ornate for her austere Prairie décor, he might not have heard the door click. But an hour after he sent Margaret Rose to bed, with his accounts complete, he stands again at the wide front window, a brandy snifter warming in his hand, the liquor searing his throat. He watches her hesitate under the splayed budding elm, shifting the heavy valise to her left hand.

She's running away. Instead of throwing open the front door, he watches Margaret's direction and when she's half a block away, follows her quietly.

She means to elope with that boy. Amsel lays the blame on Jack. How could a girl not even thirteen think of such a thing on her own? Amsel believes in Margaret's innocence as surely as he does his own corruption. Margaret is all things good, and it's his charge to preserve her, so he follows.

Instead of walking west to Hollingwood's Tudor mansion, the girl trudges east and north to the park, where the wide brown show tent sags, roped and pegged into the soft spring ground. A circle of painted trucks surrounds a licking fire where glowing shapes sing, laugh and pass a bottle. He watches for Jack, but Margaret beelines toward the farthest truck, where some darkies huddle together, joshing and laughing.

Amsel loiters behind a show truck, watching her move through flickering shadows. He draws a sharp breath, stunned as Margaret approaches one of the men, drops her valise and throws herself into his arms.

Amsel steadies himself against the truck box. When the Negro puts his arms around Margaret and lifts her off the ground, it's more than Amsel can bear and he rushes out, grabs Margaret's arm and spins her to the ground. He drives his fist toward the man's face, deflected by a raised arm. Enraged, Amsel drives back and back, punching at that dark eye cheek belly chest. A girl shrieks and cries until two Negroes pull him off. Choking with rage, glaring, Amsel dampens with shame to see he hasn't left a mark on his victim. The tall man's not breathing hard, hasn't even broken a sweat, but draws himself up to straighten his clothing. With a light in his eye, he spits on the ground by Amsel's shoe.

Margaret runs to the dark man, sobbing.

Amsel pulls away from the two who hold him and lunges one last feint, but his stumbling and shaking limbs prove he's finished. Margaret's chosen is twice Amsel's size and fit as a boxer, maybe fifty years old. Calm but ready, he stands with fists clenched. In his brown eyes, a low fire, exhaustion and resignation flicker as if this is an old fight, one he knows he'll never finish, one he dare not win.

Still shaking, Amsel brushes his face, sees a stain on his fingers, tastes it and finds it's blood. He doesn't remember the Negro hitting him, but there it is. He touches the swelling lip with his tongue. He defended Margaret and has a badge of honor, a sign to justify his outrage even as he knows he didn't win. He rushed in with nothing to his credit but rage and, what he already denies, a sinister jealousy.

He tells himself it was for honor, that it's unseemly a Negro should touch Margaret. It wasn't Jack who deceived or enticed the girl, but someone she should have known not to heed, so he doubts her innocence and raises his hand to slap her. Seeing the dark man step forward, Amsel holds back and shouts instead, commanding her home. Outraged, diminished, blustering, he expects she'll fight him, too, but instead she glances from Amsel to the other men. Damn her, she's protecting him as she picks up her valise to obey. He grabs and shoves her, calling back to the half-circled Negroes, This affair is by no means settled. Mark my words.

Walking home, Margaret pours out her defense about Cyril or Cecil or Cedric, some name Amsel casts aside as soon as he hears it. The big man carried her to the orphanage, was like a father to her when her parents played in a vaudeville troupe and she never told because Florence hates her already and what would've been the point? It was all but forgotten until tonight, when she found herself again, and a whole life she'd counted lost. She felt her heartbeat revive when he danced and decided she'd make her own way with someone who truly loves her. She says his name again. Cedric loves her.

Amsel tells her to hush, that people will hear her nonsense through their open windows. That he can't think with her constant bawling and chatter.

It horrifies him that she feels the difference, the flawed charity he gave instead of paternal love. He shrinks to think she might sense the other side, carefully tucked in its shell. That would be unbearable.

For the first time since she came to him, he thinks of sending her back to the orphanage or away to another home.

As if she senses his thought she says, I appreciate all you've done for me. You've been kind.

Kind. After all he's done, all he's felt, she makes it as small as kindness. He winces and hardens his shell to a cruel edge.

To throw yourself on a Negro that way, he chides her, deliberately twisting her confession. You're a great disappointment to me, Margaret. He goes on, denying her past and her right until she hiccups and sobs in step beside him.

Anger and indignation subside from the hollow in his chest. Amsel wants to comfort her, to comfort himself by putting his arm around her thin shoulders, but he doesn't dare put his hands on this not-his-daughter now. Not while the deep, horrific part of himself stirs.

I meant to adopt her, but she did this, he tells himself.

Brow, chin and wrist. Mind, word and deed. He calls himself to purity, to indifference and steps away from Margaret, but it's cruelty that speaks.

If that Negro is your father, he tells her, then I'll never be.

After sending Margaret to her room, he sits up all night to keep her in, and when dawn ribbons the sky with yellow and pink, he begins his Friday like any other.

But after Grayson's and The China Cup, he walks to Albert Hollingwood's office two doors south of his own. While Hollingwood creaks back in his chair, tenting his fingers into a little cathedral, Amsel tells the necessary lie he worked out during the night, having already convinced himself it's true.

Hollingwood clips a cigar and stares at the door Amsel closed behind himself. That was a peculiar story, chock full of holes and it doesn't smell right. What was Margaret doing out late at the vaudeville camp? Jack wasn't there and even if he had been, he wouldn't run off, leaving Margaret at the first sight of trouble. He saw the girl home well before midnight, Hollingwood knows, because he heard the boy come in. And that other part is preposterous. No Negro would be dim enough to put his hands on a White girl in Darkwater Creek, especially not after Monday's upheaval in East St. Louis, Illinois, where all those Negroes were attacked and the National Guard came in. That story was in all the papers, national news. Why, he and the show manager even met to discuss canceling the Negro acts, to be safe, but decided it wasn't necessary.

Maybe they should have called it off.

Hollingwood knows the Negroes of Darkwater Creek, mostly railroad porters, maids and their families. He never liked having them clustered in that settlement the Coloreds call New Eden and the Whites call Dogtown. Better had they built their shanties in Red Cloud or Franklin, but until today, he never worried. Five miles seemed a safe distance and Illinois, with its race riots, a world away.

So last night's show went on, as they say on the stage. But now this.

You'd have to know Amsel the way Hollingwood did to tell how this upset the banker. He's a cold fish, never uttering an unweighed word or allowing color to rise in his cheeks. Yet there he sat with a split lip and his voice tight as a bowstring, hands clenched into fists. Something happened, without a doubt.

Damn it all. With their business interests enmeshed, their wives being cousins and that child all but being Amsel's own daughter, Hollingwood owes a sort of family loyalty and it irks him. He doesn't like feeling obligated to anyone, especially someone who owes him everything. He lights his cigar and leans back in his chair, pondering which way to go. Amsel promised discretion but will no doubt start the rumor mill this very hour or Hollingwood could give the matter some time to shake out on its own.

What Amsel's asking is risky, though, should people find out, and it makes him wonder if the man is setting a political stage. It's no secret he covets Hollingwood's mayoral seat, but failing to warn the sitting mayor and letting things boil over would be more to Amsel's advantage. And he did appear genuinely riled.

Hollingwood sighs, weighing his own advantage, his distaste for trivial violence and the greater good of Darkwater until he tires of the taste of his cigar. Blowing one last undulation of smoke, he sets his feet on the floor, squeaks his chair around and tamps out the glowing end.

Better to put the fear of God into one traveling show darkie than to risk an East St. Louis here in Nebraska.

Grandfather Burnt Wolf told me that Kitsahuruksu shoulda died but after his enemies busted his head and peeled the hair off, he walked away and dug a cave by a stream in the Republican Valley. He covered the scabs on his head and his missing hair with mud and a handkerchief. Grandfather couldn't say if a White took his scalp like happened to Joe Chapman or if a Lakota done it.

Scalped Men usually come out at night. When I miss Joe Chapman, I wonder if he was a man or Kitsahuruksu. He liked to walk outside at night, even without a moon. I'd wake up and find his sleeping place empty and figure he'd gone and left me, the way he finally did. But those other times, he was only walking the prairie. He said the pain in his head kept him from sleeping.

If you get to know one like I guess I did, you're either lucky or unlucky, hard to say. My mother's mother said they come after naughty children like me. Burnt Wolf said the one he talked to wasn't bad, just an unfortunate irari, a brother. He also said those Kitsahuruksu speak with many voices, throwing them out of trees or stones. I'd like to learn that magic.

I start thinking maybe it's a Kitsahuruksu throwing voices into Jack's head. In the old days, people set out fry bread and soup to satisfy him so maybe if I cook up some fry bread he'll leave Jack alone.

I get flour, soda and salt from Marta, Mr. Hollingwood's fat little cook who has eyes like blue buttons and hair like long hay. She always smiles and gives me whatever I ask for and once she asked me to kiss her. It was interesting, a thing I'll try again if she wants to.

For the fry bread I mix the ingredients in a big bowl with water, my hands remembering Grandmother's. I get most of it off my hands and put it in hot popping grease in my cast-iron skillet. The bread puffs and the hot brown smell makes me miss my father, even though he sent me away those times. Love and hate for Crooked Walk shifts and hides in me like markers in a hand game. I can't figure out which to choose.

It's not the worst fry bread I ever ate but too sticky in the middle for Kitsahuruksu. A little burned on the bottom, too. He might spit it out and say, Huh, this is a poor offering. I guess I'll tease that White boy a while longer.

I got to do better for Jack so I decide on tobacco and chicken soup instead. After I kissed her again Marta made the broth with globs of melted fat floating on top and chunks of chicken big as my thumb. Puffy noodles. Carrots and peas.

That soup is a fine offering to Scalped Man, for my brother Jack, my unfortunate irari.

Sometimes I stop for Toss at George's place and let him ride on the wagon seat with me when I'm working. He's grown into a long-legged hunter who only cares about chasing prairie dogs and rabbits but I can't let him run out of my sight or take him to town like he's my dog. The only time George took Toss into Darkwater, Quoyle looked at him sideways and elbowed Dietz and laughed. He'd still be glad to see Toss running on three legs, to show who's boss.

Those two bastards break into my dreams and I wake up nights sweaty and tangled in my sheet, stomach sick, heart thudding, legs twitching. It's always knife blades flashing, gunshots ringing, tearing off Rolf's scalp or mine or Jack's with brains running out red and gray.

That night is branded on me like I'm a bawling calf. There in Voegels' barn, I acted that way, hiding behind a milk cow with my cheek against her rough hairy flank, my mouth full of belched beer and my hands clutched together the way Christians pray. The beer made my head spin but I knew the difference between hiding and fighting.

Rolf's been dead a year but I'm the same except my arms and legs are longer and my voice cracks whether I'm scared or not. Mostly I am. When he was thirteen like me, my grandfather already handled a bow and knife to hunt and fight his enemies. He had a father to learn from but I got no excuse to act the way I did.

Mr. Hollingwood thinks he's some kind of father to me but his hands smell like sweaty dollar bills and metal from coins. He teaches me how to make beer but not how to live. How to count money but not what's worth keeping. He protects me from Quoyle and Dietz like I got a chain on my leg, staked into his ground the same way I keep Toss. Alive. Wearing my life into a dry circle where nothing grows.

I got me a strong back and arms and working all day don't bother me a bit. I can do sums in my head and I like thinking about the things Maggie and Jack teach me from their school. I don't tell White Boss any of it, though. He made up his mind I'm part mule and part Wild West sideshow Indian, dumb as a post and won't ever be more.

Except I got one thing he don't count on, my memory. He tells me things he shouldn't. Other things I pretend not to see when I do. True good and true awful stories about Darkwater burn in my head and I keep them like a book only not wrote down, along with stories Grandfather and Joe Chapman told me. The Pawnee stories are hardest to keep because I'm losing the language and like Coyote they change shape in my English and the meaning twists. It's all I can do to hold the heart of what Burnt Wolf gave me, keeping the stories from turning small and White. But I keep them best I can, repeating them to myself every night.

The sun streams in the carriage house window down onto Toss and me here in my bed. I feel myself rush full of blood and wanting. Will I ever be man enough to climb on top of a girl, to make a son and raise him up? When Marta kisses me my body tells me it's ready but I got to do something to become a man. Something to make Grandfather proud, like coming out from behind the cow with a weapon.

All I got for now is my stories so I sharpen them like knives for when I can stand and tell the truth. Then I'll strike my enemy and make Grandfather proud. Then I'll be a man.

I feel lightheaded. I rub the back of my neck and shake my head to clear it, but the words don't make sense. Father is telling Quoyle and Dietz how a Negro from the show did something wrong to Maggie, something no girl should suffer. How he must be taught a lesson.

But I took Maggie home and my father knows it. She was safe and sound when she latched the door with Mr. Amsel waiting there to meet her under that tiny wall lamp in their gloomy front hall. He looked me in the eye when she closed the door, and all I could do was cuss myself for not kissing her like I meant to.

In Father's office, Dietz laughs like a crow. Quoyle tells him to hush and asks my father if he has something specific in mind.

I leave it to your discretion, but do it quickly.

That's something the great Albert Hollingwood likes to say even to me, so I know I heard those words right.

We'll take care of everything. Quoyle's voice is so oily, I look down like it might ooze under the closed door.

When they scrape back their chairs I hightail it down the hall and around the stairs, out the front door and into the street where a dog is pissing on a light post and the grocer is sweeping the walk. A flag flaps on a pole over my head and a wagon lumbers by.

Angry says, Your father's a killer, but you know that already and the nigger is in for it. Angry's voice is so loud, I look up to see if the grocer heard him, but he's bent over, brushing string and paper and gravel into a pan, sneezing at the dust a breeze puffs in his face.

A gentle woman's voice says, You're a lucky boy. After your father is dead, you'll give the orders.

I turn to see her, but there's nobody else. Shut up, shut up, I say under my breath, but a red-faced farmer stepping out of the hardware store squints and asks, What's that you say, son?

I shake my head and push a smile at him so hard my cheeks hurt, then walk south on Main.

The troupe has another performance here in Darkwater tonight, before pulling up stakes for a three-day run in Holdrege. People last night said the show's good, they'll come again tonight and then still drive to that other town to see it a third time.

It's dawning rose-blue morning in the east but I'll bet those singers and dancers are asleep in their tents and trucks, some rolled up in blankets around smoky fires. I heard it's what they do and, if I was free, traveling in a show, I'd sleep on the ground every night 'til frost crusted over me and snow came. I'd watch the moon slide over, feel the breeze stroke my face and sleep all night because nightmares need corners to hide in, to spook you from.

But you sleep in a feather bed with linen sheets in a mansion, the woman sing-songs to me. Beloved son, beloved son. Such a fortunate boy. So fortunate.

Teacher, shut up, shut up, I tell her. She repeats things and then I hear myself doing it, too. I call her Teacher because she's different, speaking up like she's in front of a class while most of the voices mumble.

I walk faster to leave Teacher behind but it's no use.

With these voices shouting, I can't go to school. My hands shake and I want to yell. Since Rolf died the voices come fast, exploding in my head, and I might need to do something crazy to make them stop. I'd better stay by myself for a while.

When my hard shoes clatter off the last bricks of Main Street and *whap-whap-whap* on the dirt road, I bend over in some shivering elm-leaf shade with my hands on my knees, looking down where the dew blackens my shoes. My heart drums and my lungs suck air.

Angry whispers, That nigger's in for it.

It's the last week of school, mandatory attendance 'til I graduate on Saturday, but Father won't let them hold my diploma if I skip. I get away with things because of who Father is, while other people suffer for what I do. I start a fight and another boy gets the blame. I tell a lie and Father stands up for me against everybody. I do get a beating, after, to teach me not to embarrass him, to make me a better man.

Father makes the world easy and hard.

My father uses hard ways to get things done and punishes people when they do wrong. It's what powerful men do and he's the mayor now and it's no different from when he whips me. Sometimes you hurt people to keep them in line, if that's what it takes.

I love him I hate him I love him.

The boy's crazy, Angry says.

Don't be unkind, Teacher reasons. He's upset.

Nothing I say makes a difference to them so I fix my mind above the voices, on the Negro. Father said he's the one billed as Easter. The tall one. Or is he the short one? Those two danced so together I can hardly separate them.

I get a sudden, sick chill and my knees almost buckle to think of my Magpie hurt, but she's not. I saw her safe with my own eyes. It's that dancer I need to worry about.

I trot along the road knowing I should go back to the vaudeville camp, but instead my feet carry me south and across the bridge, with the Republican roping along below me, fat and deep with the spring thaw and a week of afternoon showers.

He's going to let them kill the dancer, Jezebel screeches in, laughing. The same way he let them kill the German boy.

Well, he is his father's son. His father's son.

My father's son. Will I grow up to do the things people say about him? How Albert Hollingwood holds up the law just high enough to break whoever walks under it. That it's a foolish man who gets in Hollingwood's way, that you'd best give in straightaway and live to tell about what you lost. How he sends Quoyle and Dietz around like the horsemen of the Apocalypse, Quoyle with his words and Dietz with his knife.

Now this morning Albert Hollingwood said, I leave it to your discretion, but do it quickly.

I feel something like a stone in my stomach to think of that poor man rolled up in his blanket at the camp, not knowing what's coming. I should warn him. I should be somebody other than Albert Hollingwood's son. While I shimmy up to the tree house I tell myself, Somebody should go, but I know nobody will.

Under the voices, I almost can't hear the birds at the window. They start in about Kuruk, how my father chose him. I can't argue with them about that. Kuruk lights up his eyes with hope. He trusts my friend, my brother, with secrets that could destroy both of them, about the brewery and other illegal doings, information most men would only trust a son to keep.

He knows you're mad as a hatter, Angry says. He has to replace you.

I know it, I answer. He loves Kuruk like a son, but I loved him like a brother first so I don't give a damn, I don't give a damn, I tell the voices and myself while I brush and scrape loose the leaves and mold that rotted here all winter, staining the tree house floor black and brown. He's my brother and he says I'm his irari too, so I don't give a damn.

Cain was Abel's brother, and he slew him.

Damned voices.

I gather up the dead stuff, all stinking and wet and sticking to my hands, and dump it out the window.

Kicking a ratty squirrel's nest out through the trap door, I watch it separate into clumps and tumble to the ground. The tree house feels like home, with echoes and traces of Maggie and Kuruk like strong arms to hold off my loneliness. To keep me sane.

I close my eyes to listen over and through the nagging insults that never quit. Sparrows chitter and robins chirr to their friends in five-part stanzas like kids in school. A cardinal whistles, then *choo-choo-choos* and a woodpecker knocks at a tree he won't ever open. A deep breath and I open my eyes, grabbing hold of my mind to push it into what is calm and good. The river. Outside the tree house window, the Republican spreads and shines like a silver tray under a doily of branches. The rhythm, quiet and peace here can save me from the voices and troubles on the ground.

But the robins and cardinals startle, flutter above their perches and change their conversations, yeeping and chipping alarm like sparks off metal. Then mumbles and threats and bodies cracking through the underbrush like a barrel rolling downhill and the woods erupt in a flurry of wings and shouts. I pull back into shadow, watching Quoyle and Dietz shove two men ahead of them some twenty yards from the tree house, breaking a new path to the river. When their voices echo bright off the water, I know they've stopped on the river bank. I shimmy down the tree, shaking and sick but trying to be somebody Albert Hollingwood never saw coming.

The barley behind me is hidden under bales and since the Nebraska Prohibition law took hold on May 1, I'm to lie to anybody who asks, to tell them I'm no longer in the employ of my real White Boss, Mr. Albert Hollingwood, but now hauling for Mr. Raeburn Amsel. They always been in cahoots. Now even more since White Boss pretended to shut down the Heilbrau brewery.

The night of the Prohibition deadline, most of the men in town jammed into the Red Lantern to drink it dry so Marlow could restock with sarsaparilla and Coca-Cola. Under darkness, Amsel's men drove hundreds of cattle and even some horses from his western lot, north over the railroad tracks and east around Darkwater Creek. Then those cowboys turned the herd south through a shallow river bend to the old Voegel place to disguise the brewery as a cattle operation, to prove Hollingwood an honest man by midnight.

That brewery's still fermenting and bottling but you can't smell the yeast for the stink of lies and manure or hear the machinery for the chuff-banging Fordson tractors and bawling calves. The house stands empty. Hollingwood never needed it for nothing but proving he could take it.

So now, to keep White Boss and me out of jail, I gotta make twice as many hops, barley and bottle trips as I did before, with the top half of every load being hay and corn. You can be sure I don't get paid twice as much, though. I'm supposed to be grateful I even got a job.

Humming that song the vaudeville dancers sang about Jesus giving me a little broom, I'm making good time. I rein in the horses, though, and creak the wagon to a halt. They roll their eyes, flick their tails and toss their heads while I study a truck angled at the end of a curved skid. Soft clay and dust push little hills up front of the tires like the driver about lost control and slammed on the brakes, and both front doors and the cargo doors in back are a-hanging open.

Damn. It's that same truck Quoyle and Dietz shoved me in two years ago and I still dream about. My heart *ka-thumps* and my leg muscles pull tight as a jackrabbit's, ready to run. Holding my breath, I listen and my skin tingles, trying to hear danger with my whole body. Nothing at first but soon as I sigh and tell myself to slap the reins and move on, I hear voices, sharp shouts and yips like coyotes wailing.

I oughta run to save my hide but I never forgot how it feels to be caught and hurt. What if those two devils got ahold of some other kid? If old Hollingwood wasn't so cheap I'd be driving a truck and could hightail it back to town for help but with these old horses, I got no time.

For all I know, they're up to Hollingwood's business so I oughta think twice about butting in.

So I sit there and weigh the rights and wrongs and the idea of dying for a stranger.

One thing I got against White religion is it pops into my head at the worst times and shoves out my common sense. Hearing somebody in trouble, I remember Father Marquardt at Genoa and his story of the Good Sumatran.

Another missionary teacher already taught us about tigers he saw in Sumatra, fierce cats bigger than cougars with orange and black and white stripes so we settled down for a good animal story like our grandfathers told. In this one, a wounded warrior got left behind on the plains. He musta been a Kitsahuruksu, a bloody Scalped Man, because everybody who came along walked on the other side of the trail, looking away. They left him to die. Then the Sumatran tiger came along. He musta been able to change into other things like Coyote, because he took the shape of a man. Even though the warrior was from a different tribe and his head was disgusting with the brains running out, the Sumatran took care of him and when the Sumatran had to go back to being a tiger, he paid somebody else to doctor the warrior.

The priest told us Jesus's story of The Good Sumatran to teach us kindness for people who are different, a strange lesson for a White to tell Indian children in a school where they cut off our hair but that don't make it a bad story or wrong. Because Father Marquardt pretended not to hear us when we spoke Pawnee or Lakota or Ponca to each other and never beat us, he maybe even believed it himself.

So I hate to think it but I do. This is a time to change myself into a Sumatran and help whatever creature is down by the river with Quoyle and Dietz.

I hide the wagon by some elderberry bushes where the truck drivers won't see it when they come back. Wrapping the reins around a hook on the buckboard, I ask the horses to stay, thinking what a mess I'll be in if they trot off. They tilt their ears back at me and paw the ground, then drop their heads to nibble the trickle of oats I spread on the short greening grass. Standing with my hand on the bay's withers, I listen again. No sound but teeth grinding and that scares me more than the yelling did.

I pick my way slow and quiet through the dried milkweed, elderberry and woods rose, remembering like yesterday how Dietz's fists shocked my face, my ribs, my belly. The bruises were deep and pressed out of my skin for weeks, brown and purple and yellow like rotten fruit. Dietz's curved Mexican blade point tested my throat, my cheek and the arches of my bare feet, not piercing but needling the sensitive parts. All this is better to think about than how quiet it's got by the river until I hear a yell. I sigh, glad for a sign of life and fight in somebody. Maybe it's not over yet.

Soon as I top the little bluff over the river, I drop on my hands and knees and crawl, then wiggle on my belly and pull with my elbows to the edge and peer out from behind some sedge. I see four men, two Whites standing and two Negroes on their knees facing me. The bigger one lifts his chin and squints at me, then shakes his head like, No. His chest puffs up with a deep breath and he closes his eyes for what's coming. Something silver dangles from his vest, catching and throwing from the sun a blade of light that pierces my eyes. The other man looks down at the sand and he's singing words I can't make out. Dietz stomps around them and Quoyle looks up into some trees like this has nothing to do with him.

This would be a good time to be a Sumatran with stripes and teeth, to leap down and save those poor men or at least make some noise and run into the trees. Maybe Quoyle and Dietz would follow and those fellows could get away. I look over but that brush looks too thick for a fast getaway. Then there could be three on the sand.

And that's when Jack moans, not ten feet away, up on all fours in plain sight. His face is like a window wide open, his eyes locked on the four men while he rocks to and fro. He laughs, whines and says, So it is and so it will be, the man who holds the knife is not the man who holds the knife. He opens his mouth wide to scream so I crawl over, knock him down and roll him on his back. He bites me when I cover his mouth. He turns his head back and forth but I press hard. He's stronger and I only got one hand free to hold him down so he pounds me with his fists.

The voices really got him today.

Pinning him down with my chest, I whisper, It's alright, I'm your friend. Listen. It's me, Kuruk. Come back here now. Come back. I keep saying it low like a song or a rhyme until Jack slows down hitting me and his arms fall to his sides. We rolled back from the edge of the bluff but I'm scared Quoyle and Dietz heard us. I ease up on Jack's mouth and wonder if he can run.

I whisper, Coyote, it's me, Ku ruks la war´ uks ti.

Jack's forehead wrinkles and his eyes dart back and forth with questions.

Irari, you be quiet now. I'm taking my hand away but you make one noise, we're in trouble. Got it?

Jack nods. I let him go and his lip is bleeding where I pushed too hard. He still don't seem right. His lips and cheeks are slack and his eyes are flat, dark like skillets. I roll off him and he stays.

A yelp from the riverbank, then somebody laughs and talks low.

Jack startles and rolls on his belly and I put a finger to my lips. Scooting over to the edge, I spy those two Colored men lumped together on the sand bar. Dietz kicks one after the other and their heads loll down in the shallow water. Red swirls into the shallows like curly writing and dissolves in the gold water like it was never red.

Dietz bends over and rummages through those men's pockets. He yanks on that watch chain, ripping it free of the big man's vest and dangles it in front of Quoyle like bragging or asking permission. When Quoyle waves him away, Dietz tucks it in his coat pocket. Then he sheathes his knife.

Let's go, I whisper, tugging on Jack's arm so he'll follow, crawling over the short grass and soft ground toward the marsh and woods. Once I figure we're out of Dietz's hearing, we stumble up to our feet and run like hell to where the horses wait, stamping for more oats.

My friend don't want to stay on the wagon even after I get it rolling and I gotta hold his arm with one hand and slap reins with the other. I figure Quoyle and Dietz will head back to town and might overtake us so I keep on to the brewery farm, easygoing and not too fast, like I been minding my own business and never saw Quoyle or Dietz or those Colored men on the sandbar.

Jack won't settle down and his shoes banging the buckboard makes the horses nervous so I give him some corn whiskey one of the other drivers keeps under the seat. I don't think much of its kick, burn and choke but I know the light, loose feeling that comes after is just the thing to settle Jack. He takes it and swallows three times like I tell him and he don't even choke when the clear fire hits his throat. He don't even blink.

I tell him, Enough, and take the blue jar back. You're gonna be fine, Coyote. Once I unload this hay and barley, I'll take you on home.

When I hold the Mason jar between my knees to screw the lid back on, the fumes make me cough and my eyes water. He's pretty far gone not to feel that.

Jack finally finds some words. Bad weather's coming but I don't know what kind of rain.

I look up to see thunderheads piling over us like a litter of puppies.

Probably a hell of a storm coming, rain and hail and lightning, I tell him. But you'll be fine. You listen to my voice, not those others.

But I don't know what kind of rain. He sways and I grab his sleeve.

There was a knife, he says. And blood. I'm going to school.

He slides on the seat like to climb down and almost topples off the wagon before I pull him back. The corn whiskey must hit him then, because when I pull him over he slumps down behind the buckboard by my feet and he's asleep before we get to the farm.

I unload the wagon at Voegels' fast as I ever did, keeping one eye on Jack and hoping nobody notices him. The brewery workers generally stay out of sight now they're illegal so I'm in luck.

My arms and legs ease up shaking and my heart thumps down into a working rhythm. The more I think about what I saw, I wonder if those men were dead or only hurt. Maybe somebody could still do something. I cuss myself for not thinking of it sooner.

I'm sure no Good Sumatran but before I take Jack home to Darkwater, I decide I'll trot those horses to New Eden. The first person I come across there is an old man in a minister's collar and I pull up the horses in front of that Colored Jesus church to yell at him for help.

When I jump down off the wagon seat, talking before I hit the ground, he says, Son, slow down you're making no sense. When he gets the gist he turns ashy. Grabbing my arm, he hurries me up on a front porch and bangs on the door. Tell it again, he says.

I saw two Colored men on the north bank of the Republican, laying by the water.

I leave out the part about Quoyle and Dietz and when the minister asks for more, I shake my head and say that's all.

One woman runs door to door banging and shouting and people spill out into the dusty road. Women call to each other and wring their aprons, children hug themselves and stare at me and men saddle up horses.

Three Colored men, one White and that Oglala I play cards with but never talk to, they thunder out on horses while the sky gets darker and lightning flashes overhead. Little drops of rain patter on the dust. I look over at Jack to see how scared he is but he's dead drunk asleep. I wish I was.

Leaning on the wagon, relieved I don't got to carry those men alone, I break down by the wheel and cry. Racing those horses over here I got twitchy and hopeful with my guts churned up. Now I'm limp like a rag doll knowing I was probably no good and too late and even though I rather he was Pawnee, I think about Colored Jesus there in his church and wonder if he can help. Or maybe he's mad I wasn't a Good Sumatran like in his story.

Jack mumbles, Rain, rain, go away.

I gotta get him home before he wakes up but I can't move.

I crumple down onto the powdery ground and cover my head, rocking myself like a cradle until George's Aunt Sadie walks over. She pats my shoulder, takes hold of my hand and pulls me to my feet. She only comes up high as my chin but she stands on tiptoe, reaches to wipe my face dry with her apron and says, You turned to a man, today. No matter what else happens, you did a good thing and turned to a man.

Her face is broken and shining with tears and proud all at once. She makes me cry so hard, I'm ashamed. I never had nobody proud of me and no mother ever dried my tears. It feels wrong to be glad for these things, with that blood spreading in the water. But here this woman is, being a Good Sumatran to me.

I oughta wait for the New Eden men to come back but I'm afraid they got nothing but bad news and bodies. Jack's gonna wake up and I got no strength left to fight him so I drive the wagon back to Darkwater Creek, a place forever changed for me. After New Eden, Darkwater looks like sticks and paste, a toy town some rich man can stomp down in a fit and the people in it, we're only paper dolls.

Seeing Rolf killed was a terrible hard thing but now this, and I got a suspicion Mr. Hollingwood knows what Quoyle and Dietz just did. Then I look at it another way. It don't make sense. He's a hard man but what's he got to gain from killing two dancers? By the time I roll the wagon up to Jack's front porch, I believe it's nothing I can blame on White Boss but like when they came after me, Quoyle and Dietz were acting on a grudge. I believe it enough to face Albert Hollingwood and trust him with his own son and anyway, what else could I do?

I ease Jack down off the wagon seat and drape him over my shoulders. I don't usually go in by the front door but today I climb those steps and push it open today without knocking because it's not me coming in, it's young Master Jack.

Jack opens his eyes and says, What the hell. Then he falls back into dead weight and snores.

When the housekeeper flutters in I say, Master Jack is very ill, and I ease Jack down onto a big stuffed chair in the parlor.

Hollingwood thunders down those fancy inlaid wood stairs, catches one whiff of corn liquor and yells at me for getting Jack drunk. He blusters about me being a bad influence and he'll stretch my hide on the carriage house wall for a trophy.

When he winds down I explain Jack had some sort of fit and I could only settle him down that way, instead of leaving him on the road.

Jack was talking back to people who weren't there, I tell him. He tried to beat me up.

White Boss turns whiter.

I don't want him thinking his son is insane but I sure as hell can't say Jack's in shock over Quoyle and Dietz killing two men, in case White Boss did order it. I stay close to the truth, without telling him about what we saw or how long Jack's been fighting with the voices.

I knew somebody who got a fever and talked out of his head. Maybe that's it.

He sets his face hard, showing White Boss already knows about Jack's voices and it pains him. Instead of calling a servant, though, he picks up his own boy, shifts Jack's dirty, sweaty weight against his fine new suit and cradles Jack like he's a baby.

I get a big lump in my throat and swallow it down. Sir, can I help?

No. And Peter, you did fine. You brought him home and I thank you.

My eyelid twitches at my reservation name. I never shoulda given it to Hollingwood. He knows I want him to call me Kuruk. I know he never will.

He's my friend.

Yes, Jack is fortunate in your friendship. I'm fortunate. Hollingwood clears his throat and blinks, making me wonder if he ever sheds tears. Jack mumbles in his arms.

He's like a brother.

Hollingwood clears his throat. You've become quite civilized and yet you've retained the loyalty, the nobility of your race.

I catch the thorn in his slippery compliment, the one inside every good word he says about me. I'm quite good at what I do, for an Indian. I'm an exemplary noble savage, a credit to my race.

I take off my new hat and turn it in my hands, missing the old one Joe Chapman gave me, the one Quoyle keeps for evidence. It was a little too small but it was my story and I daydream about stealing it back if I figure out where it is. I let White Boss study me and wait for him to say, You may go. I play the good Indian and study the inlaid floor. What did those planks, squares and triangles of gold and brown wood look like before, when they were living, moving trees?

I smile thinking how I could set that rich man's floor on fire and watch it burn. But Jack is my friend.

Peter, you may go.

I watch Hollingwood carry Coyote up the curved staircase. When a bedroom door closes, I cross the wide bright space Whites call a foyer and let myself out the front door. Hollingwood's porch is like inside a bottle of perfume, sweet from lilacs and buzzing with bumblebees.

201

My Medicine Bear sense warns me not to go but I wonder about those two men on the sand bar and their blood curling away. Did the New Eden men find them? Are they dead?

It's his quitting time but Hollingwood's warehouse foreman has one more load for the brewery, three cases of bottles. I say I'll take them now.

After my delivery, the truck is long gone but I get scared driving past those elderberry bushes where I stopped before. I hide the wagon better this time, a ways off the main road.

Walking under our tree house, my hands sweat and my knees shake. I'd like to hide up there with Jack and Maggie and never come out but I'm afraid Quoyle and Dietz would find us even there.

I walk a different trail farther east to the river. Instead of coming out on a bluff, I stand level with the water. The Republican stretches out front of me like a bolt of gray-brown silk spread on a store counter to be measured, cut and sewed for a lady's dress. The low sun glints off its ripples like they're gold threads. Cottonwoods dip branches down, snagging and wrinkling the surface and fish flick up from underneath, setting off rings inside rings that flatten and grow apart. Leopard frogs chuckle to their mates and a cricket choir sing high and low. A mosquito buzzes by my ear.

To keep from seeing one thing, I'm noticing everything else and it's like nothing could happen here, like nothing did.

Finally I push my eyes to the sandbar about twenty feet west of me. Footprints rumple the sand but I can't see bodies or blood from here so I kick off my shoes and wade in to get closer without leaving any sign. Minnows dart around my feet to nibble and my toes stir up muck off the bottom. The cool water is a comfort until I think about that blood touching and staining my skin.

Those devils mighta shoved those men into the water but that woulda floated them in plain sight past Red Cloud. Two bodies bloating in the water would be bad business. The law would come asking questions here upstream and trace those men to the traveling show in no time. But Quoyle and Dietz are too lazy to dig graves, to bury those poor fellows along the riverbank or in the marsh. And too hard-hearted. You gotta care a little about somebody to bury him.

Maybe the folks from New Eden took the men away alive, fixed them up and hid them or carried them back to their friends at the show. Maybe there wasn't much blood and nobody died and it wasn't a nightmare I gotta suffer for the rest of my life, alongside the one with Rolf in it.

If I go to New Eden, those folks will ask new questions. How did I know the men were there? What did I see? Who did this terrible thing? I'd lie again to save myself and feel even worse than I do now. One part of me figures they're dead. Another part wants to keep hope.

The sun dips down and chills my face. I wipe my wet eyes and snotty nose on my sleeve. I want to make things right but I'm only thirteen goddamn years old, a runaway Pawnee in White territory and it's not even my world to fix. Quoyle and Dietz already got it in for me and I only live in White Boss's good graces. I got no father to protect me and no place else to go but a reservation or Indian school. I'm feeling sorry for myself and that makes me feel small.

So I do a small thing, the best I can. I swear to those men I'll remember what happened, won't let it fade or twist into nothing but a nightmare. I'll sharpen their story and keep it with Rolf's. Remembering don't seem like much but maybe someday it'll count for something.

⚪

I stole another book because the librarian said, No, yet one more time when I asked her to assign me a library card. She turned me away with the same old reasons. First, I'm a Gypsy no-account house girl for the Amsels, and second, I'm a brat to say I have no last name.

When the old hag wasn't looking, I tucked *Bible Stories and Religious Classics* in my skirt and sneaked out. It's a book they had at the orphanage, and holding it feels like hugging the little girl I was back then. The stories are warm and familiar.

Maybe the librarian's right, though, to say I'm no-account, if I'd steal a book about the Bible, but wouldn't Jesus want me to have those stories? He said Blessed are the poor, but I think this—*Beati possidentes.* Blessed are those who possess.

I don't steal much other than books. I'm as hungry for them as for food, but I know it's a sin, and a reckoning will come, one I must read my way into, to understand.

So I examine my soul. If hungering causes the stealing, then what explains the keeping? Even if I was a half-honest girl, I'd return the books because once I read a thing, I remember every line. But there is another mystery in books that runs like water under memory, a beauty beyond my eyes. Searching for it, I get half-drowned in the bubbling words, swimming down into pages for secret meanings under the swirling letters and rushing lines.

Like this story I just read, remembering each word before my eyes brush over it, from when I was little. In *Bible Stories*, Hans Christian Andersen tells about four proud brothers who thought they'd be Something. An old woman with my name, Old Margaret didn't think anything of herself and had a pure soul.

I suppose she'd never steal a book, either, but being pure already, she didn't need one.

Back to the story. The proud brothers worked like heck to do Something or be Something in this world, but they didn't amount to much, only making some bricks and buildings, meanwhile criticizing everybody. Then they died. Poor Old Margaret lived in her little brick house and nearly froze to death until, one night the people of her town were out dancing on the ice at a party. Margaret saw a storm coming and wanted to warn them, but she couldn't go down because she was too old and sick, so she set her house afire to get their attention. They ran off the ice to put out her fire, and it saved them sure enough, just as the ice broke apart behind them.

But Margaret died, too. When she got to heaven's gates, she stood talking with one of the dead proud brothers, a genius who never did anything good. An angel came and scolded him, saying he couldn't come in, but then let Margaret into heaven because she did Something by dying for all those people.

You'd think the story would end there. Heavenly rewards for the good and all that.

But then Margaret did a thing I'll never forget. She begged the angel to let the genius in because of some broken bricks she got from his brother to build her house. Some trash he didn't think twice about, not a good deed at all.

Margaret said to the angel, *It will be an act of mercy; he needs it, and this is the home of mercy.*

I can't stop swimming around those words.

Can you imagine? A home of mercy. *Domum misericordiae.*

Jack stares at the misted balcony window in his room as if he can see through it. His eyes are bloodshot and ashy pockets sink in under his eyes. Sweat beads on his upper lip and forehead and he stinks from the heat, but instead of summer cotton, he wears that black wool suit from Rolf's funeral. It makes his skin look yellow, or maybe the cast falls from the globe lamp burning beside him on this gloomy day. If not for the lamp, this chamber would be dim as a tomb.

Maggie, help me decide.

What? I squeeze his hand and his fingertips are like dry paper over sticks. His wrist bones poke out white under his skin. I remember how brown he was last summer, when he swam and played in the sun with me and Rolf and the other boys. Before.

I can't keep it straight. Are there six or seven kinds of rain?

I don't know. You tell me.

The science is unclear. Of course, first is the everyday raindrop that splats on the ground. It's center is made of dust.

I didn't know that. I lie, hoping he'll correct and remind me. Maybe being right will keep him from fading away.

He licks his lips and blinks twice. The thing that washes us is dirt. Is dirt.

That's funny, I say, and force a little laugh.

He glances at me, then back at the rain-blurred glass, his expression as flat as a tray. No, it's a scientific fact.

What's another kind?

Drizzle. The kind that doesn't fall, but makes you wet if you stand in it.

It's drizzling today, Jack. I nod at the blurry window, raise his hand and set it on my damp sleeve. Then I pat it on my frizzy, wet hair. Do you feel that?

He doesn't look, but nods. That's drizzle, alright, fog gone to extremes. Jack chortles at his own peculiar joke.

A good one. What's next?

Freezing rain, near to being ice. It solidifies when it hits something cold. And sleet, which is almost snow, but still liquid.

I never knew there were so many.

How many does that add up to? Jack lets go of me and taps each of his fingers against his thumb, counting.

Four, I tell him.

He holds up five fingers between us. Number five is hail, water tossed up into the clouds again and again, coated with layers of freezing vapor.

Hail is a good one.

Unless it knocks you on the head, Jack says.

I wait for him to laugh, but he doesn't. What's number six?

207

He sighs. I'd have to say it's snow, but that's debatable because a lot of rain begins as snow. You could say snow is the father of rain. The father of rain. The father.

He frowns.

Are you thinking about your father?

No, about rain.

Six kinds, then. Are there more?

Jack closes his eyes. This is the one I can't settle in my mind. This is the problem. There might be one more, but I can't settle it in my mind. This problem.

I pick up his hand again. Jack, you're saying things twice.

I am?

Yes. Why is that?

Well, she does. I'm sorry, I'll try not to.

Who is she?

She's nobody.

Jack leans forward and places his other hand flat on the window glass. His face nearer the outside light looks blue and it makes me think of Rolf. I shiver and tug on his hand to get him back into the yellow light. It makes him look sick, but alive.

Tell me about the seventh kind of rain.

I'm not sure it is or isn't, he says. For the first time since I sat next to him half an hour ago, Jack looks me in the eye. Help me, Maggie.

How can I help him? Maybe I can cook something he'll eat so he'll stop losing weight. Maybe I could sit and read to him to ease his mind. I'll do anything, Jack. Tell me what.

I'm stuck in the dilemma. It's phantom rain. The kind you see in the sky, but it never reaches the ground. How do we measure and prove it's there? How do I know if it is or isn't? Is or isn't?

Well, that would make seven.

Jack shakes his head and clenches his jaw. But we can't count it 'til we prove it's real. 'Til it proves itself. 'Til we prove. Jack taps his counting fingers on his knees. One-two-three-four-five-six-maybe-seven. One-two-three-four-five-six-maybe-seven.

You're repeating things, Jack.

Because she does.

Who is she?

The Teacher in my head. She's not the only one. Father says he's sending me away because I hear voices that aren't real. I may be the only one who can hear them, but they're real, I swear.

You hear voices?

Too many to count. They come with the rain or not with the rain. When people live or die. With knives and guns. Any time. Hah! I'm mad as a hatter.

You're as sane as I am.

I'm like my mother, with a delicate constitution and a fragile mind. Father says I must be taken care of.

Jack, you're not fragile. You're smart and strong and—

It's reasonable, isn't it, that if I prove the voices exist, then I'm not insane?

I can't keep up, with his mind flying everywhere. I ask, Where is your father sending you?

He waves his hand toward the window and changes his voice lower to sound like his father's. Not to Ingleside, because it's nearby and people would find out about Hollingwood's mad son. We can't have that.

Jack twists a bitter smile and goes back to his own voice. Father's telling everyone I'm so intelligent, a top boarding school is taking me early. It was true, but I'm not going there yet, if ever. I'm leaving on one of my father's trains. My mother went away on one, did you know? In a boxcar, in a casket. I hope I'll be in a passenger car, but you never know. Maybe in a boxcar. Maybe in a casket.

He settles his fingers back on his knees and taps them, one after another. One-two-three-four-five-six-maybe-seven.

I press my fingertips into my eyes to hold back tears, then dry them on my skirt. Jack, what do the voices say?

Jack is bad and Jack should die.

That's terrible. You never told me.

If you knew I heard them, you wouldn't love me. Nobody loves a lunatic.

I put one arm around his shoulders and draw him close, burying my face in his neck. His soft hair tickles my face and I whisper, But I already do.

He reaches up, feels my tears and says, Don't rain, Magpie. He pats my cheek and tugs on a lock of my hair.

Magpie? I chuckle, sniff and dry my eyes. Why do you call me that? I know, but I want him to say it again.

They have bright eyes and feathers that shine like your hair. They're smart, talk a lot and swipe things that don't belong to them. Like you.

I glance up in time to see a flicker of grin. The Jack I know is there for a few seconds, and I forgive him for calling me a carrion bird. Only books, I say, remember?

And don't forget the magpie funeral, he says. Magpie loves her friends, even when they're gone.

You always make it add up to a compliment.

I mean it that way.

He puts his arm around me, and we hold each other until Albert Hollingwood clears his throat in the doorway. I don't know how long he's been standing there or what he heard.

As I pull away, Jack whispers, Promise you'll remember the six kinds of rain? And help me decide about the seventh?

I promise.

He tugs my hair again and brushes a kiss on my cheek. I touch the spot where he finally did.

Mr. Hollingwood shifts his shoes on the creaky wood floor and checks his pocket watch as if I'm a train running late.

I stand up and smooth Jack's hair, but he stares at the droplets on the window as if I've already gone, his fingers tapping on his knees and his lips moving to a silent count.

Jack's father steps aside to let me pass, but I stop and lean close to whisper, It seems *filius est dedecori patri*. The son is a disgrace to his father.

Understanding, he draws back as if I slapped him. Latin, he says, raising his eyebrows. Where did you learn?

From books, of course. Will you tell me where you're sending him, or do you mean to hide him from everyone?

I can't hold my sassy mouth, but I'm begging him with my eyes.

He glances at the stiff pink lilies on the table beside us and lies to me. Jack will attend a prestigious and competitive school, where he'll be completely occupied with coursework and athletics. He won't have time to write. He'll meet other girls.

Albert Hollingwood brushes his eyes over me as if my clean clothes are dirty, as if by being in the same room with him, I somehow make him less.

Rich girls, I say. With soft hands and no scars? Girls with fathers and mothers, good bloodlines and fine breeding? Who speak elegant French, not patched-together Latin?

He clears his throat again and looks down at the calluses on my hands. You're an intelligent girl, Margaret Rose, and despite your circumstances you may go far. You've been a good friend to Jack, but life is uncertain. Some friendships must end.

But sir, *Amicus certus in re incerta cernitur.*

A true friend is discerned in an uncertain matter, he translates, giving me a grudging nod of respect. Then he flushes over his tight collar, shakes his head and thanks me for stopping by.

Abiit nemine salutato. Three weeks ago, my Jack went away without bidding anyone farewell.

Kuruk and I hike to the tree house to sort through Jack's books, as if we might find some secret part of him or some spell to conjure him back. Holding the one Jack loved first and best, *Our Own Weather,* Kuruk tells me of finding Jack with his voices in the thunderstorm and how they started with the Omaha tornado.

I want to scold Kuruk for keeping that secret, but it shows how trustworthy he is. How strange to read today about the 1913 storm in this very book, the one Jack reread a hundred times. Now I understand why he did. The voices had Jack before we three became friends and he's suffered all this time, studying so science could save him.

Kuruk holds the weather book tightly, his knuckles creamy white. I've never seen him cry, but today tears spill down his cheeks. Teach me to read English, he says, so we can study together, to find a way to help him.

I've offered to teach him a hundred times, and a hundred times he quietly answered, Being Pawnee is enough and, Whites did nothing but hurt us with lies in writing. Today, for love of Jack, he's willing to take his mortal enemy's writing deep into himself. We both knows what this means, what Kuruk risks by learning.

Kuruk's love is one I understand. I'll go anywhere and learn any language I need. There must be some medicine for what ails Jack. It can't only be about the rain.

I lift the book from Kuruk's hand and thumb through for a simple line, a beginning to honor his Pawnee heart. At Genoa, Kuruk learned his alphabet and simple words like *and, is, to.* I hope he remembers a little more for us to build on, because this book is no primer. The writer likes complicated sentences, but this book is Kuruk's choice. I scan for something to give him.

Here, it's something a grandfather might say.

If the new moon lies on its back, and so will hold water, it will be a dry moon.

Kuruk nods and asks, Which word is *moon?*

In the first week, I feel the pain of Jack's parting like an arrow shot from a distance, losing force until it clatters on the ground. After that, it seems the calluses on my hands spread and harden into a cast that numbs me. The loss of feeling frightens me more than pain, as if I'm suddenly old enough to die. I crave to feel something. On the inside of my arm, under the sleeve where no one will see it, I scrape my fingernail against the skin until I bleed. Barely feeling that, I steal something new, not a book but a silver razor from Mr. Amsel's bathroom shelf.

The blood trickling from the crescent slice stirs me. That first bright pain comforts me, and all day afterward the throbbing wound reminds me I'm alive. It chants without words, To love is to hurt, to hurt is to live, to live is to love. My heartbeat echoes the truth like one of my old nursery rhymes and the scarlet invites me to leave behind what I cannot bear.

Evening red and morning gray
Will set the traveler on his way
But evening gray and morning red
Will bring down rain upon his head.

Alone every night with Amsel's razor, I push the edge of feeling alive. Without it, I fear I will curl into myself, away from the void to die.

One week since my first cutting, and I cherish four parallel razor lines on my upper arm. They hold my mother and father, Jack and Cedric near. I keep them in the pain. As each wound heals and scars, I slice a new one like a covenant, watching myself bleed and sighing a sort of prayer. One by one, the lines form a script and story, a secret account of my life. A language of loss on my body, a book I can never close.

Jack's insanity confounds, angers and exhausts the man. He catches himself grieving, as if the boy had died, and reminds himself he should be grateful his son isn't old enough for conscription for the War in Europe, where he could be gassed or blown to pieces. Hollingwood sees new boys every week boarding the train for Camp Funston, the well-off ones with strapped suitcases and the poor with nothing but flour sacks slung over their shoulders. Some won't return, yet he covets their parents' pride, their honor. He struggles to keep love flowing over his shame, to hide it from his friends and workers. He constructs hard, simple lies to deflect their questions.

If the boy can recover, it may well be on The Sidis Psychotherapeutic Institute's park-like grounds. Fountains, brooks and pools where geese slide as if over glass. Gardens bursting with flowers and indoors, sitting rooms with upholstered, silk divans and chaise lounges. A place like home. Not any sort of madhouse. Not Ingleside.

It makes sense. Treat the boy as if he's sane, and he might realign himself.

Hollingwood has warned himself not to expect a quick recovery, so Boris Sidis's first update isn't a complete disappointment. The boy's at least eating three squares a day, putting back on a little weight. Besides, radical improvement after only a few weeks would suggest malingering.

He considers himself astute in matters of human nature, so it rankles that he didn't spot Jack's condition sooner, even with his wife's mother banging around in a private asylum. He's paying those monthly bills in addition to Jack's, even with Edith thirteen years dead. Yet what can he do? Constance Appling was a notable lady before her breakdown and a state hospital is unthinkable. He maintains his mother-in-law for Edith, whose cherished memory still warms him when he glances at her portrait over his desk. A gentle, good-hearted woman cursed with bad blood, born into a family of liars. He grinds his teeth, resenting how the Applings artfully concealed a long family line of lunatics and poisoned his legacy.

He recognizes now the signs he first missed, Jack's decline after that Omaha tornado. He became distracted and spent too much time alone, ostensibly studying science, then sought out low company like that orphan girl. Now he fears Jack will never be fit to assume the family business or pass on his name.

The solution glimmers in Hollingwood like a chip of glass in a dusty corner, missed until a sloping sunbeam refires it. He ought to remarry and beget sons more like himself, this time from a mother of sound body and mind. His heart snags on Jack, though, as he refolds Sidis's most recent letter into its envelope. Instead of daydreaming about the next Mrs. Albert Hollingwood, he'll hope Sidis is correct, that Jack's problem isn't inherited.

Four years ago, they shared both a train car to New York and their first discussion about insanity and heredity. Dr. Boris Sidis offered novel ideas about consciousness and put little stock in hydropathy and electrical stimulation, standard treatments of the day. He admitted to providing them, simply to attract and reassure his patients and ease them into psychiatric care. Hollingwood immediately appreciated the man's business acumen and has since respected the trim little man with the broad, bow-like moustache, even if he is a Jew. He, like Hollingwood, discerns what people want and what they need, knowing they're rarely the same thing. Sidis knows that to succeed, you provide both.

To businessmen and bootleggers alike, Hollingwood presents himself as an educated man, despite his half-earned college degree. That first day on the train, and in his correspondence since, Sidis has always spoken to him as a peer, respecting Hollingwood's life experience and insight into human behavior. With no tone of condescension, Sidis explained as he would to another doctor how he experimented on himself, using his right, amblyopic eye for statistical analysis. He posited a secondary, subwaking self, based in his other eye's experience of reality, to suggest what the diseased eye couldn't see. This subwaking self, he claimed, perceives things the primary waking self cannot ascertain, and is the key to human sanity. He called it a highway of suggestion that, once connected to the conscious mind, restores the self to stability.

Sidis's theory intrigued Hollingwood even then, concerned as he already was about Jack. Flattered by the esteemed man's attention, he sustained ongoing correspondence with Sidis, who regularly and good-naturedly challenged Hollingwood's cherished beliefs about eugenics and insanity. After he confided in the doctor about Jack, Sidis shared his paper *Neurosis and Eugenics*, reassuring him that imbalances of the mind are not inherited, but learned and based in fear.

Hollingwood drums his fingers on the desk and gazes at Edith's portrait, hoping Sidis is correct. If what is learned can be unlearned, the boy might recover. The details of Sidis's theory are fuzzy for Hollingwood in hindsight, but limited by his own sort of half-blindness, he chose to trust the doctor, to send Jack to Maplewood Farms.

He opens the manila envelope Sidis sent in response to Hollingwood's first telegram about Jack, two months ago. He spreads its contents over his desk in a ritual that's the closest thing he can manage to prayer, foregone since he escorted Edith's body to Rosehill. He rereads Sidis's written favor, that although he'd never taken a child patient at his institute, he welcomed Jack into his family's care. A believer in the pure potential of children, Sidis guided his own son into Harvard at age eleven, which gives Hollingwood hope.

Sidis included a photograph of the gabled main house, where he and his wife reside with the patients, and an illustrated booklet. Paging through it, Hollingwood admires the luxurious drawing and dining rooms. He pictures Jack tossing smooth stones into the goldfish pond or closing his eyes to sleep in the carpeted chamber with its private bath. Good Lord, Hollingwood chuckles, he'll be so spoiled, he may never return. He thanks heaven Edith isn't here today, to hear Jack raving about voices in his head, but if she were, she'd approve Hollingwood's generous provision for her boy.

That being said, he hopes that at one hundred dollars per week, Jack's convalescence won't last long. A good value, though, he reminds himself, buying both care and confidentiality. For Jack to have any sort of future, this whole affair must remain unheard of in Darkwater Creek. Hollingwood concocted a story about Jack summering with distant relatives back East, learning to sail and play polo before his early admission to Blue Ridge Academy. Far better to be envied than pitied, after all, and rumors of lunacy are unequivocally bad for business.

Hollingwood eases back in his rolling chair and ponders the one loose end, that Indian boy. He demonstrates good character and cares about Jack. Already complicit in

218

Hollingwood's hidden-in-plain-sight bootlegging enterprise at the German farm, he may be persuaded to keep one more secret. And if Sidis is right, Peter may not be ingrained with the hot-blooded savagery Hollingwood, at a tender age, learned to fear.

In the wild railroad town of North Platte, where the Union Pacific tracks met the end of the Texas Cattle Trail, he watched his father grow wealthy from iron and beef. At nine years old, Albert traced a finger over the greasy news report of Little Big Horn and hundreds ravaged by Sioux. For months, the hair prickled on his scalp and arms as he pictured Indians creeping in to slaughter him in his bed. Half a lifetime later, Jack's future rests in the forge-scarred hands of a runaway Indian child. Hollingwood finds this coincidence more terrifying than ironic.

He considers setting the clever boy on a westbound train, to make his fortune in California. If not that, one letter to Indian Affairs would return Peter to Oklahoma, where someone on the reservation would claim him. Both ideas have merit, but leave too many loose ends. Who's to say the rascal wouldn't demand more money or return with a vengeance if he's unhappy, bringing state prohibition agents or worse?

Hollingwood paces the room and rubs the back of his neck. Trading a life for something or someone of greater value, he's done this often enough, it seems not so much a moral offense as a business strategy. In this case, a murmured suggestion to Quoyle would ensure Jack's secret and it would be a small price to pay to protect his flesh and blood.

Peter was a runaway once, and folks would naturally assume he is again. He has no family to even question where he's gone and while this fact simplifies the matter,

Hollingwood feels it as somehow more troubling. Then there's the boy himself. He's proven to be strong and loyal, sincere and honest and—unlike Jack—clear in his mind, even if he is illiterate and superstitious. He's reliable, ready to learn from Hollingwood's experience and quick to help in ways Jack never was. It's comforting, yet alarming, to realize his paternal affection for this untamed, unpredictable boy. Settling back down into his creaking, rolling leather chair, he licks a thumb and turns the booklet pages, picturing Jack on those grounds, missing home and almost certainly missing Peter. The two chum together like brothers and Jack might completely unhinge, should Peter disappear. He might not believe any runaway story, either.

Damn it all. Hollingwood shakes his head, frustrated with his uncharacteristic waffling. Gusting out a breath to clear his mind, he smacks his desktop.

Peter's only a boy, he mutters, and I've yet to sink so low, to cause the death of a child, that situation with the Voegels notwithstanding. He ponders how Quoyle and Dietz botched that simple business transaction. Those two. Hardly worth the trouble they cause, and yet, without them . . . but that's water under the bridge.

Hollingwood scratches his beard and smooths his moustache. He'd best keep Peter safe and near, to encourage Jack's recovery, or all Jack will come home to is that ornery half-breed, Maggie. But how to further befriend and obligate the Indian boy? Deepen his trust with paternal attention. Increase his pay. Teach him to drive, something every boy yearns for, and promote him to driving a truck for deliveries. Let him even chauffeur, from time to time. Involve him in work with more serious legal penalties, if he turns his coat. And give him some fun, time off and some extra coins for matinee picture shows. Maybe old Jose at Amsel's ranch can teach Peter to break and ride horses, like a real Indian. And when he's a little older, have Quoyle introduce him to the girls out at Muriel Roquette's.

Hollingwood refolds the Sidis literature, locks it in a drawer and pockets the key. Having reasoned it through, he sees the benefit as clearly as if through his magnifying glass. He'll take the high ground.

Selecting a Cuban from his humidor, he snips it with his gold cigar cutter and, after sniffing the sweet, unburned leaves, he strikes a match. A little cough clears the scorch of sulphur from his throat and he puffs, rewarding himself for resolving a ticklish dilemma.

Magpie *yak-yak*s on a branch over the thickening river, then tugs the last dry mulberries off twigs. The winter sun inches farther south each day, chilling the ground and the water and the bird.

Coyote, scant as an old deer hide, snuffles and scratches the freezing ground. He tenses up for burrowed, sleeping mice he can smell but can't see. He swings his head to see his mate and nips at a limp, bloody ground squirrel caught in her teeth. He sniffs the air for rabbit but the sharp breeze following the river doesn't tell him anything.

The female Coyote drops her prize and both turn to watch the gaunt ghost of Bear. He snaps and lumbers out of the brush down onto a sandbar. Stepping in so heavy, he cracks through the fringe of ice to follow the bank. Splashing, Bear lifts and lowers his glossy black head and snuffles for remembered plums.

Bear being in this place is more than a dream, but less than a shadow—a quick sun-silvering off the tips of his fur are his only sign. To see him you best look away because like many real things in this place he is, but also is not.

In Coyote's memory, in Magpie's shining black eye and in the bony bedrock under the loess, Bear remains.

Elsiver Dietz stomps his boots up my carriage house stairs, busts into my room and rousts me out of bed near midnight, shining a bright light in my eyes. He howls out, Where the hell's that mutt a yours? Then he laughs until brown spit dribbles out the side of his mouth.

I jump up like I touched a live wire, thinking he's come to hang me but it turns out Regal Quoyle sent that jackass to put me to work. There's bodies piling up at the train station, dead soldiers in wood caskets coming back from the War, and nearly a half dozen every week wrapped in linen at the undertaker's, the Spanish influenza dead. So they figure, who better to dig graves than the local Indian?

Dietz is a foul man, swearing and spitting snuff all the while he prods me with a stick like I'm livestock. He humiliates me because he can't kill me. He stands by with a gun while I work like I'm a prisoner and he's my guard, drinking himself mean and telling me ugly stories about women he says he took. Come sunrise, he warns me to be back the next night, by eleven. Quoyle came by after the first night, polite and reasonable, explaining I got to work at night because folks are so wracked with mourning and deep in shock from all the death it's too disturbing to see graves dug in broad daylight.

When I tell White Boss what Quoyle and Dietz got me doing all night, thinking he'll stand up for me, it seems he don't mind. I think it tickles him somehow, to see me taken down a notch. When I say, You must have more important things for me to do, he says, Not at night, Peter. Then he grins, bites on his cigar and tells me I should consider it my contribution to the War. He reminds me of the thousands of dollars he's contributed to the County War Memorial, because we must honor the courageous dead. And all I got to do is dig a few holes. Is that asking so much?

When he stops talking, I guess he notices my clenched fists and jaw because he puffs some smoke and says, For your contribution to the community, Peter, I'll double your pay.

I want to tell him where to stuff his money but then I think how much sooner I'll be able to buy that piece of land on Lovely Creek, out by New Eden. That roll of dollar bills in the coffee can I buried will fatten up twice as fast. I got a dream of a little farm, some land I'll get back for the Pawnee, to make my life my own. A place outside town where Hollingwood can't boss me. I picture a field of corn, some painted horses and a brown milk cow.

Seeing I'm not as grateful as he likes me to be, Hollingwood reminds me how important I am to his operation and how I got a shining future as his *protégé*. That someday I could become a manager. He tells me to buck up, not to lose heart in these difficult times. At least I still got my health in this horrible epidemic.

He smiles and asks if I'd like to move into one of his nice empty bedrooms in his house but I stretch a smile back and say, No thank you, sir, I'm fine where I am. That old carriage house is all the home I need. A single fellow like myself, I need my privacy.

He squints at me and says, Peter, do you have a girl? Or do you need me to get you one?

My face gets red and hot but I stick out my chin and say, I can see to that myself, sir. Thanks, anyway.

He grins. Hah! Good man, he says.

But move into his house? I'd sooner dig myself a grave. At least there, I'd get a good night's sleep. If only I could get this cemetery clay scrubbed out from under my fingernails, I wouldn't mind so much. But I console myself with this—digging those holes night after night builds up my arms and shoulders, making me stronger for when Quoyle and Dietz come after me. Doing nothing but carrying dirty money for Hollingwood was making me soft.

That's most of what I do, now, since I got tall and shave and can pass for grown. Hollingwood taught me to drive and I take his cars, the older ones nobody will notice, across the county and even up to Lincoln to deliver the whiskey he makes in his new still at the Voegel farm. It's a lot more profitable than the beer and so pure, the rich folks in Lincoln can't get enough. About twice a week I meet slick-haired fellows in shiny suits who take crates of Hollingwood's liquor and give me leather satchels fat with cash. I got a nice shirt and trousers and a haircut so I can carry those satchels into banks for deposit in White Boss's accounts, without folks getting too suspicious of me. The first time, I think they wondered how an Indian got so much money but Hollingwood musta warned them I was coming. Since those tellers got to know me, most treat me nearly as good as a White man.

Last time I left the First National, I bought a newspaper from a kid on the corner. I can make out most words now so I could read in the *Lincoln Star* how influenza hit my old Oklahoma reservation hard. That story set off a dream of my father in a fever-sweat, dying, and I woke up desperate to steal one of Hollingwood's cars and drive to Pawnee. But I knew better. That would be the last driving I'd ever do.

Since then, even when I'm awake, Pawnee faces and names I forgot years ago, they bubble up in my mind. The old woman who mended Crooked Walk's shirts after my mother died. Some little kid named Stewart Blue Horse who liked to sit on a rusty bicycle. The fat friendly fellow who worked at the Agency store and gave me free pickles. The snub-nosed teacher who kicked me out of the Pawnee school. Seeing them so sudden and clear outside of dreaming I wonder if they got sick and died and now come back to steal back a little of their lives from my memory.

If it wasn't for Maggie meeting me out at the tree house, I'd feel like a whole different and lost person. Being with her ties me to the ground, the river and our Coyote Jack, the one we miss together.

George comes by sometimes, asking me out to visit his Auntie at New Eden for some chicken and pie. It unsettled me to go there the first time, after the awful thing happened by the river but nobody asked me about it again. I guess for those folks every day has enough new sorrow in it without going backwards to borrow more. Last month George's oldest cousin, a boy our age, ran off from there and lied about being eighteen so he could join the Army. I thought about doing that to get away from Hollingwood and the crimes he got me tangled up in. But I learned already, there's no going away from who you are. You got to dig the grave laid out in front of you.

∞

Armistice. Since October 22, the state prohibits our public gathering in groups of twelve or more, but the beleaguered and quarantined people of Darkwater come together anyway to feel the sun, shout and throw hats in the air. We forget for a moment our other war, the one we fight in our bedrooms by lamplight.

Darkwater Creek lost seven boys overseas, five of them in one battle. Three of them, I remember from school. One studied mathematics to become an engineer, while the other two farmed with their fathers and begrudged the classroom time. They all teased us girls, went to church and probably did things they shouldn't, drinking, rolling made-your-owns and pulling pranks. I hope so, because now they can do nothing, having died in a war I'd be hard pressed to explain to their mothers.

Our spontaneous, illegal celebration for the end of their blood-boughten war drains into a greater fear, the way rain rushes downhill to a river. Some boys who survived Europe are dying where they should be safe, at Camp Grant in Illinois and Camp Funston in Kansas. No mustard gas or bullets there, only influenza. Soldiers and civilians face the same enemy now, on home ground.

Our first civilian casualty was Mrs. Otto Wimmers. Adelaide, with the red cheeks and creamy alto voice, carried pie and jam to her brother at Camp Funston, then carried influenza home. Two days later, she fell into a fever and infected her family. Her husband and baby survived, but the two closest to my age died within a week.

It's a unique quality of this strain, unlike the Russian flu of '89, to prefer children and adults while often excusing infants and older folks. Following a disease course of fever, cough, purple skin discoloration and bleeding from the eyes, nose and mouth, this season's influenza is written up in the papers as a nasty character, gruesome and horrible. I find it exotic and mysterious and, while others turn away, I observe, resolved to untangle influenza's morbid mysteries. Each time a patient struggles to live, I touch Jack's cut through my sleeve and pretend he's with me in that throbbing. Silently, I discuss with him what's happening, as if it's an experiment. I struggle to hold a scientific mind, but the disease is relentless.

Influenza's sickrooms and deathbeds create scenes more like a church than a laboratory, more emotional than rational. Washing hands and lighting lamps. Speaking words of comfort. Filling, emptying and cleansing vessels. Unfolding and folding cloths. Preparing last meals. Hearing desperate confessions, pleadings and whispered prayers.

And yet, while I can't prove the existence of a soul, it's a mystery more intriguing than the disease itself to hear a breath exhale and not return, carrying with it the facial expressions, gestures, quirks and language unique to that person. It covers me with a holy, terrible feeling and makes my hands tremble every time. As every new death echoes the ones before, I feel Rolf join every new one who dies, to flutter over me like moths in candlelight.

Dr. Reed, who treats me with grumpy respect since the horrible night with Rolf, called me off the sidewalk in late October into a house of six flu patients to make soup and wash linens. With the school doors locked indefinitely, I'm glad for the occupation. I am Dr. Reed's Little Resident, and together we face what he calls The Exponential Dread, the sick piled in wagons and clustered on his brown lawn. Between house calls, he quizzes me on medical Latin and tutors from his old edition of Henry Gray's *Anatomy*.

In a flat pasture, the doctor teaches me how to leverage all my ninety pounds down on the clutch, reverse or brake pedal, how to manage the spark advance and throttle, and how to angle the clutch lever of his Model T. He says that compared to managing those complicated controls, an appendectomy or any other surgery will seem simple. I like driving so he can catch a few winks between house calls. Lack of sleep appears to be the hardest part of being a physician, but as exhausted as he is, Dr. Reed insists I rest every eight hours on the dot, even if I'm in the car. He claims it's for selfish reasons, because in all of Darkwater Creek, no one else is brave enough to stand beside him in this epidemic.

I say, Poor Doctor, that I am his best hope.

My work of mercy and the doctor's favor earned my banishment from the Amsel house. Florence, after years of puzzling over the conundrum, at last found cause and proclaimed me an influenza carrier, Darkwater's own Typhoid Mary. She didn't even let me pack my things. While Florence ranted, Mr. Amsel stood aside looking pitiful and Mrs. Endicott carried my bundle to the doorstep. That Raeburn Amsel is a terrible coward. I regret I ever longed for his fatherly concern. Seeing me cast out, Adolf piddled on the slate tiles and Greta wailed for her Mama Maggie, which touched my heart but didn't improve my case with her mother.

A true outcast now, without even the figment of parents, I sleep where I must. Sometimes I'm in Dr. Reed's storeroom on a cot, at others in a patient's parlor chair. Now and again, I'm in Kuruk's bed while he snores on a pallet on his floor. I'm careful to come and go in darkness there, because if anyone discovers me in the carriage house, I'll be considered not only a dirty Gypsy no-account, but also a wanton.

Kuruk is a comfort to me, but we are still as children together, innocent. If we can't sleep, we retell stories about Jack's Coyote tricks and hope he's surviving insanity and influenza, wherever his father's hidden him. I help Kuruk with his reading, which he's growing to love, and we laugh together at the awkward palefaces and redskins in James Fenimore Cooper. I lose count, now. It's been two or three nights since I last rested in Kuruk's room.

The child on the bed is dying. I ask Dr. Reed if our patient's cyanosis, choking and outpouring of blood indicate that influenza attacks not only the lungs, but also the heart. After I speak, I realize how hard-hearted I must sound, with the mother sitting there, weeping.

Instead of shaming me, he peers over his glasses and nods. Girl, you'll make a physician yet, he says. The first thing is to understand your enemy.

I have many of those, and disease may be the least of them. I lied to Dr. Reed this morning, telling him I slept a full eight hours in the Ford, but nightmares of Quoyle, Dietz and Rolf kept me fitful and awake. A quivering sensation in my belly and limbs would take over my hands if I let it, and it's all I can do not to watch for the little boy's soul over his body as he exhales. I'm sure it's circling there, with all the others.

While I nurse a man named John Taylor, a laborer at the brickyard, Quoyle and Dietz pound on the door of his little house. They push past me into the sickroom and stand over John's bed. John coughs and sweats and is gray as the sheet I tucked around him, but they harangue him for his ten-dollar obligation to Albert Hollingwood. An amount that doubles with interest into twenty, at midnight.

I step near Elsiver Dietz and touch his arm to reason with him.

He shoves me against the wall. The knife he had at John's throat he turns on me when he says, Don't touch me again, bitch.

Quoyle stretches a thin smile and says, She's merely playing doctor. No need for threats.

I'm caught like a sleeve on a nail, Dietz's insult pinning me where I stand. Shame for nothing I ever did knifes my stomach and chest and spills hot over my face. Quoyle grasps my arm and leads me to a corner.

Dietz is uncouth, Quoyle says. His rudeness is unforgivable.

He leans over me, thick arms hemming me in like fences. He reeks of spicy hair pomade and a sickening smell like raw chicken left out of the icebox. I shrink into the corner as he sniffs my neck and my hair.

Ah, he inhales, There it is.

Pressing his lips to my cheek, he flicks his tongue, tasting.

I duck and shove against his chest, but he's tall and wide and strong. He laughs and presses me smaller.

Furious, I sense how he loves the struggle. Swallowing and closing my eyes, I lower my hands and pull my anger backwards, into the throb and pain where I cut my arm. Mother, Father, Cedric, Rolf, Jack. I fall through the red, to hide myself in that deep place where I decide, where I hold the blade.

But even from there I hear his whisper, You are unfortunately beautiful, and smell the hard licorice clicking against his teeth. Sweet and forbidden, he calls me, the essence of dreams. He rests a hand on my breast, to weigh and measure me. I press myself deeper and smaller.

Dietz coughs and demands, Do you want me to kill him or not?

Quoyle whispers, Later, and backs away.

I hold on to the rhythm of my heartbeat, watching from a deep distance to see how they will hurt John.

Turning to his man, Quoyle shakes his head and sighs, Enough. To John, who's gasping and graying into blue, he says, Pay, or I'll climb on your daughter to get it. Understood?

The two men clatter back into their night.

In one-breath syllables, the man in the bed makes his dying request, that I take his last ten dollars from the cigar box under the bed. An hour after I seal those bills in an envelope and write on it *Regal Quoyle,* John dies in a hiccup of blood. My knees shaking, I keep my promise to slip the envelope under Quoyle's door, well before midnight.

My fervent prayer, fed by fear and rage, is for Albert Hollingwood, Regal Quoyle and Elsiver Dietz to contract influenza, choke on their own blood and die. But day after day, heavenly retribution stalls and justice eludes me. All three scoundrels walk about with both impunity and immunity.

As evil is so concentrated and justice so dilute, I borrow a scalpel from Dr. Reed's medical cabinet. I wrap it in gauze and tuck it in my right boot, close at hand. An answer for Quoyle, should he demand one.

Pleading for God to bring about my enemies' bloody suffocations, I grow impatient. I wonder if I should wreak vengeance on the world with more than a scalpel. But after fitful nights and bloody dreams, each morning I make rounds with the doctor and ask myself if justice and vengeance are truly my heart's desire. Medicine is strenuous, a calculated and relentless work of mercy. It feeds on the ethic of *nil nocere*, to do no harm, even to one's enemies.

What an appalling state of affairs. To alleviate suffering, must I suffer all? I'd hold a remedy in one hand and a sword in the other, if I could, but from Dr. Reed I've already learned one must choose to either shed blood or staunch it. I suspect I am, by the world's usual calculations, too young to discern this matter. But the truth is clear as the oozing, split skin on my soap-dried hands. Those don't appear to belong to a girl, either.

So I scrub, rinse, wring and hang linens spotted with my own blood, leaving them to flap and freeze solid in the subzero wind. I comfort the dying, then bathe and bundle them in clean sheets for hasty burial. When the pleasant prospect of murder flushes my cheeks, I choose Dr. Reed's ideal, instead, to survive this disease and become a healer.

I fear if I don't choose medicine, my fiery heart will fall into retribution. I would rather be an angel than a devil, after all, should I drown in the sorrow that floods our little brick streets.

In mid-December, when Kuruk erupts into a fever on the floor at my feet, I fear I've proven Florence a sibyl, carrying influenza to the last one who loves me. Dr. Reed says, Posh to that, he'd have caught it sooner or later. He relieves me of my volunteer duties so I may nurse my friend.

Kuruk's lungs gurgle with fluid and his skin blues like stacked slate along the river. Although they're useless treatments, because I have no real remedy I rub my friend's chest with Vancoa and dose him with Dr. Pierce's Golden Medical Discovery from Nader's Pharmacy. Over his little coal stove, I lace chicken soup with onions and garlic and dribble the broth between his chattering teeth. I pray and rage and beg for Kuruk's life, calling on his Tirawa and my Jehovah, who must be the same god, after all.

I doze with my hands on his and my head tucked near his chest. In my dreams, his watery breaths become the river we both love. We build a raft from the broken walls of our tree house and float not east, the way the river flows, but against the current to the setting sun. I wake up, fearful it's a bad omen.

At midnight on his second night, near the time when other patients turn purple, leak blood from their eyes and die, my Kuruk calms into slow, shallow breathing. His skin loses its bluish cast and his body unknots from its battle spasm. I cry, biting my lip, as he slides from deathly unconsciousness into restful sleep, and stretch out beside him. Soon his skin cools to match mine and my breaths synchronize with his. With my rough fingers on his cheek, I fall into an exhausted sleep, empty of dreams.

George Dakin finds me north of town two days later. He's thin and haggard after his own bout with the flu, which took one of his sisters, Katherine, but spared the rest of his family for mourning. He tells me the disease has crept in upon Florence, despite her efforts to bar the door. She's dying and asks for me.

The tuberculosis surely weakened her lungs and I'm sorry now to have judged her a malingerer. When I ask George if others in the house are ill, he says Adolph looks feverish, abed with his mother, but she'll let no one touch him.

On the polished oak and slate floors, Florence's Frank-Lloyd-Wright pride and joy, my shoes echo as if the house is deserted. Treating me like a guest, Greta leads me down the hallway to her mother's room. Only nine years old, like many other Darkwater children, she now looks more like a little old person than a child. Her hair is thin and her skin pale. Dark circles hollow out her eyes. I press a hand to her forehead, but she's cool and dry.

I've been sitting up with them, she says.

Where's your father?

He's . . . I don't know.

Useless. I finish her sentence, but then see I've hurt her, that she loves her father as I once wished I could.

I'm sorry, I say, realizing that when her mother dies, Raeburn Amsel will be all Greta has. He's afraid, I tell her. Everyone's afraid, because they don't understand. The influenza brings out the worst in us, especially ignorance.

Greta likes it when I speak Latin, so I teach her as we stand in the hallway, *Timenda causa est nescire*, Greta. Ignorance is the cause of fear.

After she repeats it, I tell her, You don't need to be afraid, because you're not ignorant, right?

She shrugs and says, I don't know much.

You know enough. Now, go sleep a little while I check on them. You need to stay strong, to stay well.

And Adolph? Greta's eyes redden. You'll save my brother? I wouldn't want to live without him.

It strikes me that she doesn't say the same about Florence, but I understand. She feels the same way about Adolph as I feel about Kuruk and Jack.

Because, she adds, brushing blonde hair out of her eyes, parents die. You know that, but a little brother shouldn't.

He shouldn't, I tell her, but influenza is cruel. I'll do what I can.

I wish I could talk to her as if she's a child, but this epidemic has made a caricature of childhood. Instead of lying, I tell her she's strong enough to deal with whatever happens, even Adolph's death.

I'll still have you, won't I, Mama Maggie?

I nod, kiss her forehead and send her to her room.

Florence's arms are loose around her boy, who nestles against her in his sweat-soaked cotton gown. It's hard to say which one is more ill. Surprised Florence will allow it, and considering it a bad sign that she does, I feel the boy's damp forehead. It's cool, but his face is dark and his breaths, fast and shallow. It won't be long for him.

Florence's blonde hair lies shredded over her pillow, and this alarms me too, that her vanity is gone.

She studies me as I touch her burning cheek.

You came.

I nod and pull a chair to the bedside, with nothing to do for her or for Adolph. I clench my useless hands, hating being merely a witness, with no sheets to wash or soup to simmer. No safe distance. Panic bubbles up, but I push it back down. The red foam bubbles swelling and popping on their blue lips, these are familiar signs, but here I can't hover, detached, as the nurse.

Their dying pierces me and I feel how much I love them. Then, how useless love can be and how painful when it's not returned.

Florence's cough shakes Adolph in her arms. He doesn't react.

I take a damp rag from the bedside table and dab Florence's lips. Little red stains seep in the corners of her eyes, as if she's weeping blood and it reminds me of the story of a statue that did the same. That was a miracle.

My boy is dying.

I want to offer her something both good and true. He's unconscious, I say. He's in no pain.

She brushes his head with her lips. That's a mercy.

George said you asked for me.

She flinches as if I pinched her, and things fall back where they always were. I never could say the right thing and this is no exception. My good intentions carry me away, though, and I touch her hands, where they lock around Adolph. I say, Thank you for taking me in, for not leaving me at the orphanage. It was a good life here, with you.

She shakes her head. That was Raeburn's choice. I never wanted you. You've brought nothing but trouble to this house.

It makes me smile. Here, even at death's door, Florence won't flatter me. She won't even patronize God with a last-minute flurry of kindness. I realize, too late, the value of her unflinching honesty.

She twists her mouth in what might be a half-smile and tries to shrug inside her nightgown. I'm not much for charity, she admits, or for mothering. But she turns her head to Adolph like an instinct and inhales with a wheeze, as if seeking his scent behind the urine and sweat.

Florence, you love your children. You're a loving mother.

It's the first time I've addressed her by her first name. She blinks, then nods. A red tear trickles down her cheek.

I can almost let her die in peace, but my good intentions fail me and I blurt it out. What is it about me, the part you couldn't love?

She winces and shakes her head, sighing, Oh, Margaret.

What is it? I'm cruel to insist, but I can't help myself. Tears rush up and trail down my face. I'm ashamed to feel a need so deep, it would wring the truth from a dying woman. But if she doesn't tell me, I'll never know what makes me unlovable. This could be my last chance.

She raises a hand and if she could, I think she'd slap me. I'd almost welcome it, now.

It was the darkness, she says. Mine and yours.

It's not much of an answer and I almost press her for more. But her hand drops and I find enough compassion in my cold tight heart to let her go at her word. I lean back in my chair and draw on my clinical way, like a winter coat.

I wait. Her breathing slows and she slips beyond me, beyond her husband and children, sliding into somewhere else. I think about the mother she wasn't willing to be to me and the daughter I couldn't be to her. And yet, she called me here today.

As Florence's grip on him releases, Adolph's dead weight unfolds into my lap. I catch and gather his light body, realizing that while I tried to claim his mother, he slipped away, another moth drawn to invisible light.

I lay out Adolph on the chaise in the corner, with his hands folded on his chest. He's as perfect in death as he was in life, self-contained and peaceful. I cry over him. I adjust his nightgown, call him little brother, brush back his hair and kiss his forehead.

For Florence, I rifle through her wardrobe for a dress and plunder her vanity table for cosmetics. I bathe her with a warm, wet cloth and dress her in the blue gown Mr. Amsel just brought from New York, unworn. I brush and arrange her hair in her favorite style, raising her head to coil the chignon and heating an iron for the tendrils on the sides. I dab the stains from the corners of her eyes and powder her lids, then brighten her face with rouge. I touch her lips with a color nothing like blood.

Leaving Florence, I walk down the echoing hallway for Greta, who sleeps.

Strange to remember it now, but I do. Freda the orphanage cook recited this German proverb on every stormy day, while she simmered hambone and white bean soup.

Eine Elster allein ist immer ein Zeichen von
ungünstigem Wetter;
denn bei kalter und stürmischer Witterung verläßt
immer nur

Eine Elster das Nest, um Nahrung zu suchen.
Fliegen sie aber beide zusammen,
so deutet dies auf warme und milde Witterung,
wie sie besonders zum Fischfang günstig ist.

A magpie alone is always a sign of bad weather;
because in cold and stormy weather
only one magpie leaves the nest to look for food.
If both fly together,
this indicates warm and mild weather,
particularly favorable for fishing.

Having wished her dead for so long, Amsel reeled
with a peculiar mixture of shock and guilt when influenza
finally took Florence. Coming home to find Margaret in
the house, cradling Greta, and his wife and son lying dead
. . . he must have seemed a madman, weeping and laughing,
pacing the hallway outside the room where the bodies lay,
pulling at his beard and calling out their names. Shouting
at Margaret and Greta, berating them for not seeking him
out in time, even though he was intentionally driving,
driving for hours on dark country roads beyond anyone
calling him home. Knowing his wife was dying, not trusting
himself to act the sorrowful husband, because Florence
knew him too well.

Now, seven months later, he grieves over Adolph, if
not the boy's mother. To the world, he is bereft of both and

he lets people pity him for his double loss, although after the epidemic, there's little pity to spare in Darkwater Creek. He's one widower among twenty, and many families lost at least one child. You wouldn't know it to look at the cemetery. Few graves are marked, but for nailed white wooden crosses among the old stones.

Despite the shortages and backlogged orders in Omaha, Florence Wolcott Amsel's grave boasts a black granite stone shipped overnight on Hollingwood's train. Engraved with Beloved Wife and Mother, he says aloud, so she can hear. Doesn't that count for something? Amsel rubs his forehead and frowns. God, he thinks, this trying to pacify the dead is a runaway horse to insanity. And, according to Pastor, Florence won't hear a thing until the Last Judgment.

He reconsiders Adolph's diminutive gray stone. It should be something more grand, to last for hundreds of years. After all, it will be the boy's only achievement, the only sign he was ever here. He might have been an attorney or a medical doctor, but none of that potential survived the epidemic. Stone, though, that will endure. Amsel pictures a marble angel over his son. Not one who weeps, but one with a trumpet like the brass one Adolph loved to toot, rattling Florence's nerves. And there he lies, beside his mother . . .

Amsel misses the boy more than he expected to, not having seen him every day of his short life. So young, he was primarily his mother's concern, while Amsel provided and looked to the day when they might do whatever it is fathers and sons do. Amsel's own father never spent time with him, but Amsel would have been a better father. No doubt about that. When he was at home, between his weeks of business travel, he walked with the boy down by the river or through his acres of pastureland. Amsel listened to him recite his alphabet and Bible verses, and he'd tell Adolph stories of his own childhood. Just last summer, he took the child with him to Omaha to the stockyards, but the boy was flighty, wanting to run everywhere, too young to appreciate the opportunity to learn. He preferred climbing trees.

As Amsel refills his brandy, the late summer evening thickens into night between the oaks and maples, and the cicadas trill and buzz beyond his open study window. There, at the corner of his sight, he spies a shade of Adolph climbing that damned apple tree, the one he fell out of countless times.

Amsel raises his glass and whispers a toast. You were a good boy, Adolph. My only son.

Downing the brown liquid, he feels prickling and pressure around his eyes, but no tears come. He pours another and tosses it back. From the drawer beside him, he takes a photo of Florence and studies it, to deepen his feelings for her, indulge them and root them out.

Again, he senses her spirit in the house, her whispered accusations.

But I did love you, he insists aloud. I built this house to your design. You chased me to marry you, and I did. When I longed for Annabelle, I went to your bed. I gave up my heart's desire for you. If that's not love, then . . .

He finishes off his drink, silently conceding such a thing isn't love.

Well, he says. Almost crumpling her picture in his hand, he looks back out the window, but Adolph doesn't return.

He feels not exactly guilty, but rather, genuinely sorry for his wife. He always told himself Florence never suspected his unfaithful heart, but how could she not? He thought he was clever, but women are wise and Florence was wiser than most.

He sighs, but can't put his wife back in the drawer.

I took care of you, all those years with consumption, he says, offering his last defense. I kept my vows.

He waits for the feeling of love and the void of loss, or even forgiveness, but they don't come. The eyes of the woman in the photograph are focused somewhere else. He imagines that she, too, ponders her little sister, Annabelle.

In the first months after her funeral, like a child he suspects his morbid hopes held enough power to accomplish his will. But he reassures himself that, by God, the epidemic wasn't his doing. And what married man hasn't wondered what it would like to be free again? There was no seriousness, no malice there. He never truly wished anyone dead. Did he go running after Annabelle, to steal her from her husband? No. There's the proof.

For good measure, he asks God to forgive him for errors of imagination.

In this manner, Amsel gradually absolves himself through reason and faith. He washes away any residual stain in his study, in the fuzzy-edged space between prayer and intoxication.

In summer, he notes that so many died and mourning is so commonplace, nobody grieves for long. He decides he's waited a decent seven months to show respect, but life must go on. He notes with bitterness, had Annabelle been faithful, now would be their time. He has no photograph of her to tear into pieces and can only imagine her with her victorious Naval officer, home from the war. As if tipping an inkwell, he blots her face and body from his mind. But he could remarry. The idea quickens him.

He keeps his routine, noting how strange it is, how little has changed. He keeps the Junghans alarm, the bath, the barber and breakfast at the China Cup. Then work, and home to the supper Mrs. Endicott leaves warming in the oven, with Greta eagerly awaiting her father and Margaret joining them at table.

Yes, most everyone around him has eased out of mourning and back into time. Humans can only bend so far, for so long, under the weight of the dead. At some point, they must leave the cemetery to carry on with business, travel, love and sex.

Amsel notes that June weddings are quiet this year, but brides still carry flowers. No longer Victorians, he tells himself, we Americans don't wear crape and mourning bands on our sleeves. Like engines, we turn over and drive into tomorrow.

The old idea stirs and uncoils again, but over his steaming coffee at the China Cup, he raises his eyebrows in mock surprise and sits back in his chair. My, my, he murmurs, I never considered that.

Calling the idea into the light as a new creation, Raeburn Amsel ponders and calculates.

It makes perfect sense. He already loves Margaret, and she must feel some affection for him, to come back into his home and stay. She's like Annabelle was in the early days, innocent and lovely. And faithful, proven in her devotion to the community during the epidemic.

He pretends he's never imagined himself alone with the girl he shelters, the orphan in his house. He tells himself he's never hoped to stroke her honey-colored skin.

He takes a deep breath, imagining how it might be to marry for love and to finally give Margaret Rose his last name.

He smiles to remember how, before she mourned, his ward craved his attention. She always treasured his little gifts and leaned near for his touch. Margaret's love for Greta is clear, as well, and the girl already calls her Mama Maggie.

Yes, she's young, only fourteen, but the signs of womanhood have been on her for quite some time, although he pretends he hardly noticed before today. He'll begin at once, grooming her for a future beyond her station. Abiding love, comfort, luxury and children. Leadership in the community. But he must take care not to forfeit another future to indecision.

Margaret will be his love and, as soon as it's legal, his wife.

It is reasonable. It is the natural progression.

Yes, Amsel pronounces, setting down his coffee cup, it is good.

In two years, I never got one letter from Jack. I fear the influenza took him or, if he's alive, he's forgotten me.

People here don't appear to miss Jack, because they're heavy with missing all the ones who died. His father never once brought him home for Christmas or summer holidays. If anyone asks, he reports what a star pupil Jack has become at that Blue Ridge Academy and how he races sailboats on the ocean off the Hamptons all summer. But Albert Hollingwood lies as easily as breathing. I wouldn't put it past him to bury his son in an unmarked grave and never tell a soul, if it was better for business to be rid of his crazy son.

With Jack gone for so long, I still think of him every day, but I'm different after watching death come and come back for more. I'm tired and hard and determined to go to a good medical school, to be a doctor. I don't know if I love Jack the same way, when I can't see his eyes or hear his voice. When maybe he's loving somebody else, some rich pale girl with blonde curls. Maybe I love him now more like he's a brother, one who died in the epidemic. One I mourn.

I must have some hope left for Jack, because coming back from my bath, I'm wondering if he's falling asleep now, wherever he is. I press the bedroom door shut behind me, but before it can click, Mr. Amsel pushes it open. He's smiling flat and cool the way he was when he tried to kiss me an hour ago and I pushed him off. Men can be such a nuisance, always pushing in, cornering.

Margaret, my dear. He sounds a little angry.

I tie my robe around me and glance over the floor for my slippers. I wonder what I've done wrong or if Greta is ill. He's been sloppy and strange lately, too familiar. And drinking more, even during the day.

He closes the door and locks it with a key I've never seen.

Crossing my arms, my fingers brush through my sleeve against the fresh cuts in my arm.

His fingers tap his brow, chin and chest in that tic of his, before he steps closer to stroke my cheek.

Beautiful, he whispers.

I swallow and look at the floor. My mind flies around the room like a trapped sparrow. I prayed this wouldn't happen and now it is and what do I do?

My heart pounds me bold and I step around him, reaching for the door and shaking it in its frame. I call as loud as I can for Greta.

He puts an arm around me and pulls me across the room as he slides the key into his pocket. Then he touches my upper lip.

This curve, it's exquisite, and when you blush that way . . .

I call for Greta again, and she shuffles in the hallway. Mama Maggie?

Go back to your room, dear, Amsel tells her.

No, Greta, don't go. I need you to find a key. I'm locked in.

Greta! Go!

She's a good daughter, and I feel sick as her footsteps pad away.

Not you, I say. Not this.

I understand what he wants, but all I can think of is Quoyle fencing me in, breathing threats, dogs in the street and cattle riding each other. I doubt myself, wondering what it is about me that makes this happen. What did I do? I should have stayed with Kuruk, but Greta begged me.

I say it louder to make him understand, No. Greta!

I call her three times, but she doesn't come.

He pulls at my crossed arms to unlock them and cups my chin. Margaret, you're beautiful, I can't stay away.

I shove him and snap at his hand with my teeth, like the dog he must think I am.

He laughs and pushes me back toward the bed. He's holding my arm where it's already cut and it hurts worse than when I sliced it. I reach into the red, taking pain to make myself strong. Pulling away, I reach for the bedside tabletop behind me, knocking my hairbrush and mirror to the floor. I feel the razor blade I use to cut myself and it will do, but it slips between my fingers and falls with the rest.

He's telling me this is love, that he'll teach me everything. That we will marry.

This isn't love, I argue. Leave me alone.

When I threaten to tell someone, he laughs.

Who would take your word over mine? His voice is hollow as a vase in winter.

He's herding me the way he corners livestock. My feet slip on the floor and I duck under his arm, but this gives him the advantage to turn me, to lift my nightgown.

The only thing left on top of the bedside table is the porcelain cardinal, his gift. My fingers curl around it but it's too smooth to harm. Even its tail and the bit of branch it sits on are rounded, fired with scarlet-and-brown glaze.

Beautiful.

He grabs my hips and pulls me against himself.

With one blow, I crack that porcelain bird on the table and its edges fly free like little birds out of that one. The chunk I grip is sharp as a blade.

I wrench sideways, spin and wave it between us. Stop, or I'll cut you.

My heart is a drum, beating up into my ears, but his sigh is louder.

He hesitates. I see his face, then Quoyle's, then both together. I remember the smell of licorice.

My dear girl, Amsel croons, I love you. Now Florence is gone, you'll be my wife, the mother of my children. I'll teach you everything. We'll start tonight.

Quoyle said, Later. Now another voice, another man.

Amsel or Quoyle or whoever this is smiles like a blind beggar, like he can't see me or the red, glassy blade I'm waving in his face. He unbuttons his trousers and I swing, slashing open the back of his hand.

He startles, then laughs as if I gave him a gift.

Why do they laugh?

The blood fills in the shallow curve and courses down in a long drop. He lifts his hand and licks the blood away.

Of course, you're surprised, he says, and you're a good girl, so you think you should fight. But it's me. It's the right thing, not like what you wanted with Jack or that Negro. This is right and pure.

His voice coos nonsense, as sweet and calm as the day he came to the orphanage.

Trust me, he says. He parts his clothes and I look away. I won't make it real by seeing.

Stop calling me beautiful. I shout again for Greta to find a key, to let me out, as he yanks open my robe.

I swing the cardinal blade at his face, but he clamps me in his arms. I'm too close now to strike him, my clenched fists trapped near my face.

He kisses my wet cheek, scratching me with his beard, whispering, Beauty, beauty. His words are gentle, but his hands crush and bruise me. He smells like camphor and sweat and liquor.

He's squeezing the air out of me. When I say, No, all I have left is a whisper.

He calls me Annabelle.

I clench what's left of the cardinal. Where his finger traced my beauty, from my cheek down to the corner of my mouth, I follow that line with the blade of the broken bird, laying open my own skin, freeing my blood. Falling into the hot red pulse.

It relieves me, to be the cause. I control the pain, and my blood flowing down is like a sigh. If only it will be enough, my blood offering. While I trace the line, I stare into his eyes. Darkness closes my vision and I struggle for air.

See? I whisper. Beautiful Margaret Rose.

He's not looking joyful now. His grip loosens and he mutters, Don't.

With my arms free, I raise the bird again, this time higher, and retrace in parallel the arc he drew, that line of beauty he loves. I press deeper across my cheekbone, to my lip.

I love the shock on his face, but my smile hurts so, I could faint. He backs off and it's my turn to laugh, gasping, taking in the beautiful air he forced out of me.

You're insane. Stop it now.

The dark pulse drops back out of my eyes and I'm clear.

Look at me, Father, I'm beautiful.

He wants to look away, but he can't. I'm not your father.

There, I call out, pointing at him. Finally, you say something true.

I press the broken bird to the pulse point on my wrist like a weapon until he backs away, digs in his pocket and unlocks the door.

My God, he says, pale and shaking, his trousers still unbuttoned and his shirt splattered red. Greta presses into the room, cries out and reaches for me. As he pushes out, he tucks and refastens his clothes behind his daughter.

Stay away, he orders her. She's gone mad. He grabs her and pulls her out of the room.

I hurry to close the door behind him, frantic for a key of my own. All I can do is lean against the door.

They whisper. Greta argues while they clatter down the short stairway. In the hush that follows, I look inside the broken cardinal where it must have been white. Now it's red, too, from his blood and mine. Again I press the tip of its razor edge to the blue-green vein in my wrist. While I consider, my breath goes in and out, catching in silent sobs. Should I let more blood, or keep it in? I crave the strength and escape of pain, but when I touch my sticky, flayed cheek, I decide it's enough. What's left of the bird clatters to the floor.

I rest my head back against the door, waiting while beauty throbs and flows away. What little I had, whatever trouble pulsed under my skin, will never show itself again.

Downstairs, a door slams. Amsel's car kicks to a start and coughs, then rumbles away.

The cold slate hall, the bedrooms, even the downstairs room are silent, emptied by what I've done. I frightened Amsel out of his own home, but I'm sorry for Greta. I call for her, in case she's hiding. No answer.

Passing through her abandoned bedroom, I rummage through Florence's bathroom vanity for scissors. In front of her mirror, I chop that bloody stranger's hair as short as a boy's, but the long, dark chunks stick to the blood on my hands. When I rub them free in long red streaks against my nightgown, they drift to the black-and-white hexagoned floor, scattering and shining like a magpie's feathers.

In the framed oval glass, the last of Margaret Rose is gone. What a relief. That nobody, she was nothing but trouble.

She trudges alone, her hair chopped off in mourning and blood running down her throat.

The boy on the horse slows down behind the walking girl, watching her weave from side to side, stumbling.

He calls out, Are you alright?

She doesn't answer.

He reins the horse around in front of her, blocking her way. He recognizes her eyes behind the dark, clotting blood and her beautiful hair molted away and says, Maggie? Maggie Rose?

She shakes her head, but says, George. You came.

He nods and slides down from the horse's back.

Who did this to you?

She laughs as if her mind is gone.

Nobody.

He helps her onto the horse. She rides in front of him to New Eden, where kindness bathes and bandages her. It burns her bloody nightgown and dresses her in clean calico.

When kindness asks if she wants to go home, she says she has no father, no family.

Who is this girl? The boy's aunt demands to know, but he lies.

I never saw her before.

He's grateful she never came with him to New Eden. He lies because she babbled and cried between his arms while he held the reins. She said, Forced. Hurt. Fought. And then, No, again and again, No.

He won't imagine what happened to his friend, but guesses who's likely behind it.

Washing her blood off his hands, watching it swirl in the bottom of the white porcelain dishpan, George knows the only kindness he can give is to take her away. Because whoever started this may not be finished. They're never finished.

He dreams up something and lies to his aunt again. She told me she's from Hastings. I'll take her, find where she belongs.

His aunt studies him, her lips pursed and her eyebrows almost meeting in a knot. Not on that horse, you won't, she mutters. And I know you're lying, George Dakin.

He leans over her, because he's grown tall in the last year, even as other boys his age died and fell into the ground. He kisses her on her gray hair.

Auntie, it's the truth.

Take the old pickup, she says, shrugging and waving him off. And the gas can beside it, in case you run out. You're not fooling anybody. But I never knew you to lie, so you must have a reason.

He doesn't say his reason, the one he feels so hard it hurts. He must save this girl he's been in love with for a year. It's a reason, but it's not reasonable. It doesn't add up, he knows, and George is good at math. He sees the equation in front of him. On horseback, between Darkwater and New Eden, he studied the problem and muttered under his breath about calculating the finite variables, but he knows. For a girl with nothing, and a boy like himself weighed down with a family, the solution is always zero.

He can't keep her safe in Darkwater. He'll help his Maggie disappear, if that's what it takes to save her. Even if he's left with nothing.

It's a hot June night with no breeze but for what chuffs in the side windows of the pickup, air smelling like fuel, a hot radiator and dust. Maggie sleeps beside him, her head lolling back on the seat, rocking back and forth as he eases over bumps and through hollows in the road. It's a rough ride, but she doesn't wake up because he takes it slow. Aunt Sadie gave her something strong for pain. Those cuts are deep. They need stitches, if not surgery.

He's looking for a doctor's house when they pull into Hastings three hours later.

The new Mary Lanning Hospital isn't a good idea, he says under his breath, because those tall columns in front took money to set them up, and money means people with connections and questions. Police, newspapers and community leaders.

He won't have Maggie waking up where they'll make her tell and send her back. He needs somebody quiet and safe, maybe a woman doctor who can guess what happened and will know what to do for Maggie. If there is such a person in this town.

He stops in front of a house where an old man dozes on his porch, bare-chested in a rocking chair. It's that hot of a night, and George is glad to find another person who couldn't sleep because of the heat.

After George asks, the old man sees the girl sleeping in the pickup. He spits on the ground, points and says, Three blocks that way, then four to the north. A white house with a curved wrap-around porch. A lady doctor. She's peculiar, but she saved some in the epidemic. That's something.

George thanks him and climbs back into the truck, easing the heavy door almost shut and holding it so the heavy banging noise doesn't wake her. He glances over, seeing her lips part and hearing her moan when he squeaks to a stop at intersections. The moon tumbles light onto her face. The side he can see is still the girl he knows. The other, wrecked side is a secret swathed in cotton and gauze.

His stomach lurches as he sees the numbers painted on the doorpost. Both glad and sorry to find the doctor's house, he stops the truck and thinks, Maybe I will stay.

But his father's not well and one sister is dead. His mother leans on her only son. The crops, the livestock. The books to balance and food for the table. These are his concerns.

He's angry, thinking he must leave her in this condition. He wants to fight for her. I'll find who did this and take care of it, he whispers. But there's no getting around money and power to set things right. No remedy, but to make her disappear.

He swallows hard and gets out, and when he opens the door beside Maggie, she slumps into his arms. She's soft and bruised, like an apple left to rot on the ground, so he tries to hold her with no pressure. It's hard, because she struggles weakly against his help, shifting and crying, No, no, no.

He shushes her. It's okay. It's just me, George.

He doesn't say the greater thing, I love you.

Bearing her slight frame, he stands beside the truck and hums an old song she likes, about children wading in the water, God's gonna trouble the water, until she calms and lifts her arms around his neck.

Like a condemned man, he carries her up the steps to the door where he rings the bell. He eases her into a porch rocking chair and he settles her head on a pillow. He tucks his own shirt around her against the midnight chill and bends over to kiss her forehead. An electric porch light flicks on, startling him. In its falling yellow light he sees a missed freckle of blood on Maggie's chin. He licks his thumb and dabs it away.

Hurrying back to the truck, he curses, jams his hands in his pockets and kicks a loose stone. Even though he's becoming one, George hates all men tonight.

He shouldn't look back at the porch, because he might change his mind, but he can't drive away until somebody else holds her. He leans against the passenger pickup door and waits.

The backlit shadow of a woman behind the screen door reassures him. He points to the girl he loves and when the screen door squeaks open and a woman steps into the light, he calls out softly, I'm not the one who hurt her. His face flushes with shame, anyway.

The woman calls back, I know, son. If you were, you wouldn't be here. They never bring them. They never come.

Sick at heart, he watches her kneel in front of the rocking chair. She murmurs to Maggie. He can't make out the words, but the sound eases him. He gets into the pickup and goes. It will have to be enough.

K. Lyn Wurth

∞

Reading in the *Post* about those two Brits, Alcock and Brown, flying across the Atlantic in their Vimy-Vickers made up my mind for me about being a pilot. I can't think of anything better than getting up there where the weather's born. To study it, sure, but to get lost in all that space. It must be powerful quiet up there, and water-blue.

The newspaper ink is so fresh it makes my eyes water and blackens my fingertips. It's late afternoon and the Exeter library windows let in long slabs of light that cut across rows of tables, lighting up dust motes like thousands of little Vimys and Jennys doing loop-the-loops. I read the whole article a second time, then a third, 'til I almost feel the ice, the sleet, the fog in my face.

I skim the other pages the way I do every day to be ready for Dr. Paul's Morals and Ethics in Today's World lecture. I never know what he'll ask. A Hotel Biltmore jewel theft, pearls and a twenty-carat diamond vanished from a lobby safety deposit box. A New York doctor on trial for killing his old wife with a lead pipe. Villa's rebel Mexican army recruits 5,000 men. And President Wilson at the Paris Peace Conference, arguing about how to make Germany pay.

On page ten, I find this.

ORPHAN GONE, FEARED SLAIN
A Bloody Scene

DARKWATER CREEK, Neb, June 13 — On Thursday morning, Mr. Raeburn Amsel, a banker and cattleman, reported to the local sheriff that his ward and household servant is missing. Margaret Rose, 14 years old, is feared to have suffered harm, as her blood and hair were found in the Amsel home. A local Indian boy has been questioned extensively in the case. Kuruk Sky Seeing, 15 years old, has not been charged. Mr. Amsel, who was reportedly out of town when the mysterious events occurred, is not considered a suspect.

A rushing noise fills my ears and dark spots flood my eyes, so I rest my head on my crossed arms. The ink fumes burn in my nose like smoke, but I breathe in and out slowly, the way Dr. Sidis taught me.

Magpie. Missing. Blood. Hair.

A voice in my head says, You did this.

No, I whisper. I love her.

I wrote I love you on all those letters I sent to her, the ones I got back, stamped RETURNED TO WRITER UNCLAIMED.

Albert Hollingwood bosses the Postmaster in Darkwater Creek.

Magpie. Missing. Blood. Hair.

You did this.

No.

But maybe I did. In April at Grandfather Appling's house in Chicago, where we meet once a year on my Easter holiday, I asked Father, Did Maggie Rose survive the influenza?

His jaw tightened up the way it does when I say something wrong, and he looked down at the brown grass where little green blades were poking through. Then that

woman Velda, the one he plans to marry and the reason I
never go home because she's afraid of crazy people, lost her
hat in the wind and he ran after it.

Here is his answer.

You did this because you couldn't leave well enough
alone. You made Father angry.

Magpie. Missing. Blood. Hair.

I hate him, I hate him with all my heart. He knows
the one thing, the one person I love and made her disappear.
Maybe even killed her. Not with his own hands, but at his
word, the way he does.

Quoyle. Dietz. How many is this now?

But Jack, you did this.

I rub the hot tears out of my eyes and off my face.
Then I tear the article out of the newspaper page, fold it
and put it in my jacket pocket.

I could send a telegram home to Darkwater Creek
to ask somebody for the truth, but the only person who
would tell me is Kuruk. And he can't read or write.

I swear I will never go home, even if Father changes
his mind and sends for me. Even if he stops being ashamed
to call me his son.

Magpie. Missing. Blood. Hair.

I did this.

I ask God, Find and save her.

And please kill Quoyle, Dietz and Father.

But forgive me for wishing my father dead.

And forgive me for killing Maggie Rose.

Finally, I ask God for wings to leave this earth, its
tree houses and rivers and love letters and missing girls
behind. To let me live in the sky, above the voices in the
rain. Just let me be over the rain.

The voices and the idea of her blood make the reading space seem too wide and open. Leaving my chair, I wander deep into the stacks, turning angle after angle to lose myself. I slide to the floor like a shadow to cry and think and cry some more.

When I come out, the light through the library windows is soft, its warm slab cooled into gray. I missed the closing chime and stayed too long. At the front desk, all the lights are off. The library doors are locked and the librarian's gone from his high perch, ink stamper and card files as if I'm no more than a ghost in the book stacks.

I pop the inside latch and step into the freshly fallen night, so deep violet the lilacs dissolve into it, but I can smell them while I follow the glowing walkway lampposts to my dormitory room.

As I walk, I say, Yes, it's me. I did this. It's my fault.

I take care to keep the voices quiet so I don't have another breakdown and leave Exeter, the way I left Blue Ridge. Because, as Father says, this country has only a few top schools that will take a boy with problems, and my reputation precedes me. I take the guilt onto myself, because sometimes this satisfies the voices.

They are satisfied now, so they leave me empty and cold in blessed silence except for my shoes scraping on hardwood in my room. It's hard to say because I let my clock run down, but the other boys might be in the dining hall or at evening convocation. Most of them have gone to the places they call home, to fathers and mothers for the summer, but not me. Exeter scheduled its first summer session this year, and Father enrolled me. After that, I'm to Chicago for five weeks with Grandfather, the same as every summer since I went mad.

The model I built of a Curtiss JN-4 dangles from a string over my bed, spinning in a breeze from the open window. I take my old copy of *Our Own Weather* from the headboard bookshelf, the one Father mailed to me last year, writing how Kuruk pestered him 'til he did. I tuck the news story I tore from the *Post* between the pages where I underlined, *But then all signs of rain fail in dry weather. The familiar maxim is perfectly true: the signs do appear, and yet the rain does not come.*

Lying down on my coverlet, I keep my finger between those pages, touching the newspaper words as if I'm touching Maggie Rose. Even after I close my eyes, I keep myself safe in the Jenny over my bed. Flying with Magpie through and over the rain.

∞

They came for me while I was sleeping so Maggie being gone still feels like a bad dream. The blood and her hair on the black-and-white tile and the bright lights in my eyes while they yelled at me. But she's gone in all my walking-around hours, too, proving it really happened.

My grandfather told how Ready-to-Give, the god of the north, rewarded hunters and poor boys who were brave. He told me to show respect to the gods of the heavens and earth. He said Ready-to-Give, Kawaharu, should inspire me to find my Medicine Bear courage. But since Maggie disappeared, I'm scared all the time. I drop things and can't sleep very good. Nothing helps me but standing in the river, listening to the water lap and the leaves shush, picturing an old ghost bear who wades in the water beside me and sniffs for berries along the bank. I'm not so lonesome there with She Who Holds You, feeling her ripple cool around me.

The night the law men came, I thought for sure they'd hang me for Maggie's murder but I guess Quoyle and Dietz got something else in mind for me. They still got my hat and that made-up story about Rolf so I keep out of their way, close to White Boss, who hasn't changed his mind about me yet. It's all I can do to keep him happy. I'd run off but I got to be here if Maggie or Jack come home.

After they questioned me and let me go, I added Maggie to my Remembering, the story I keep in my head of all the terrible things I can't tell. Things I saw that Quoyle and Dietz would come after me for, if they knew I saw them. Even if I was a good writer—and I am not—I wouldn't put my Remembering on paper where the words could get into somebody else and back to those scoundrels, to get me killed.

In my Remembering I keep folks who died in secret for getting in the way or being poor or wrong. From what I saw, not one deserved dying that way so I keep their stories in my head. I tell them in a whisper every night before I go to sleep the way Grandfather would tell stories, always the same words in the same order, never forgetting any part. Rolf's in there, not the first and not the last, and now Margaret Rose. I don't know if I need to add Jack, my Coyote, my irari. I hope not but he seems gone to me. I never saw him once since White Boss sent him off to school and I don't believe the way he brags about his son. But I got no proof to put him in the Remembering yet. If I did, I'd need to quit White Boss and leave town. I won't stand to work for him another day if I find he's hurt Coyote.

The Remembering is the only way I know how to be brave and I'm the only one to keep those stories sharp. It is my destiny and I follow it like a river flowing, even when it feels like it could drown me. Because the only thing worse than dying is people forgetting why you died, like you were never a person.

A story can hold power even if it's not on paper. Like the one Grandfather got from his father, who got it from a Kitkehahki named Thief. It tells of a girl who could bring Buffalo to her tribe by swinging away to the west so far nobody could see her. She went too far and got lost, but the animals saved her.

It's a good story, showing how friends help each other and if you see Coyote, Magpie or Buffalo, the others aren't far away. It gives me some hope. Maybe a girl who is missing can come back. It worries me, though, that in Thief's story Coyote never came home.

I get a knot in my stomach thinking how this isn't an animal world or a Pawnee world but a White one where stories got bad or uncertain endings. Like in my Remembering, people disappear and nobody knows where, or nobody's telling. So in this story, even if the girl does come back, will Coyote find his way?

A preview of Seven Kinds of Rain's sequel

Remember
How
It Rained

River Saga · Book Two

a novel by

K. Lyn Wurth

The quality of mercy is not strain'd,
It droppeth us the gentle rain from heaven
Upon the place beneath . . .
Though justice be thy plea, consider this,
That, in the course of justice, none of us
Should see salvation: we do pray for mercy . . .
— The Merchant of Venice, Act 4, Scene 1

⟲

May, 1934

The last swallow of beer is warm and when I raise the empty bottle to signal for another, it leaves a third wet ring on the bar. So I've probably had enough, if I plan to fly this afternoon, but still, I need another for social and business reasons. I'm not done persuading these farmers. The bartender obliges and I slide him a quarter with a dime for his trouble.

A Colored fellow pulls open the screen door. He doesn't step in, but calls, You gentlemen better take a look at this. He nods to the west, steps back and lets the door slam. That's when I notice the east wind flapping his trouser legs and shirt tail around to the front of him. He steps into the street, flattens a hand above his eyes and shakes his head, saying loud, Lord help us.

So all five of us with nothing better to do than drink beer on an afternoon amble outside. The bartender is last.

One says, You guess it's grasshoppers? I heard they're getting clouds of 'em in Oklahoma.

Nah, only a thunderstorm.

There's no only in that monster. If it's a storm cloud, it's full of rain and that can't be bad, says the one who's been nursing the same beer for two hours. He slaps his knee and smiles at me, cackling, See, we don't need your high-falutin' science.

The way it's dragging on the ground, looks to be a tornado, says the bartender.

I don't say a word. I'm a guest in this town and since I said I went to college, my opinion counts for shit, anyway. I size up the situation and draw this sudden conclusion; that black cloud dragging over the ground and billowing thick like rubber-tire smoke doesn't need a name. Since that tornado picked me up and threw me against a wall when I was nine, I know a fellow has to survive the weather first, to classify it later.

And I am, after all, a sort of weatherman.

The cloud of whatever-it-is rumbles. The other drinkers hot-foot it all different directions home, while the bartender yanks open the screen door, dashes into the bar and lets it slam behind him, yelling, Velma!

I'm nobody's concern, just another vagrant, or worse, a shyster. And what have I been trying to sell them, pitching a story I practiced a hundred times, one-part science and nine-parts luck? The very thing that cloud may carry, bearing down on us from heaven above.

The wind sucks upwards and shifts, coming more from the south and blowing grit in my eye.

Even without the dust, I wouldn't see her from here, but I squint, turn and look toward where my Eaglerock plane is staked and tied down north of town. Even if I got to her, there's no hangar here in Springfield to wheel her into, and no time to tarp her. Magpie will have to fend for herself. I glance around and there's not one building I'd bet a dollar on against the oncoming weather. A panicked coyote dashes past me, north up Main Street. That's a bad sign, and I wish I could follow him to whatever hole he's got in mind. Then somebody speaks up behind me.

Unless you plan to watch it kill you, come along, the Colored man says, so I still have one friend left in the world.

When he turns and runs west down a side street, even though I don't see the sense in running into the wind, I do, too. There's something about his certainty I can follow.

He's holding down his straw hat against the shifting wind and I'm hard pressed to keep up, with the gusts beating me back and forth. We run to a pale sandstone building set up high, marked with a Freemason "G", a carpenter's square and compasses. It looks solid enough. Two sets of steps climb to meet each other at the front door, but a storm door slants below them, to the cellar. We each grab one door handle and yank hard. His comes open so he goes down the stone steps into the hole first. I can't help myself. Sure as Lot's wife, I turn and look to see the black cloud take its first bite of Springfield, the far end of that side street with its houses and trees disappearing as if down a dark throat. I can tell now it's not rain, not a thunderstorm or tornado, but dust. I've heard of these storms, they're plentiful in this drought, but I've not been caught in one before today.

I plunge into the cool earth like a child being gladly unborn. The door behind me slams us into dim safety, dulling the sound. A slice of light divides the cellar doors and dull daylight filters through eight grimy cellar windows.

Ramsey, he says to me in the dark. Reverend Josiah Ramsey.

And although, for the benefit of my sales pitch back in the bar I'd conjured the name Dr. Joseph Abernathy, to this man I tell the truth, Jack Hollingwood. I thank him for saving me.

The reverend says, You're not saved yet. You just got another chance.

I wonder if he means physical or spiritual salvation. Then a familiar voice in my head snarls, Hello again, Jack.

I think, how can it be Hello when you never once said goodbye, or left me the hell alone in twenty-one years?

My eyes seek out shapes in the dim light. There's a bedroll leaning against one wall and I guess this man's been living down here. So he's a bum like me. When the reverend ties a bandanna over his nose and mouth, I dig out my handkerchief and cover mine. We hunker down in the southwest corner, our backs to what's coming, in case the sandstone isn't stacked as strong as you'd expect from Freemasons.

The lights between the doors and the windows go dark, as if somebody pressed a button on a wall. The wind passes like a train and I'm feeling like a boy again, but in all the wrong ways. More voices kick up in my head and I almost yell back at them, but I fear scaring the kind pastor out into the gale. Instead, I shut my old terror-memory down and cover my mouth with my hand, telling myself it's not the same storm that almost killed me. Nothing like the one that first woke up the voices, back in Omaha, 1913.

The air in the cellar thickens up from dust sifting in around the door. My eyes water, but because I'm stubborn, determined to see what's coming for me, I shut them too late. The grit feels big as gravel under my lids and I wonder if eyes can bleed. Our cotton rags can't keep the fine dust from our lungs and within an hour, we're both coughing and gagging until we settle into panting, shallow breaths to move enough air so we don't pass out, but not so much we suffocate, either.

We don't talk because words are air.

I think about that full beer I left on the bar and imagine I'm swallowing it, but my throat is so sticky, I choke.

No light moves over the window glass to mark the days. The cellar keeps a steady cool damp, like one long night. We can only wait in a space with no mark of time, listening to the wind whistle and whine and scream. I count my heartbeats into minutes and hours, but soon the numbers don't mean anything. I let them go.

I sleep and dream and wake in the wailing dark and wonder if I'm dreaming.

I wonder if the mad-dashing Coyote made it back to his den, or if this black blizzard sucked his breath away.

It's two days before the silence leans in like a new kind of roar, and our ears keep ringing. We shoulder open the storm doors of the Freemasons' cellar, blown topsoil weighing them down and drifted like snow against the ground-level windows. No wonder it was so dark down there. It's bright outdoors now, and our dust-scalded eyes squint and shed tears against the light.

I feel I have risen from my grave, Rev. Ramsey croaks.

Gusts of wind still sift dirt-snakes around our feet as we kick through the dunes and debris looking for a place to get water, beer, anything to drink. The bartender is watching us come, so he steps out and waves us both in.

This here sure is a mess, he says, setting two bottles in front of us. Three fellas got lost in the storm. We ain't found them yet.

Three that were here?

No, three others, high school boys. They went out looking for a little girl who was at home the whole time, hiding under her bed.

We drink and shake our heads and cough while he talks about the damage done. The wheat crop lost again for another year. How Baca County will never recover from this and goddamn the wind, it won't lay all the way down. How you can't see more than a mile with dust hanging in the air like fog.

My hands turn muddy, slipping, trembling around the brown wet bottle I press against my cracked lips, loving that beer like a girl I can't stop kissing.

After we quench our thirst and the bartender runs out of stories, Rev. Ramsey asks to come with me to the farm where I left my airplane. He saw me fly in the day before the dust storm and offers to help. Who knows what condition she'll be in, he says. You might need another man.

I'll be glad if anything's left.

We cross a field as dusty-gray as the face of the moon, drifts and crests covering any wheat or alfalfa planted this spring. In this third year of drought, there probably wasn't much to begin with. We pass out of the sunlit, choking heat, through a grove of elms and oaks and maples with dull, tattered leaves sagging under little loads of dirt. Here and there, fresh limbs hang, broken by the wind and snow-like burden of soil.

At the farmstead, a cast-iron hand pump marks a drifted-over, covered well. A skinny German Shepherd pup licks at the spout. I find an old dish pan blown up against the house and pump some water for the dog, who drinks until his belly rounds like a drum. Magpie is behind the house, or was, when I left her. I can't bear to look, not yet. I scratch the grubby dog's ears and call him Sandy, to call him something. Sometimes you need a dog.

269

Stalling, I knock on the front door. The bachelor farmer I met two days before, who rented me his yard, leans against the doorframe. He's pale and feverish, wheezing, probably from dust pneumonia. Delirious, he thinks we've come to take his farm. He swings a limp fist at my head before he staggers back inside, onto a wooden chair, yelling for that nigger to get out of his house.

I tell him nobody wants his farm and this man's a Baptist reverend, so watch his mouth.

He calms down then, covers his face with his hands and lets us to lead him to his bed. Reverend Ramsey opens a can of soup and heats it up on the gas stove. We both sit by the old man's bed, steadying his hand so the spoon gets to his mouth. We get him to drink some water, too, and he falls asleep.

I've put it off as long as I can, not glancing through windows at the back of the house, afraid of what I'll see. But when I go out the back kitchen door, I find Magpie whole. Battered and filthy, but for the most part, unbroken.

The wind-blown sand blasted bits of black-and-white paint off her fuselage, struts and wings, but because I tied her facing west, she didn't roll. I can almost picture her lifting, straining against her staked ropes to rise like a blinded bird while the wind pummeled her, with me huddled like a prairie dog underground. One of her incidence wire bolts sprung free when the spiraling winds twisted her planes, but I can fix it. The worst part is, dust as fine as baking powder is packed solid between the engine cylinder fins on all nine cylinders. I start picking those spaces clean with a screwdriver, blowing and brushing away what I can. I can only clean the outside of her Wright J-5 engine, making it a risk to fly, but I have to get her to Colorado Springs. At the

Alexander plant, the mechanics will have to open her up to discover how far inside her engine the black blizzard has filtered. They can touch up her paint, too, and make her pretty again.

Rev. Ramsey uses an old coffee can to scoop dirt out of the cockpit and passenger seat. He clears his throat by singing hymns, both of us punctuating the verses with coughs and retches as the dust storm's filth works out of our lungs. His steady baritone clears and cools like water as we work.

When he digs out my supply crates, Reverend Ramsey asks me what exactly it is I do with those chemicals stowed inside Magpie. I explain to him the simple chemistry of rain, and the elusive equation that will draw atmospheric water down to earth.

So it's not just hocus-pocus? A confidence game?

I tell him, Some days I wonder, but I think I'm close to a breakthrough. The theory is solid, but there's no way to test variables in a lab setting, so I keep experimenting in the air with different chemicals and processes. It takes a lot of money, I tell him. I don't promise the farmers anything. I only ask them to help fund my experiments, whatever they can afford.

I show him my notebooks, with the data I keep. He peers at the pages and nods.

You don't look like a poor man, flying a pretty plane like this. Why are you taking poor folks' money?

She was prettier two days ago, I say, running a hand over her pitted prop, but not nearly as pretty as the girl I named her for. And I admit it. I'm only as poor as I choose to be. My father . . . well, he has money, but it's dirty money, so I don't like to take it. And I try to give back a little hope, and maybe some rainfall, for anybody who'll bet on my experiments.

A gambler with a conscience.

I squint at him and he looks back at me with his red-rimmed, irritated eyes and smiles. It's only then I remember Colored Jesus, in that painting in the church back in New Eden, and in my dream. I tell him about it, the way Jesus carried those chains, and ask him if he's ever seen anything similar. He shrugs, but his half-smile hints that what he sees when he closes his eyes to pray is too sacred for words, or too sacred to share with an unbelieving White fellow like me.

I ask, Besides, don't even the best grifters get caught in their games?

He shakes his head and says, I'm not casting stones. I've been promoting intangible goods for thirty years. You can't exactly bottle the Holy Ghost. God the Father scares most people, and Jesus on the cross, he's a tough sell. Folks like him better when he's healing and telling stories to the children. But all in all . . .

The Reverend wheezes, coughs and spits a glob of black mud on the ground before saying, Selling salvation is hard work, even on an easy day. And with this destruction, topsoil and people scattered to the winds, a fellow'd think, maybe even hope, this is the end of days, for something to preach about. But it's worse, I think, a long season we best get used to.

I offer him a ride to Colorado Springs, for his help, with a clear warning Magpie may or may not be safe for flight. He says he figures he's in more danger on the ground, but no thank you, anyway. His sister lives in Santa Fe, and she wrote she has a bed and a job for him there. Without me asking him for it, he spreads his big warm hands on my head to grant a blessing. I get an ache in my chest I haven't felt since I was a boy, when I walked double-time to stay in step with my father, holding his hand.

Remember
How
It Rained

River Saga · Book Two

Coming soon to
Amazon, barnesandnoble.com
and other fine book retailers

⬭

Acknowledgements

In my first novel, *The Darkwater Liar's Account*, I entered a geographical place dear to my childhood heart, the Republican River Valley of Nebraska. In *Seven Kinds of Rain* and its sequel, *Remember How It Rained*, I explore the history of the land my grandparents loved, sweat over, and struggled to pay for. I remember how Henry and Laura loved that little plot of ground in the Republican River Valley, planting corn, alfalfa and apricot trees. These novels echo the unspoken truth, that before my grandparents were born, their beloved land was stolen by our government. The Pawnee Native American tribe, removed by the United States government to Oklahoma reservation territory in the 1800s, preceded American settlers in the region that would become the states of Nebraska and Kansas. They were killed or removed and deprived of every right promised by our Constitution, because they were not considered to be human beings. To this day, many of their ancestors are buried along that river valley, if their graves have not been plundered or desecrated by settlers, souvenir hunters or anthropologists. This is the preface to my personal and family story. It is the preface to most of ours.

In this way Kuruk, the dispossessed Pawnee child, earned a firm right to be in my story of White power, privilege and success on the early twentieth-century Great Plains. The child Margaret is much like my grandmother, abandoned by her parents to be a servant for those who considered themselves her betters. Jack is the uneasy heir and product of privilege. Among these three, I trace a less-told story of what happened to the young and innocent, after the West was taken from its first peoples.

As I researched Pawnee history, culture and myth, the character of Kuruk grew large in the heart of this novel. Yet, the constraints and biases of written history nearly obscured him. I found scant records of a nation rapidly dismantled, forcibly removed from their traditional lands, robbed of language and deprived of their hunting and agriculture. Entire tribal generations of young Native children were killed, lost to devastating epidemics, forcibly adopted into White families or removed from their families and cultures to be "saved" by Indian boarding schools. These lost generations interrupted the flow of the Pawnee legacy and their original voices. Many who suffered still bear trauma that reaches down the generations. Yet the Pawnee Nation survives. History lives.

Without personal ancestry or community connection to the Pawnee tribe, I resorted to the late-18th and early-19th century anthropologist-translators, George Amos Dorsey and George Bird Grinnell. Their books provide the Pawnee and Cherokee traditional stories central to Kuruk's battered, but durable, Native identity. Alexander Lesser's *The Pawnee Ghost Dance Hand Game* is an important source for some song and ceremonial details that color Kuruk's memories. I appreciate these sources, but wrote with an uneasy sense of distance from Pawnee history. I longed for immediacy and the voices behind the translations, lost to time and my own culture.

As a student of Great Plains and Western literature, a writer who loves the West and one who's lived in the region almost all of my life, I've studied much of what my country cherishes in its version of Western expansion. I love the American archetypes of the tough pioneer woman, cowboy, sodbuster, gold miner, fur trapper, dance-hall girl, trader and explorer. I love the covered wagon (my great-grandfather, Charles Willcoxon, was born in one), buffalo and tall prairie grass, both the real and the symbolic, in my experience of America.

Yet, I also recognize my own culture's dehumanization and enslavement of diverse peoples and, maybe most destructive of all, the deep and stubborn silences, the gaps in the Western narratives we hold dear. Too often, the only images we keep are dehumanizing distortions that reinforce our sense of entitlement and power. Stereotypes of Native cultures and persons are offensive, destructive, widespread and popular in sports, movies, television and in print. I ask my readers to consider the harm these images inflict on contemporary Native tribes and individuals. I work against their recurrence in my own mind and writing.

Even as we reconsider the deeper, violent meanings at the core of our cherished images, we must also ponder the gaps. Our culture's most deadly assaults on Native survival may be our omissions, the perpetual pretense that there are no lives or voices of value but those of the White majority. This gap solidified my (admittedly ironic, and not lightly made) decision to give a voice to Kuruk, a child of injustice, in a particular time and place where Native people are not usually mentioned. I hope Kuruk's inclusion leads to a wider, more just retelling of history.

For firsthand testimonies and stories about Native experiences, I encourage my readers to seek out Native authors. Sherman Alexie, Dee Brown, Louise Erdrich, Wilma Mankiller, N. Scott Momaday, and Anna Lee Walters are a few of the talented Native writers, activists and scholars whose works have inspired me to try to break stereotypes and question recorded interracial histories. *Wičazo Ša Review: A Journal of Native American Studies*, edited by Dr. James Riding In, Native American activist and professor of American Indian Studies at Arizona State University, enriched my understanding of the complexity of Native American history and modern tribal cultures.

The 2015 Standing Bear Conference at The Center for Great Plains Studies in Lincoln, Nebraska was my most recent opportunity to be quiet, listen and learn to reconsider my own assumptions about race and Western American history. At that conference, folklorist and author Roger Welsch's personal story of his involvement in the repatriation of Pawnee remains to Nebraska touched my heart. His devotion to the Pawnee tribe, who adopted him as one of their own, added nuance and depth to Kuruk's experience of his ancestors. David Wishart was another presenter at that conference. His book, *An Unspeakable Sadness: The Dispossession of the Nebraska Indians*, provided historical and geographical background for my Nebraska Pawnee research, localizing vague, national policies of destruction against Natives into vivid regional detail.

A number of important people and institutions supported me in my 2014 research trips along the Republican River in Nebraska. Thanks to the Franklin Public Library, Red Cloud's Webster County Historical Museum and the Auld Public Library for regional history resources I couldn't find anywhere else. The Willa Cather Memorial Prairie, 612 acres of never-plowed Nebraska ground, transported me to a time and place I could not have imagined without it. Thanks to the The Willa Cather Foundation for preserving the prairie in its pristine beauty, along with the Cather houses, which sheltered me and inspired my period architecture descriptions in these novels. The Pawnee Indian Museum and archaeological site near Republic, Kansas, gave me a glimpse of the life of Kuruk's ancestors. A visiting Kansas State University archaeologist, Donna C. Roper, Ph.D., was supervising students in reverently closing an earth lodge archaeological dig there at the time of my visit. She shared with me her insights into everyday Pawnee life on that site in the early 1800s. I was sorry to hear of her passing in 2015, and appreciate my brief opportunity to learn from her. I made a few new friends on those trips along the river. The Red Brick Café in Red Cloud, Nebraska was a highlight, with Tracy and Tom's excellent breakfasts, hospitality and interest in this project providing delicious, much-needed sustenance.

I thank Lori Handelman, Ph.D., for her thoughtful, courageous editing and enthusiasm for my story and its characters. Nanette Day, thank you for sharpening my perspective on, if not changing my habits with, comma usage. You're an amazing and tolerant proofreader, and you elevated my stylistic quirks. Carmen Peone, I appreciate your thoughtful comments on Native issues, as treated in this text. I thank Keith Williams for his generosity in allowing his Mr. Magpie photo on both book covers. Vin Downes, one of my favorite musicians, kindly permits use of his guitar recording, "Unweaving," in my book trailers. Music from his album, *Unlike the Stars*, frequently forms the sound track for my writing, and I encourage your support for this talented artist. Thank you, Vin.

Last, but first in my heart, I list the friends and family who sustain me in my work. David, my husband, serves as my best friend, my most ardent supporter and my patron, without whom I couldn't write a word, let alone publish. He makes me laugh and offers genuine comfort when my health issues overwhelm, and reminds me of my joy and purpose. My mother, Beverly, to whom *Seven Kinds of Rain* is dedicated, is truly my first and most devoted reader. She loves to talk with me about the writing process, and cheers me on through the exhilaration and exhaustion phases of being a woman and a writer. Who could write a word without such love?

My writing is an exercise in gratitude, born of mercy that has flowed to me from the day of my birth. I can't say, "Thank you," often enough to those who bear me up and lighten my burdens. Thank you for reading. Whatever race of child you may be, I hope you find yourself in my stories. I hope they light a path toward the justice, wisdom, respect and love our Creator intends all children to share.

∞

Sources Consulted

Allen, William Francis, Charles Pickard Ware, and Lucy McKim Garrison. *Slave Songs of the United States*. New York: A. Simpson, 1867. Print.

Bekoff, Marc. "Animal Emotions, Wild Justice And Why They Matter: Grieving Magpies, A Pissy Baboon, And Empathic Elephants." *Emotion, Space and Society* 2.2 (2009): 82-85. Print.

Carson, Gerald. "The Rainmakers." *Natural History* Sept. 1985: 20-28. Print.

Clarke, F.W. "An Ode to Pluviculture; Or, The Rhyme of the Rain Machine." *Life* 5 Nov. 1891: 260. Print.

Cook, Hull. *Fifty Years a Country Doctor*. Lincoln, Neb.: U of Nebraska, 1998. Print.

Denham, Michael Aislabie. *A Collection of Proverbs and Popular Sayings Relating to the Seasons, the Weather, and Agricultural Pursuits*. London: Printed for the Percy Society by T. Richards, 1846. Print.

Devil Clouds. Perf. David Bristow, Harl Dalstrom, Donna Caniglia. NET Foundation for Television, 2013. Film.

Dorsey, George Amos. *The Pawnee, Mythology Part I.* Baltimore, MD: Carnegie Institution of Washington, 1906. Print.

Dorsey, James Owen, and Francis Flesche. *The Cegiha Language the Speech of the Omaha and Ponka Tribes of the Siouan Linguistic Family of North American Indians.* Washington: Govt. Print. Off., 1890. Print.

Embe. *Stiya, a Carlisle Indian Girl at Home: Founded on the Author's Actual Observations.* Cambridge Mass.: Printed at the Riverside, 1891. Print.

Ferguson, Frank. Interview by Unknown Interviewer. 3-part document of Ferguson family record; 1935 and 1979, found at NOAA.gov

Fletcher, Alice C., and James R. Murie. *The Hako: A Pawnee Ceremony.* Washington: Govt. Print. Off., 1904. Print.

Franklin, Nebraska 1879-2003: The Best of the Good Life. Kearncy, NE: LIPS Printing Service, 2005. Print.

Grinnell, George Bird. *Pawnee Hero Stories and Folk-tales: With Notes on the Origin, Customs, and Character of the Pawnee People.* Lincoln, Neb.: U of Nebraska, 1961. Print.

Harrison Miller, Betty. Interview by Unknown Interviewer. Personal reminiscence of Republican River Flood, 1935, at South Fork Nebraska; found on NOAA.gov site.

Herder, Nicole Beaulieu. *Best-loved Negro Spirituals: Complete Lyrics to 178 Songs of Faith*. Mineola, N.Y.: Dover Publications, 2001. Print.

Hittman, Michael, and Don Lynch. *Wovoka and the Ghost Dance*. Expanded ed. Lincoln: U of Nebraska, 1997. Print.

Jones, M. *Bible Stories for Little Children*. London: T. Nelson and Sons, 1871. Print.

Leahy, J.F. *Leahy's Hotel Guide and Railway Distance Map of the State of Kansas*. Chicago: American Hotel Register, 1934. Print.

Leahy, J.F. *Leahy's Hotel Guide and Railway Distance Map of the State of Oklahoma*. Chicago: American Hotel Register, 1934. Print.

Lesser, Alexander. *The Pawnee Ghost Dance Hand Game: Ghost Dance Revival and Ethnic Identity*. Lincoln: U of Nebraska, 1996. Print.

Mason, B. J. *Clouds, Rain, and Rainmaking*. 2d ed. Cambridge Eng.: Cambridge UP, 1975. Print.

McCall, Malvern M., and Richard C. McCall. *Nebraska Farm Life: WWI to WWII*. San Jose, Calif.: Writer's Showcase, 2002. Print.

Mooney, James. *Myths of the Cherokee: From Nineteenth Annual Report of the Bureau of American Ethnology 1897-98, Part I*. [1900]. Washington: Smithsonian

Institution. Bureau of American Ethnology, 1900. Print. p. 3-568, 569*-576

Nasar, Sylvia. *A Beautiful Mind.* Waterville, Me.: Thorndike, 2002. Print.

Nobody. Perf. Arthur Collins. Excelsior, 1905. Audio Recording.

Okrent, Daniel. *Last Call: The Rise and Fall of Prohibition.* New York: Scribner, 2010. Print.

Osler, William. *The Principles and Practice of Medicine.* New York: D. Appleton & Company, 1895. Print.

Oswell, Kate F., and Charles B. Gilbert. The *American School Readers: Primer.* New York: Macmillan, 1911. Print.

Pound, Louise. *Nebraska Folklore.* Lincoln: U of Nebraska, 1959. Print.

Price, J. C. *The Republican Pawnee Village. Republic, KS*: Private., 1900. Print. Introduction and an Archaeological and Historical Commentary, copyright 2013 by Donna C. Roper. Booklet obtained at Pawnee Historical Site near Republic, KS.

Rawleigh's Almanac, Cookbook & Medical Guide, 1895-1910. Freeport, IL, 1909. Print.

Richardson, Lewis F. *Weather Prediction by Numerical Process.* New York: Cambridge UP, 1922. Print.

Riding In, James, ed. *Wičazo Ša Review: A Journal of Native American Studies.* Univ Of Minnesota, 1985-2016. Print. (past editors, Elizabeth Cook-Lynn, Roger Buffalohead, and William Willard)

Shaw, Napier. *The Air & Its Ways. The Rede Lecture, 1921, in the University of Cambridge, with Other Contributions to Meteorology, Etc.* Cambridge: Cambridge, 1923. Print.

Skinner, Charles Montgomery. *American Myths and Legends.* Philadelphia & London: J.B. Lippincott, 1903. Print.

Spence, Clark C. *The Rainmakers: American "pluviculture" to World War II.* Lincoln: U of Nebraska, 1980. Print.

TEDTalks: Eleanor Longden—The Voices in My Head. Perf. Eleanor Longden. TED, 2013. Film.

TEDTalks: Elyn Saks—A Tale of Mental Illness...from the Inside. Perf. Elyn Saks. TED, 2012. Film.

Townsend, Jeff. *Making Rain in America: A History.* Lubbock: International Center for Arid and Semi-arid Land Studies, Texas Tech U, 1975. Print.

Ubelaker, Douglas H., and Herman J. Viola. "An Historical Character Mythologized: The Scalped Man in Arikara and Pawnee Folkore, by Douglas R. Parks." *Plains Indian Studies: A Collection of Essays in Honor of John C. Ewers and Waldo R. Wedel.* Washington: Smithsonian Institution, 1982. 47-48. Print.

Wells, Philip P. *Bible Stories and Religious Classics*. S.l.: S.n., 1903. Print.

Weltfish, Gene. *The Lost Universe: Pawnee Life and Culture*. Lincoln, Neb.: U of Nebraska, 1977. Print. Reprint of *The Lost Universe with a closing chapter on "The Universe Regained"*.

"Prostitution in Grand Island, Nebraska, 1870-1913." Western History Association Conference. Venue Unknown, San Diego. 1 Oct. 1978. Lecture.

Wilmot, Marlene Harvey. *Bluff-to-bluff: The 1935 Republican Valley Flood*. Greeley, CO: Wilmot Ventures, 1995. Print.

Wilmot, Marlene Harvey. *Bluff-to-bluff, Too!: The 1935 Republican Valley Flood*. Greeley, CO: Wilmot Ventures, 1996. Print.

Wishart, David J. *An Unspeakable Sadness the Dispossession of the Nebraska Indians*. Lincoln, Neb.: U of Nebraska, 1994. Print.

Wright, Blanche Fisher. *The Real Mother Goose*. Chicago: Rand, McNally, 1916. Print.

Wyeth, N. C. *An Autobiography of Buffalo Bill*. New York: Cosmopolitan Book, 1920. Print.

Zoch, Richmond T., ed. "Rivers and Floods." *Monthly Weather Review* 63.6 (1935): 198-201. Print.

About the Author

K. Lyn (Kelly) Wurth writes short fiction and novels about Great Plains and Western experience, history, health and family life. Her first novel, *The Darkwater Liar's Account*, also unfolds in her family's home state of Nebraska. Her short fiction has been published in Women Writing the West's *Laura Journal*, *The Broadkill Review*, *The Examined Life Journal*, *St. Anthony Messenger* and an anthology, *The Arduous Touch: Women's Voices in Healthcare*. Inspired by a lifetime of Great Plains and Rocky Mountain experience, Kelly now writes in rural Iowa, where she lives with her husband, David.

CPSIA information can be obtained
at www.ICGtesting.com
Printed in the USA
FFOW04n0414130916
27516FF